MOONLIGHT BEACH

PRAISE FOR TAMMY L. GRACE

"I had planned on an early night but couldn't put this book down until I finished it around 3am. Like her other books, this one features fascinating characters with a plot that mimics real life in the best way. My recommendation: it's time to read every book Tammy L Grace has written."

— *Carolyn, review of Beach Haven*

"This book is a clean, simple romance with a background story very similar to the works of Debbie Macomber. If you like Macomber's books you will like this one. A holiday tale filled with dogs, holiday fun, and the joy of giving will warm your heart.

— *Avid Mystery Reader, review of A Season for Hope: A Christmas Novella*

"This book was just as enchanting as the others. Hardships with the love of a special group of friends. I recommend the series as a must read. I loved every exciting moment. A new author for me. She's fabulous."

—Maggie!, review of Pieces of Home: A Hometown Harbor Novel (Book 4)

"Tammy is an amazing author, she reminds me of Debbie Macomber… Delightful, heartwarming...just down to earth."

— Plee, review of A Promise of Home: A Hometown Harbor Novel (Book 3)

"This was an entertaining and relaxing novel. Tammy Grace has a simple yet compelling way of drawing the reader into the lives of her characters. It was a pleasure to read a story that didn't rely on theatrical tricks, unrealistic events or steamy sex scenes to fill up the pages. Her characters and plot were strong enough to hold the reader's interest."

—MrsQ125, review of Finding Home: A Hometown Harbor Novel (Book 1)

"This is a beautifully written story of loss, grief, forgiveness and healing. I believe anyone could relate to the situations and feelings represented here. This is a read that will stay with you long after you've completed the book."

—Cassidy Hop, review of Finally Home: A Hometown Harbor Novel (Book 5)

"Killer Music is a clever and well-crafted whodunit. The vivid and colorful characters shine as the author gradually reveals their hidden secrets—an absorbing page-turning read."

— Jason Deas, bestselling author of Pushed and Birdsongs

"I could not put this book down! It was so well written & a suspenseful read! This is definitely a 5-star story! I'm hoping there will be a sequel!"

—Colleen, review of Killer Music

"This is the best book yet by this author. The plot was well crafted with an unanticipated ending. I like to try to leap ahead and see if I can accurately guess the outcome. I was able to predict some of the plot but not the actual details which made reading the last several chapters quite engrossing."

—0001PW, review of Deadly Connection

Moonlight Beach
A Novel By
Tammy L. Grace

www.tammylgrace.com
Facebook: https://www.facebook.com/tammylgrace.books
Twitter: @TammyLGrace
Instagram: @authortammylgrace
Published in the United States by Lone Mountain Press, Nevada
ISBN 978-1-945591-18-1 (eBook)
ISBN 978-1-945591-19-8 (Print)
FIRST EDITION
Printed in the United States of America

ALSO BY TAMMY L. GRACE

Hometown Harbor Series

Hometown Harbor: The Beginning prequel

Finding Home

Home Blooms

A Promise of Home

Pieces of Home

Finally Home

Forever Home

Hometown Harbor Series Books 1-3

Cooper Harrington Detective Series

Killer Music

Deadly Connection

Dead Wrong

Cooper Harrington Detective Novels Books 1-3

Christmas Stories

A Season for Hope (Christmas in Silver Falls Book 1)

The Magic of the Season (Christmas in Silver Falls Book 2)

Christmas in Snow Valley

Christmas Sisters (Soul Sisters at Cedar Mountain Lodge Book 1)

Christmas Wishes (Soul Sisters at Cedar Mountain Lodge Book 3)

Glass Beach Cottage Series

Beach Haven

Writing as Casey Wilson

A Dog's Hope

A Dog's Chance

Tammy would love to connect with readers on social media and her website at www.tammylgrace.com. Remember to subscribe to her mailing list and you'll receive the fun interview she did with the dogs from her Hometown Harbor Series as an exclusive gift only available to her subscribers. **Subscribe here: https://wp.me/P9umIy-e**

Follow Tammy on Facebook and click over and follow Tammy on BookBub and major retailers by clicking the follow buttons on her pages.

Drink tea, read books, & be happy

MOONLIGHT BEACH

GLASS BEACH COTTAGE SERIES BOOK 2

TAMMY L. GRACE

LONE MOUNTAIN PRESS

1

It was three o'clock in the morning and instead of sleeping, Lily sat on the couch, staring at the television tuned to a black and white movie with the sound muted, listening to the clock tick away minutes, adding to the hours Mel had been missing. She petted her dog, Fritz, while the puppy, Bodie, burrowed into her lap. With each stroke across Fritz's golden back, she tried to calm the sense of dread that had taken residence in her chest since yesterday when Mel hadn't come home.

It had been a Wednesday like any other, until it wasn't. She and Mel had worked on cleaning the cottages and Mel took off for the library after they enjoyed an early lunch on the deck. Lily had been wracking her brain since last night, replaying their conversations and looking for any hint that Mel had intended to run away. It paid to have a friend in the Chief of Police, Jeff, who she had met when she first moved to Driftwood Bay. Lily had spent most of the evening in Jeff's office, brainstorming possibilities with him and aiding the investigation—the one that shouldn't even technically be going on since Mel was an adult. They had just celebrated her birthday two weeks ago.

Jeff's wife, Donna, who was the town librarian, first introduced Lily to the young woman. Mel had been volunteering at the library while living in the local shelter. Her father had died in action in the Middle East and then her mother had committed suicide the following year, leaving Mel to the whims of the foster care system. She had not had an easy life and when they suggested Lily could give her a stable environment and present it as an exchange for helping her with the cottages, she was reluctant. Now, after a few months, she had grown close to Mel, and was filled with worry at her disappearance.

Since Jeff was familiar with Mel and her situation, he had bent the guidelines that required a seventy-two-hour wait before the police would consider a person to be missing. Unlike most nineteen-year-olds, Mel had no cell phone and the bike Lily let her use was still locked up in the rack by the library. Donna had joined them at the police department late last night and had broken down in tears when they explained that Mel hadn't come home and her bike was still at the library. She, too, had no sense that Mel was looking to run away or leave Driftwood Bay.

Lily was convinced Mel hadn't left on her own, but there was a tiny thread of doubt that pulled at the back of her mind. Mel had been living at Glass Beach Cottage for such a short time and to say she was tight-lipped would be an understatement. Mel hadn't had an easy life and Lily didn't know her entire history, only that she had no family and had lived at the shelter in Driftwood Bay.

When Donna and Jeff had approached Lily about letting Mel stay with her and giving her a job cleaning the cottages, she had let her heart override the warning signals in her brain. She wasn't looking for drama. She'd had enough of that to last her a lifetime. But hearing the heartbreaking story of the young woman who had no family and volunteered at the library, where Donna had befriended her, led Lily to agree to the plan.

She never expected to form an attachment to the young woman with the harsh exterior. Mel was a tough cookie and having been through what she had suffered, Lily suspected that was how she had survived. Her reluctance to trust, to form relationships, to let anyone get too close, made sense. She was wary and not someone who would strike up a conversation with strangers, so if she didn't run away, how did anyone get close enough to take her?

Questions, scenarios, and possibilities swirled through Lily's mind. Her eyes stung and her head throbbed. She needed to sleep, but couldn't turn off her brain.

To complicate matters, Lily was flying to Virginia tomorrow morning. The thought of leaving without knowing where Mel was or if she was safe, sent a shudder through her. While never exuding much joy, Mel had seemed content at Glass Beach Cottage and had just revealed her first glimmer of excitement when they had discussed her classes at Driftwood Community College while at the Labor Day barbecue.

Mel's first class was set for today and Lily had little hope she would be there. Donna had worked her magic and secured a scholarship for Mel, who would be taking three classes this semester. Mel wanted to take more, but Donna convinced her to start slow and increase her load next semester, once she had a handle on a new routine. "I wonder if the idea of college spooked her and she couldn't face it?" Lily looked at Fritz as if expecting an answer. Bodie was fast asleep, cuddled in her lap.

The golden retriever answered in his own way, gazing at her with his gentle eyes and giving her hand a quick lick. Lily concentrated on taking deep breaths, comforted by the calmness of the dogs, willing her mind to quiet. She focused on approaching the situation more professionally and less personally, letting her law enforcement instincts assess the case, rather than her maternal ones.

Jeff tasked his detectives with gathering any camera footage of the area surrounding the library. Driftwood Bay was a far cry from the big city and they didn't have traffic cameras or other coverage throughout the town. Most of their cameras were dedicated to tourism and beautiful views of the coastal areas. The library had a camera on the main entrance, but not the side door that Mel always used.

Mel was obsessed with daily routines and Lily couldn't fathom her ignoring the patterns that served to stabilize her. With all the trauma Mel had endured in her short life, Lily assumed the routines comforted her and gave her a sense of control. Lily's heart ached for the young woman, and she murmured another quick prayer for her safety.

She had searched through Mel's bedroom last night and found nothing amiss. The book she had been reading was still by her bedside and her meager wardrobe hung in her closet. All her toiletries were in place in the bathroom. Nothing seemed to be missing except the clothes she wore and her backpack.

The aching band across the back of her head tightened and pain shot down into her neck. She hadn't slept a wink since trying to go to bed hours earlier. Despite her habit of securing the property, Lily had left the house unlocked, hoping Mel might return, and she didn't want her to be locked out or embarrassed to ring the bell. Lily hadn't been in a hurry to have an extra key made, since she was never away when Mel was expected at home.

She let her eyes close as she continued to pet Fritz, now asleep, his head resting next to Bodie, the puppy he had come to love like a brother. Her mind continued to churn as she willed herself to remember to call the cleaning service and ask them to handle cleaning the cottages today. She didn't know what, if any, news she might get from the police and wanted to spend all her time helping to find Mel.

When today's guests checked out, she'd be free until next week. With her trip to her mother's annual memorial in Arlington, she had made sure she wouldn't have guests for a few days. Mac, the local veterinarian Lily had been spending time with, was taking the dogs to his place and Donna had planned to have Mel stay with her and Jeff for the long weekend. There was no way Lily could miss the memorial service or a chance to visit with her son, Kevin, but a part of her didn't feel right leaving if Mel was still missing.

It was moments like these when she missed Gary's calmness and his way of approaching difficulties, his confidence assuring her that they would handle it, no matter what. Though her husband had passed more than two years before, she still longed for his strong shoulders and comforting words.

Sun filtering through the large window looking out over the backyard, woke Lily. She startled when she opened her eyes, not expecting to sleep at all and then surprised to wake up on the couch. She groaned when she moved her head from the slumped position she had slept in and tried to stretch her neck and back.

"I'm getting too old for sleeping on the couch," she muttered, as she led the dogs to the kitchen. She put grounds and water in the coffee maker, and as the coffee brewed, checked her phone for any updates from Jeff or Donna, but found nothing. There was a text from Cyndy, Mac's sister who owned a gift shop and helped Lily decorate the cottages and, in the process, they had grown quite close. Cyndy wanted Lily to know she was thinking of her and praying for Mel.

Lily poured a cup and paced around the island counter a few times as she gulped down the hot elixir, while willing the guests to wake up early and hit the road, so she could be free of them. After, she had a quick shower, then headed downstairs with the dogs, taking little care to be quiet as they tromped past the cottages and hit the trail that led to the beach. She didn't want to deprive the dogs of their morning routine, and the way she was feeling, she needed a bit of Vitamin Sea, as some of her guests like to refer to it, to ease her worries.

Fritz and Bodie ran along the edge of the water, playing and chasing each other, while she basked in the view that never failed to soothe her. The gentle lap of the water, the serenity of the horizon meeting the sea, the cool sand on her feet, and the sunlight dancing on the water served to calm her mind as she soaked in the tranquility and breathed the salty air.

She let the boys romp a bit more, each of them tugging on bits of driftwood and sticks they found, before signaling them it was time to go. They cocked their heads and gave her confused looks. They hadn't had their usual amount of beach time, but still hurried to follow Lily.

She let them frolic in the yard while she fixed their breakfast, guiltily hoping their activity would prod her guests out of bed. She hollered for her furry friends to come upstairs and they bounded to the deck. Feeling jittery from coffee and nerves, she nursed a cup of tea. Food was out of the question.

As she savored the view, she saw a bit of action down at the cottages. She checked her phone, anxious for an update on Mel, but found no new messages. While she waited for the guests to depart, she concentrated on packing her suitcase for Friday morning.

Fritz and Bodie watched as she selected clothes, with Fritz's eyes full of wariness. He was smart enough to understand the appearance of her suitcase was oftentimes a precursor to her leaving. "I won't be gone long, Fritzie." She petted his head to reassure him. Mac will take good care of you and Bodie and you'll get to play with Sherlock." Fritz's eyes lifted at the sound of the name of Mac's faithful golden retriever, who had become his best friend.

Lily forced herself to concentrate on her packing, knowing

how pointless it was to worry about where Mel was and what could be happening to her. She finished the chore and wheeled her suitcase to the entryway, ready for tomorrow morning's early trip.

Downstairs she found the guests in the process of loading their luggage and getting ready to leave. She wished them safe travels and breathed a sigh of relief when the last couple's tail-lights disappeared. After herding the dogs into their enclosure, she hurried upstairs, gathered her things, and headed to town to find out what the police had learned about Mel.

But instead of turning at the intersection for the police station, she drove past it. Jeff would have called her if there was news. She'd do a little sleuthing on her own.

2

Lily continued down the road a couple of miles and turned into a parking lot. She eyed the nondescript building that served as the local homeless shelter, on the edge of a small industrial area and separated from the nearest residential area by a wide swath of forested acreage.

She knew the police had probably already visited the shelter where Mel had stayed, but wanted to see it for herself. She made her way to the office. Behind the front desk, a young woman, with strands of once vibrant green lingering in her hair, lifted her eyes, giving Lily an uninterested glance.

Lily smiled at the apathetic receptionist. "Hi, I'm new in town and was wondering about volunteer opportunities here." Organizations like this one protected their clients and might not share much information if she came right out and asked about Mel. Without changing her expression, the woman picked up the phone and escorted Lily to a small office tucked into a corner, with a nameplate labeling it the director's office. Lily took in the papers and folders covering a desk and small table, and plastic bins stacked on two worn chairs in front of the desk.

A woman with dark circles under her eyes and her hair held

back from her face in a messy ponytail smiled at Lily and extended her hand. "I'm Carly Morgan. You'll have to excuse the mess. I'm in the midst of our annual fundraiser and it's a busy time." She leaned her head toward the front office and added, "Amber said you're interested in volunteering?"

Lily nodded. "I've got some time on my hands and thought I'd make myself useful. I toured the library and wanted to do the same here before I make a decision on what would be the best fit."

Carly blew out a breath that ruffled her bangs. "We run on a shoestring budget around here, so help is always welcome. We have beds for twenty-four people, do a meal service in cooperation with some other charities, and try to get these folks some help and set up to support themselves. Most of them can only stay here ninety days, so it's a bit of a revolving door."

Carly's desk phone rang and she held up a finger to Lily as she plucked the receiver from the cradle. Lily turned her attention to the office and examined an evacuation map posted by the doorway. She studied the drawing noting a large common room, the kitchen, some classrooms, and the dormitory areas, separated for males and females, including shower and bathroom facilities.

Carly hung up the phone and said, "I'll give you the nickel tour and explain a bit as we move through the building." She motioned Lily to follow her and led her down the hallway toward the common room.

Lily concentrated on summing up the clients she saw as they traversed the hallway and nodded at Carly with an occasional word of understanding. Carly rambled on about grant funding and how they were always struggling to find money to keep the place going. Their quest for funding and locating permanent housing for their clients were her main worries.

A lecture was taking place in one of the classrooms. Lily scanned the residents seated at tables and noted they were all elderly. "One of the young women who volunteered at the library mentioned the shelter," said Lily.

Carly nodded. "That had to be Mel. She's a bookworm and volunteers there. Thankfully, she was able to find a permanent housing solution and a job, from what I understand. I was so glad for that. This is no place for a nice young woman like her." Carly's shoulders sagged. "Now, if only there was hope for Sally. She's another young woman on her own that needs more help than we can offer." Carly moved her eyes to the side and Lily saw a young woman walking toward them, a spiky shock of dark hair atop her pale face.

"Hey, Sally. How are you today?" Carly asked.

The girl shrugged her shoulders and rolled her eyes. "Same as I always am. I'll never be like your little pet, Mel." Sally sneered at the director.

That tingle, deep in her gut that she had learned years ago not to ignore, drew Lily to take note of Sally.

Carly's eyes narrowed. "I hope you're on your way outside to work on those weeds and get those flowers in the ground. You also need to store your cellphone in the office. Remember, you lost your privilege to use it."

She rolled her eyes. "You need to chill. I'll get it done." Sally smirked as she continued down the hall. "I heard Mel ran away. So, maybe she's not such a good girl after all."

Lily's eyes stayed glued to the back of the brassy young woman. The only way Sally would know about Mel being gone was if she had been in contact with her recently. Carly let out a frustrated sigh, and they kept walking. "Some days are harder than others. She's on thin ice for violating curfew again. Sally is on the verge of a forced transfer to Seattle. She needs services we just don't have here in Driftwood Bay."

They continued to the common room where a few people were watching television and one was on a computer, then back to the front office, where Lily looked at her watch. "Oh, my, I need to get moving. Thanks so much for the tour and I'll be in touch once I make a decision on volunteering."

Carly thanked her for coming, her tired eyes displaying her disappointment in not engaging Lily as a volunteer on the spot. Lily hurried outside, scanning the area for Sally. She spotted her next to a fence, leaning against a tree.

Lily made her way to her, coughing at the stench of cigarette smoke surrounding the young woman. "You mentioned Mel. She's the one who told me about volunteer opportunities here. I met her at the library. Do you still see Mel often?"

Sally scoffed. "Like I would hang out with her? We don't exactly run in the same circles."

Lily nodded while taking note of the bulge of her cell phone in her pocket. "Ah, well, you mentioned she had run away, so it seems like you know quite a bit about her."

Sally's forehead creased as she glared at Lily. "I just heard about it. What's it to you, anyway?"

"She doesn't seem like the type to run away. She's always at the library and enjoys volunteering there. Who told you she had run away?"

Carly turned and picked up the hoe that was resting against the tree. She shrugged as she buried it into the soil. "I can't remember exactly. I need to get back to this or Ms. Carly will have a meltdown."

Lily nodded. "Have a good day, Sally." She met the young woman's harsh eyes and held them, until Sally looked away and back at the ground.

Lily strolled back to her car, giving Sally a smile and a wave as she pulled onto the street. Everything about Sally screamed she was lying and Lily was certain she knew more about Mel than she was saying. She sped through the few miles to downtown and parked in front of the police station.

One thing Lily knew, after what she saw, she didn't want to volunteer there and wasn't surprised that they had a hard time finding volunteers. Between the apathetic receptionist and the lack of organization, she wanted nothing to do with the place and imagined any prospects would feel the same way.

She found Jeff in his office, glued to his computer screen. Lily raised her brows and slid into the chair in front of his desk. "Any luck?"

He frowned. "Not yet. We're checking hospitals every shift." He didn't mention morgues, but Lily knew from all her years as a police officer that they would also be checking them.

"I may have something. A young woman at the shelter named Sally. I was just there and she has a chip on her shoulder when it comes to Mel. I'm certain she knows more than she's saying. Sally knew Mel had run away and clammed up when I asked her about it. She also has a cell phone, which was supposed to be off limits and has a street-wise attitude. The director mentioned she needs more services than they can offer here and she violated curfew. I think she's not only homeless, but possibly involved with something more serious."

Jeff grinned. "I take it you just happened by the shelter?"

She shrugged. "I'm always looking for opportunities to volunteer."

He scribbled on his notepad. "I'll look into it straightaway."

"I hate leaving with her missing, but I can't miss this trip." Lily's heart ached for Mel. The last thing she needed was another person in her life abandoning her.

"I told you, Donna and I will take good care of Mel while you're gone. We were going to anyway." He sighed and leaned back in his chair. "This just adds an extra level of concern."

Lily sighed and shook her head. "She seemed to be doing so well. I'm still not convinced she ran away. She's excited about school and I didn't notice her being upset. There's something we're missing."

"I promise to keep in touch and update you with any news. The minute we find her, I'll text you no matter what time it is."

Jeff's intercom buzzed and he glanced at the telephone on his desk. "I've got to take this. You gonna be okay?"

Lily nodded. "Yep. I have to leave for the airport at four in the morning. I'll text you when I land, but will be in the air until early afternoon your time."

"Got it," he said, picking up the phone.

Lily left the office with a heavy heart. With her mind focused on Mel, she drove the few blocks to the library and texted Donna to see if she could meet for a few minutes at the café. Lily didn't want to draw attention to Mel's absence or have anyone she worked with overhear their conversation.

Lily ordered each of them a bowl of soup and a pot of tea and soon after it arrived, Donna came through the door. She looked as tired as Lily felt, but her brows arched with curiosity. Lily shook her head. "I just left Jeff's office and there's still no word." She motioned Donna to help herself to lunch.

"Ah, thanks for this. I haven't felt like eating anything, but that soup looks delicious."

Lily nodded. "Same with me. I wanted to give you a key to the house, just in case Mel needs to get back in to get her things." Tears stung her eyes as she fumbled for the extra key in the pocket of her purse. "I've been meaning to give it to Mel and keep forgetting."

Donna nodded. "Jeff's doing all he can. I'm sure they'll find her soon."

"I'll email you my itinerary, just in case you need it. I should have my cell phone with me at all times, but that way you'll have my hotel and flight information. I'll be home Tuesday afternoon."

They finished their lunch, with only a few words of conversation. Lily didn't have the energy to focus on small talk and Donna was in a rush to get back to work. Outside, Donna hugged Lily goodbye. "Try to enjoy your time with your son. I know it's impossible not to worry about Mel, but trust we'll do everything we can."

Lily squeezed Donna's hand and nodded. "I trust you. If you find her, make sure she knows I had to go for my mom's memorial. I don't want her to think I deserted her."

Donna smiled. "I will. She'll understand. Don't worry."

Despite the exhaustion from worrying and very little sleep, Lily tossed and turned all night. Mac had brought takeout over for dinner and spent a few hours visiting, before taking the dogs back to his house. It was the first night since she'd moved to Driftwood Bay that she didn't have the comfort of her faithful companion, Fritz. He and Bodie were no doubt having a fun time on their adventure at Mac's house, with Sherlock and Mac's other animals.

She finally fell asleep close to midnight and when the shuttle driver picked her up at four o'clock, she was already exhausted and the day hadn't even begun. The airport was teeming with people for early morning flights. While she waited in endless lines, she scanned faces in the crowd, hoping to find Mel.

Without money or a cell phone, Lily couldn't imagine Mel would be at the airport with a ticket, but stranger things had happened. She couldn't shake the possibility of human trafficking, which sent a chill through her. She scanned every face that walked by her and studied the posture and gait of anyone close to Mel's age. She knew traffickers often disguised women as men, so scrutinized everyone. It gave her something to do while she stood in line waiting to make her way to her gate.

The whole process, while irritating and inefficient, was uneventful and soon she was seated in her cramped window seat, inserting her earbuds, hoping to drown out the noise of the plane and her fellow passengers and drift off to sleep for the next five hours. She texted Kevin to let him know she was on the plane and shut off her phone.

As the plane climbed higher into the clouds, she shut her eyes. The stress of the last few days caught up with her and before they reached their cruising altitude, she was fast asleep.

3

Kevin's flight had already landed and Lily found him at the baggage terminal waiting for her. As she hugged him, tears stung her eyes. "It's so good to see you. I've missed you."

He squeezed her tight before releasing his grip. "I've missed you too, Mom." He smiled and grabbed her bag for her. "I'm starving, shall we grab something to eat?"

Lily had chosen a hotel with a shuttle, so they took the free ride and checked in before venturing out for a late lunch. She texted Donna and Jeff to let them know she had landed. Over lunch, Lily shared Mel's disappearance with Kevin.

His forehead creased and his face filled with concern as she expressed her worry about Mel. "I'm sorry, Mom. Do you think they'll find her?"

She shrugged. "I hope so. I truly don't think she ran away. I'm worried, but Jeff is doing everything possible and he'll call the moment he knows anything." She gripped his shoulder and added, "I want to hear all about you and school." She pushed Mel's situation to the back of her mind, intent on being present for her son and enjoying their time together.

She loved listening to the excitement in his voice and seeing him smile when he told her about his classes that had just begun last week. The exuberance of youth and his enthusiasm was contagious. He liked most of his professors, save for one, who Kevin thought was full of himself. "I've got my flight home for Thanksgiving and wanted to book my tickets for Christmas. I'm off for almost an entire month."

"That's terrific. Just use my credit card and let me know when you're arriving and I'll put it on my calendar. I've already got your Thanksgiving trip down. That will be here before we know it. Cyndy has invited us to her house, so you won't have to contend with my cooking. She's an excellent cook." Lily laughed, but saw the relief in her son's eyes.

"I miss Fritz, too. It'll be great to be there and spend time with him and meet Bodie."

They finished their meal, walked a few blocks, where she darted into a market and picked up a bundle of white roses. They made their way to the Metro station and took the quick trip to Arlington Cemetery. It was one of Lily's favorite places to visit and was always at the top of her list. Although somber and moving, it was a peaceful venue, over six hundred acres, always beautifully manicured, and an essential reminder of the enormous sacrifices made by the men and women who had paid the ultimate price for freedom.

They took a shuttle to the Tomb of the Unknown Soldier and watched the military guard as he marched back and forth in front of it. Lily ran a finger under her sunglasses and swallowed the lump in her throat. This place never failed to evoke emotion, but today she found it especially hard to hold back tears as she witnessed the Changing of the Guard.

She looked out at the vast green lawns and the orderly rows of white gravestones as far as she could see. They lingered for a few minutes and then boarded the shuttle that took them through the winding roadways to Section Sixty-four and the Pentagon Group Burial Marker.

The imposing granite structure had been placed to pay tribute to all those lost on Flight 77 and at the Pentagon. Despite Arlington always being a place Lily visited, now it held an even more special significance. This was where part of her mother was.

Some of her remains, mingled with the others who had perished from the plane and the Pentagon were laid to rest here. Lily and Kevin approached the large octagon shaped monument. She went to the panel she had visited many times before and let her fingers trace over the letters. It was always surreal to see her name—Barbara S. Todd, with the diamond next to her name indicating she had been a passenger on the plane. Her actual gravestone was in Davidson, North Carolina, along with Lily's dad. They had purchased plots years ago and wanted to be buried in a beautiful cemetery there.

Lily closed her eyes as those old memories came into focus. The majority of her mother's remains had been interred in North Carolina, where her dad visited each week until just a few short months later, when Lily undertook the grim task of having the mason add the date of death to Robert Todd's headstone. She didn't think she would survive. She wouldn't have, without Gary.

She placed the roses near the base, amid the plants surrounding the monument. Kevin ran his fingers over his grandma's name and then took his mother's hand. "I know I was so little when it happened, but I have memories of her playing with me. I still miss her. And Grandpa."

Lily nodded, unsure of her voice and whispered. "Me too."

Kevin turned to his mother. "Sometimes, I'm not sure if my memories are real or just from all the stories you've told me about them. It's fuzzy, sort of."

"You weren't even two yet, so I would imagine some of your

memories are from photos and the stories we have told you." She put her arm around his shoulder. "It doesn't matter. She and Grandpa loved you more than anything. They were so excited to have their first grandchild and they would be so proud of the young man you are today." Tears rolled down her cheeks. "I hate that they missed out on you growing up."

They stood together for a few minutes, the breeze rustling through the trees and wicking away the sweat at the back of Lily's neck. She admired the view from the raised area, looking across to the massive Pentagon. The place where her mother had endured the last few moments of life. She couldn't help but think of the terror she must have felt, knowing she was going to die. Despite all the years that had passed, the thought of her mother suffering, shook Lily to the core.

She blamed, and always would, the terrorists for not only her mother's death, but for killing her father. The stress of it had been too much for him. She knew time had a way of easing the pain and grief and that some survivors found solace in forgiving those that had engineered the attacks, but she wasn't one of them. The burning hatred she still felt for those men, and all who had helped them, would never leave her. It wouldn't die until she did.

That same loathing filled her when she thought about the scum, along with his girlfriend, who had killed Gary. Evil criminals had been the ones responsible for taking three of the people she loved most from her. Although law enforcement had been her life's work and a true calling, she was happy to be away from it. Working as she had, in the Virginia State Capitol, she didn't encounter many street criminals, but after Gary was killed, her tolerance for lawbreakers had dwindled. The constant reminders of Gary had been unbearable, but she felt herself becoming more and more cynical.

She needed to step away from seeing the worst of humankind. At the time she retired and chose to move, she knew it felt right, but now, having been absent from the only career she had known, she realized it was not only about escaping her memories, but saving herself. Despite still missing Gary and their life together, living in Driftwood Bay as an innkeeper allowed her to engage with people in a pleasant environment without the volatility of the criminal element always present in their daily duties and discussions.

She would always mourn the unexpected and tragic loss of her mother and would return here every September to honor her and all the others. Now, at least, she took some comfort knowing her parents were together, under a beautiful tree, overlooking the quaint town they had chosen to make their home, where they had worked for the local school district. They had loved Davidson and had moved there in preparation for their retirement years. Sadly, neither of them was able to enjoy those golden years they had planned.

Tears clouded her view and she did nothing to stop their escape as they leaked from under her sunglasses. Another year here without Gary and she felt just as weak as she had last year. He had been her strength and had taken care of the logistics related to their trip each year. All she had to do was hang onto his arm and she could get through anything. Now, she didn't have him.

She took a long breath and glanced at her handsome son, whose profile reminded her of his dad. Gary would be so proud of him. She was so thankful Kevin was with her today. It was almost like having Gary next to her. Her heart swelled, knowing part of Gary would forever live on in their beloved son.

She squeezed Kevin's hand and led the way toward the shuttle. She rested against the back of the seat and let the breeze dry her cheeks as they made their way to the exit.

Anguish and exhaustion settled over her. This was just the beginning. She had to get through the actual memorial. Tired, she begged off Kevin's suggestion of dinner and opted for a nap and room service. She checked her phone once more, hoping for news of Mel, but seeing none, shut her eyes and willed herself to think of her mom happy, enjoying her garden, instead of the terror Lily imagined as her plane fell from the sky, destined to crash.

4

Thankful to be on the ground in Seattle, but anxious to get inside the terminal, Lily stood at her window seat, hunched forward under the low ceiling of the cramped plane, as she waited her turn to get off the long flight from Washington, D.C. She dug into the pocket of her purse to turn on her cell phone.

After it powered on, she heard the chime of a text alert. She gasped when she read the screen, drawing inquisitive looks from everyone around her. It was from Jeff. He had found Mel and she was safe. He and Donna would keep her at their house and would fill her in on the whole story when she arrived back in Driftwood Bay.

The tension she had been holding in her shoulders eased as relief flooded through her. Tears stung her eyes when she thought of the awful outcome she had been expecting. Her finger hovered over the green button next to Jeff's name, but the line started moving and she needed to get to the terminal. She didn't want to miss her shuttle and thought it best to call him when she was in a less crowded place.

Along with being anxious to hear about Mel, she was

emotionally drained after the memorial and saying goodbye to Kevin at the airport. Not wanting to leave him, she had gripped him in a long and tight hug. The hassle of travel was always physically exhausting and she wasn't looking forward to following the crowd to baggage claim and taking the shuttle back to Driftwood Bay. Despite it being mid-afternoon in Seattle, she was feeling the three-hour difference and was thankful she wouldn't have to drive and could doze on the way home.

As she waited for the people in the rows in front of her, who seemed to be moving at a glacial pace, she reflected on the weekend. The ceremony, as always, was somber and thoughtful. She had listened as they read the names of all 184 people who perished and rang a bell for each one. The choir did a beautiful job singing the national anthem and "God Bless America" and Lily had endured yet another rendition of "Taps" from the military band.

She and Kevin had spent the weekend playing tourist, visiting memorials and museums, and trying to make a pleasant visit out of the trip. They had spent last night at the Pentagon Memorial, where there was a small reception for the family members of those lost. The view of the benches that she always thought resembled wings, with the pools of water beneath them, glowing with a golden light at night, never failed to bring tears to her eyes. She and Gary had visited the memorial in late spring several times, and she loved it when all the crepe myrtle trees that grew among the memorial benches were heavy with beautiful white blossoms. Her mom would have appreciated them. Oh, how she wished her mom was still here. Lily could have used her over these last few years.

Lily's sister, Wendy, had promised to be there this year, but as usual, something more pressing or exciting came up and Wendy didn't show. Lily followed Wendy on social media and her sister's posts advertised a lavish lifestyle and a self-absorbed woman. She had become accustomed to Wendy's lack of dependability and her thoughtless and selfish attitude. It no longer surprised her, only filled her heart with sadness. Since the death of her parents, Lily had conditioned herself not to expect much from Wendy.

As she trudged behind the other passengers making their way to baggage claim, she fought back the sting of tears. Being in Virginia had churned up old memories, along with regrets and guilt. The memorial always whipped up feelings of loss and sorrow, not just of her mom, but her dad and now, Gary.

Although she didn't make a trip to her old stomping grounds in Richmond, instead staying in Arlington, Gary had weighed on her mind. She and Kevin had visited the Law Enforcement Memorial, leaving a flower for Gary. They ate out, went to a movie, and enjoyed a walk through Rock Creek Park and on the mall. They did all the things Gary always enjoyed, but without him there, it wasn't the same.

Although Kevin seemed happy and was doing well in school, her heart had hurt when she said goodbye and realized again what she had left behind when she made the decision to move all the way across the country to the coast of Washington. She tried not to beat herself up about it, but a mother's sense of responsibility to her child was strong. When she shifted her thought patterns in a logical direction, she knew it made little sense to stay in Richmond, two hours away from Kevin's college, just so she could be closer to him, but those heartstrings tugged at her.

She was adjusting to her new life and running her late uncle's Glass Beach Cottage property. It just hurt to say goodbye and realize how alone she was. Kevin was her only family that mattered. She swallowed against the lump in her throat as she told herself how quickly the days would pass until Thanksgiving, when Kevin would visit.

She looked up at the digital board with her flight number and the baggage claim information. As she made her way to it, she gazed over the crowd, watching loved ones greeting passengers with hugs. She smiled at a young family reunited with what anyone could see were loving parents and grandparents and her throat tightened. She took a deep breath and kept walking, feeling her solitary vulnerability.

She turned her head, saw a man smiling at her and did a double-take. "Mac?" She stopped in her tracks, looking at him, standing near the carousel, a huge grin on his face.

"Surprise," he said, reaching for her hand. "I thought you could use a chauffeur to Driftwood Bay."

A tingle of warmth traveled from Mac's hand all the way to Lily's toes. His kindness and thoughtfulness lifted her spirits and reminded her she had found more than just a new vocation in Driftwood Bay. She and Mac had been spending more and more time together, sharing their love of golden retrievers, and enjoying each other's company over the summer months.

Lily let out a long breath and her shoulders relaxed. "You have no idea how happy I am to see you. I was wading in the pool of self-pity as I came through the airport." She tightened her grip on his hand. "I was feeling quite lonely."

Bags started filling the carousel and she darted her eyes to the commotion to watch for her black bag in a sea of black bags. "You point it out and I'll snag it for you," said Mac.

"It's got a bright pink ribbon tied to the handle to make it easier to see." She kept an eye on the bags toppling from the dark hole and down the chute. "How are the boys?"

"They did great. Sherlock loved having them at the house to keep him company. All three of them are at your place, awaiting your return."

"I've missed them." She kept her eyes focused on the action, stopping short of telling him she had missed him, too. "Have you seen Mel?"

"Not yet. Jeff gave me the rundown. That's the other reason I thought it would be nice to come and meet you. I knew you'd be concerned about her." He moved a step closer to the carousel. "I'm sure she's anxious to get back to your place and the routine. When you're both settled in, we'll plan dinner at my house. She can visit the llamas and let the dogs run free."

She pointed at a bag on the stainless-steel chute. "There it is."

Mac muscled his way to the edge of the throng of passengers and snagged the bag as soon as it thumped onto the carousel. He wheeled it over and linked his arm in Lily's, leading the way to the parking garage.

As they left the airport, Mac explained Mel had been found in a rough neighborhood in South Park, south of Seattle, about two hours from Driftwood Bay. "Jeff said you were right about Sally being involved. Seems she remembered Mel talking about trying to find her aunt, her mom's sister, who used to live in Oak Harbor. Sally convinced Mel she had located her and then tricked her into going with her as Mel was leaving the library. Sally and her two creepy friends, both of whom have been arrested and are known drug dealers, picked up Mel and the two men locked her in a storage unit, using her to deliver drugs for them."

Lily gasped and brought her hand to her mouth. "Is that all they did to her?" She held her breath and closed her eyes.

Mac placed a reassuring hand on her arm. "There were no signs of any type of abuse. She was dirty, hungry, and tired from living in such horrid conditions for the last week, but unharmed. She was checked over in Seattle and Jeff drove over and picked her up himself, along with Donna."

Lily nodded. "That's a relief, but this is the last thing that poor girl needed. It makes me want to go and knock the living daylights out of Sally. I knew she was involved."

As they inched along I-5, snarled with afternoon traffic, Mac explained everything he knew about Mel's disappearance. "It took her a few days to get her bearings and Jeff said her quick thinking and calmness helped get her rescued. The two men would come and let her out of the shed, giving her a backpack and telling her where to go to meet up with buyers. It was usually parks and other public places. They threatened her and told her they would be watching her and she had to complete their jobs to see her aunt."

Lily's jaw tightened. "Sick bastards."

Mac continued and explained Mel noticed a library branch on one of her walks and the idea of using the book drop to get help formed. She made note of the streets and the name of the storage shed business. The park was the one common place she always made a delivery. She had no paper or pen, so she scoured the sidewalks and streets for anything she could use and collected an old flyer and discarded pen on one of her outings. The men collected the backpack each day, so she had no place to hide the contraband.

"She elected to hide the items in a planter in the park and at her first opportunity, when she had to wait near the women's restroom, which provided a moment of privacy, she wrote down that she had been abducted and provided the business name and the cross streets, along with her name and asked them to contact Donna at the Driftwood Bay Library. That day, on her way back to the storage shed she timed her steps so that she passed behind a group of people walking by the book drop at the library and slipped the note in the box."

Mac changed lanes and increased his speed as the traffic became lighter. "It took until the next morning when the librarian found the note. She immediately contacted Donna and that set things in motion with Jeff contacting the Seattle Police."

"She's one smart girl. I'm just relieved she wasn't physically harmed. They could have easily killed her." Lily shook her head and sighed.

"From what Jeff said, Mel was quiet and cooperative with them, playing along with the idea that they would take her to her aunt, but having figured out the moment they locked her in the shed, that wasn't going to happen. She was just buying time until she could figure a way out."

Lily jolted from the seat and dug into her purse. "I forgot to text Kevin." She tapped out a message to let him know she had landed and that she would share more details about Mel later.

She smiled at his response, telling her he loved her that he couldn't wait to see her again in November.

"I'm so relieved Mel is back. Thank you for coming to get me and for filling me in. The ride home will give me time to come to terms with it. I'm concerned for Mel and what this will do to her."

He reached for her hand and squeezed it. "Just be there for her. We know she's tough. She'll heal from this. Jeff and Donna said to take your time and collect her later tonight after you've had a chance to get settled."

Lily leaned her head back against the headrest and closed her eyes as she listened to happier stories of the vet clinic and her dogs. Frazzled from the emotions of the last week, his calm voice soothed her, as did the weight of his hand against hers.

5

When the car stopped, Lily woke. It took her a few moments to get her bearings. She smiled when she saw Mac had parked in front of Noni's. He grinned as he opened the door. "I called in an order to pick up, so you wouldn't have to worry about dinner."

Realizing how lucky she was to have found such a thoughtful friend, she watched him as he disappeared inside the building. She had missed Mac while she had been away. They had texted with each other a few times and she had considered telling Kevin she had been spending time with Mac, but never found the right moment. She'd have to do it before Thanksgiving, so he wouldn't be surprised.

Truth was, she wasn't sure how to describe their relationship. Friendship, sure, but it felt like it was shifting into something more significant. She enjoyed being with him and despite only knowing him for the last few months, felt as if she had known him forever. Being with him was such a comfort and he made her feel not so alone.

A few minutes later, he returned with a large bag he placed in the backseat. The aroma drifting from it, made Lily's stomach growl. She had been too anxious for breakfast before the flight, opting for only a cup of tea, and until now, had forgotten she hadn't eaten since dinner last night.

He parked in her driveway and sent her inside, offering to bring in her luggage and their takeout, so she could greet the dogs. She hurried to the door, anxious to see Fritz and Bodie.

Mac had left them in the yard, where they had access to the downstairs via the doggy door, but when she stepped into the kitchen, she saw all three of the happy faced goldens staring at her from the deck. Their tails swept from side to side, the arcs picking up speed as she moved to unlock the door. Fritz and Bodie were a bundle of wiggles as they dove into her arms and even Sherlock joined in the fun, pushing his nose under her arm, not to be left out of the furry group hug.

By the time Mac put her suitcase in her bedroom and came into the kitchen with the bag from Noni's, Lily was still sitting on the floor, letting the three dogs maul her with snuggles and licks.

She smiled up at him. "I've missed these silly guys. It's great to be home."

He chuckled as he removed the containers from the bag and retrieved plates from the cabinet. "It would seem the feeling is mutual. I know I'm glad to have you back here. Like Sherlock, I missed you this last week."

He offered her his hand and she disengaged herself from the heap of golden canines, who knew more of her secrets than any of her human friends. She went to the pantry and poured kibble into their bowls. After she added a topper she knew they loved to each of the bowls, she motioned the dogs to their dinner, while she slid into a chair at the counter, savoring the delicious aroma of tomato sauce and garlic from her own plate.

As she ate the tender chicken parmesan and nibbled at the pillows of cheese ravioli drizzled with a garlic and butter sauce, she relaxed. Every bite was delicious and knowing Mel was safe, she was able to enjoy the meal, chatting with Mac while the dogs lounged across the floor after finishing their dinner.

She reached for more garlic bread. "I hope Mel is able to work through what happened and focus on her coursework. She seemed so excited about it."

Mac nodded as he finished his last bite. "The poor kid. She seemed like she was starting to settle in. I'm curious what Jeff found out after talking with the police in Seattle."

Lily's cell phone chimed and her brows lifted when she saw the screen. "It's Jeff. He wants to know if he can stop by." She hurried to wipe her hands on a napkin and tapped in a reply.

A few minutes later, her phone alerted her to Jeff's arrival, picked up by one of her security cameras. She went to the door and led him into the kitchen. He took her up on the offer of a glass of iced tea and took a chair next to Mac.

"Mel is finally sleeping, so I thought it would be a good time to fill you in on what happened."

Lily placed his glass in front of him and nodded. "Mac told me about Sally's involvement and the two men, who are now in custody, along with how Mel managed to get help. She's a smart one."

"That she is. Sally has also been arrested. She was on thin ice as it was with her curfew violations at the shelter and was on probation. She tested positive for drug use, so she's going back to jail."

Jeff went on to explain the two men who abducted Mel were low level street dealers, who will most likely turn on their boss and the police are hoping to work their way up the chain and find out more about the people at the top of the drug business. "Mel was embarrassed and upset that she had fallen for the story about her aunt. They took advantage of her desire to connect with family and used that to entice her."

Lily's eyes narrowed. "That was all Sally's doing. I'm sure that while Mel was at the shelter, she confided in her or said things that helped Sally use it against her and conspire with her scummy friends. Have you looked into the aunt and tried to find her?"

Jeff's face fell. "I spent the afternoon doing just that. Mel told me social services could never find her and she didn't have any information about her that we could use. No birthdate or address, just the vague location of Oak Harbor."

"From the look on your face, I'd say you found her and the news isn't good." Lily ran her fingers over the handle of her fork as she waited for Jeff to share the story.

"I'm afraid you're right. It took some doing, but I was able to work through the system and databases and confirmed late this afternoon that her aunt died two years ago. She was living in Oregon at the time and it was ruled an accidental overdose, as it seems she was addicted to opioids."

Mac blew out his breath and hung his head. Lily leaned back in her chair and slammed her fist on the counter. "The hits just keep on coming for her, don't they?"

"I'll tell her tomorrow, after she's had a good night's rest," said Jeff. She was exhausted, but Donna managed to get some food into her after Mel had a shower, so we thought it best to let her sleep. We'll bring her over in the morning. Donna talked to the people at the college and picked up her assignments, explaining she had a family emergency and they were very understanding."

"I'm going to call that doctor my friend recommended and see if I can convince Mel to go. She needs someone to talk to, a professional."

Jeff signaled his agreement as he finished his tea. "We can get her free help through the victims of crime funding. I can put her in touch with an advocate. The young men involved were on probation, so they'll be going to jail and the police in Seattle are trying to get them to give up who they're working for. The charges for abducting Mel will be part of that package that the prosecutor will negotiate. If it goes to court, it won't be until next year."

Lily nodded her understanding and retrieved the pitcher of tea to refill Jeff's glass. "I'll talk to Mel and suggest she meet with the advocate. She's a stubborn one, so I'm not sure she'll do it. Maybe if Donna works on her a bit, between the two of us we can convince her?"

He took an Italian wedding cookie from the container Mac passed to him. "Speaking of Donna, we were thinking it might be best if we can figure out some transportation for Mel to and from the library and also school, so she's not on her own."

"Good idea. I'm sure she'll feel vulnerable and I know I'd feel better if she wasn't out by herself on her bike," said Lily. "All three of her classes are on Thursday, so that will make things less complicated. I think she needs a cell phone. I'm going to get her one and add her to my plan. I'll get on that tomorrow. I've got guests arriving Thursday and if Mel feels up to going to her classes, that would be her first day." Mac's cookies looked so good, she plucked one for herself.

Jeff stood and said, "I better get back."

Lily walked him to the door. "Thanks for everything, Jeff. I'm so glad you were able to bring her back and I'll do everything I can to help her through this. Whatever we have to do to make sure she feels safe, I'll make it work." The dogs had followed her and she shooed them back into the kitchen, where Mac was clearing their dishes.

He turned from the sink, wiping his hands on a towel. "Dishes are done and leftovers are in the fridge."

She smiled and reached for his hand. "Thank you, again. For the ride, for dinner, for everything."

He squeezed her hand. "You need some rest. Sherlock and I are going to get home and if Mel is up to it, let's plan something at my house this weekend. Maybe Sunday?"

"That sounds great. I'll keep you posted." She held his eyes for a moment longer than usual.

He inched closer and brushed his lips against hers. "I'm so glad you're home." He squeezed her hand. "I'll see myself out. You get some rest."

That whisper of a kiss conveyed so much. It was the only time she had kissed another man since marrying Gary. Her feelings for Mac had deepened and the kiss made it clear he shared those same feelings. Part of her craved that closeness and wanted to melt into him, just let him hold her. That part that longed for him fought against the guilt that plagued her, thinking she was betraying Gary. She never imagined finding someone special again, yet here she was. She felt so conflicted and was going to have to figure out what to do, but right now she was too tired. She just knew having him in her life made her happier.

Lily woke early and wasn't sure if she was still adjusting to the time change or if the anticipation of seeing and talking to Mel was the cause. Regardless, she typed an email to Kevin, explaining Mel's ordeal and then unpacked the suitcase she had been too tired to tackle last night and tossed in a load of laundry. While her coffee brewed, she took the dogs down to the beach, ready to get back to their morning routine.

Their romping and wagging along the trail made it clear they were thrilled at the idea of heading to the beach. She sat on her favorite log and let the two run into the water along the shore. Like past mornings, she felt at peace watching the brilliant golden light rise above the water. The first rays of the day shimmered across the water, dancing as the gentle waves rolled toward her, delivering the hope and promise of a new day. A new beginning. A new chance.

Sunrise at the beach was her special time. Along with the tranquility and peace the morning view provided, she sensed Gary's calming presence. Like a comforting arm around her shoulders, she savored her mornings. The gentle breeze, the cool, coarse sand, and the soft sound of the water lapping along the shore reassured her.

When she had first arrived in Driftwood Bay and made the trek each morning, she could have sworn Gary was sitting next to her. There were times she felt his hand in hers, the warmth of his strong shoulder next to her, and smelled his woodsy scent mixed with citrus shampoo. The sensations defied logic and made no sense, but she clung to them. They brought her such comfort she didn't care that it seemed crazy.

She had lived for each morning since that first visit. It was like getting to spend secret time with Gary. Logically she knew it was impossible, but she chose to feel only with her heart and let the phenomenon she couldn't explain comfort her.

But since that evening she had spent at Mac's watching the sun sink into the water from the bluff, when she had heard Gary's voice in the rustle of the breeze and listened as he bid her farewell, the sensations were fleeting and many mornings absent altogether. She longed for him, with her eyes closed and her mind open, searching for the slightest of signs that he was there—but as much as she tried, she hadn't felt any signs of his physical presence since that night.

Instead, she sensed the calmness and protection he always provided. While the feel of his body next to hers was no longer there, she remained alert for the tiny signs she believed he sent her. The glimmer of light that flashed across the water, the cool breeze that ruffled her hair, the one star that twinkled a bit brighter than all the others, the scent of his favorite apple pie baking in the oven, and the comfort of Fritz resting against her, all served to remind her that he'd always be there.

She hated that he had said goodbye when she hadn't been

ready to let him go. Maybe he knew she would be okay. She had Fritz and Bodie, now Mel, along with Cyndy and Mac. Maybe Gary knew something she didn't. He had left her when she had been at Mac's. That had to mean he trusted Mac to be there for her.

Mac had certainly proved to be trustworthy and kind. Beneath their easy-going friendship and bonding over the dogs, there was the flutter of attraction. Was she ready for something beyond friendship? That was a complicated question.

Her phone chimed and she dug it out of her pocket. She scrolled to the motion alert from the camera system and smiled when she saw Mac placing a box she recognized from the bakery on her front porch. Before she could text him to thank him, her phone dinged again with a text from Mac wishing her a good morning and prescribing she and Mel eat two donuts and then call him with the results.

She hollered for the dogs, who from the looks of their muddy paws and faces would need a bath. They hurried home, where she gave them each a quick hose down and dried them off before leaving them to rest on the deck. She retrieved the box of pastries and sent her thanks to Mac before jumping in the shower.

She put in a call to Dr. Clay, the therapist her friend had suggested, and explained Mel's situation to the receptionist. After a brief hold, she returned and told Lily Dr. Clay did some pro bono work with victims of crime and would be happy to see Mel on Friday for an initial evaluation and visit. Lily booked the appointment and hoped Mel would agree to it.

She had just brewed a pot of tea when the doorbell rang. She opened the door to Donna and Mel. Bodie and Fritz rushed toward Mel, tails in full swing as they circled around her. "Come in, please. I'm so glad you're home." Lily put an arm around Mel's shoulders and felt her flinch.

"Mac dropped off some bakery goodies for us."

Donna handed Lily her key. "I've got to get to work. I told Mel to take the rest of this week off so she could concentrate on her classes and get caught up and she can start back on her volunteer schedule next week."

"That sounds great. We'll have plenty to do around here, won't we?" Lily smiled at Mel and was rewarded with a shrug.

Donna's eyes conveyed her sympathy as she waved a hand to say goodbye and disappeared out the front door.

Lily twirled the key ring around her finger. "This is your key to the house." She passed the rhinestone covered dragonfly to Mel.

Her dark eyes widened. "You trust me with a key?"

"Of course. I want you to be able to get in, if I'm ever out and about when you get home. I know you'll keep it safe and secure." Lily took a step forward and then turned back to Mel. "I try to keep my keys in the same place, to keep track of them, but if you happen to lose it, just let me know and we can get the locks changed."

Mel followed Lily into the kitchen and accepted her offer of tea. Lily noticed Mel's brows raise at the selection of pastries and donuts stacked in the box on the island counter. She passed her a plate and nodded toward the box.

Mel selected a huge cinnamon roll dripping in cream cheese frosting. Lily handed her a fork and a stack of napkins and chose an almond croissant for herself. The dogs stuck next to Mel resting their heads as close to her feet as possible.

After they each had a few bites, Lily refreshed their mugs of tea. "I know you've been through a horrible ordeal and I don't want to cause you any further pain. I do want you to know you have some options. First off, I hope you'll come with me today and pick out a cell phone. I can add you on my plan and use it as a business expense, since you're helping me here with the cottages. Secondly, there is a doctor, a therapist, who is willing to see you for free because she likes to give back to the community and she can take you on Friday. She comes highly recommended and it would just be you, not a group setting. I know Jeff said there is also a counselor available through the victims of crime funding, so you also have that option. Lastly, and this one is non-negotiable, we're going to arrange to drive you to school and to the library for a few weeks. I don't feel comfortable with you on your own just yet."

Mel took a slow sip from her mug. "The phone sounds like a good idea. I'm not so sure about a therapist or a counselor, and I'll put up with you giving me rides, but not forever. I'm going to be okay." Her voice cracked a bit on the last word and her eyes filled with tears. "I'm so mad I fell for Sally's stupid lies. I'm normally so careful, but when she mentioned Aunt Tricia, all logic flew out of my brain. I just wanted to find her and have a family again."

Lily reached across the counter and patted her arm. "Jeff told me about your aunt. I'm so very sorry she passed away without you getting to reconnect with her. Jeff said she was living near Seaside. I thought maybe this spring we could take a drive down there and you could take her some flowers."

Mel's eyes widened and her lip quivered. She nodded and whispered, "Thank you, I'd like that." She reached for her fork and stuffed another piece of the cinnamon roll in her mouth.

"Sometimes, family isn't always related by blood. You'll always have a place here and although we aren't related," she glanced down at the dogs, "you can see we've missed you terribly."

Mel swallowed hard and reached for her mug. The loud gulps reminded Lily of the dry lump stuck in her own throat. Mel was a tough nut, but the thought of her suffering alone and afraid broke Lily's heart. She hoped, with time, all the cracks caused by the insurmountable losses Mel had endured would heal, and Lily wanted to be part of the remedy.

Lily finished another bite of the flaky croissant. "Well, when you're ready, we can head into town and find you a phone. I need to run by the market and restock the fridge and pick up a few things. We've got guests coming Thursday, so we've got today and tomorrow off."

Mel nodded, swigged down the last of her tea and took her plate to the sink. "I'll just run downstairs and change my clothes." The dogs followed after her, making Lily smile as she put the rest of the pastries in storage containers.

Lily started a load of laundry and left the dogs downstairs before grabbing her shopping list and shepherding Mel into the garage. When she reached the end of the street, Mel reached across the console and clutched her wrist. "We need to go back. I don't think I locked the downstairs door." Her breath caught as she hurried to get the words out.

"I'm certain it's locked." As Lily turned toward Mel, her forehead creased with concern.

Mel's face had become pale and her hands trembled as she shook her head. "No, I need to check it. I checked the front door, but not the downstairs."

Lily recognized Mel's distress and made a U-turn, noticing Mel's breathing calmed the closer they got to the house. Lily let Mel go through the gate with the keypad to the back of the house, understanding she had to be the one to confirm it.

Minutes later Mel returned to the passenger seat, with a weak smile. "Sorry, it was locked. I just couldn't remember."

"Not to worry. Better safe than sorry, right?" Lily pulled away from the house, glancing at Mel's legs, jiggling against the seat.

"It's normal to feel a bit jumpy after what you've been through. That's why it might be a good idea to talk to someone about what you're feeling and experiencing."

Mel nodded, but didn't commit to anything. They made quick work of their errands, with Lily convincing Mel to let her treat her to a few new shirts and jeans for school, and on the drive home Mel read the instruction manual for her new phone. While Lily put the groceries away and fixed lunch, Mel set her phone to charge on the desk. As soon as Mel finished lunch, she went downstairs to start on her homework. The dogs were at her heels and followed her into her bedroom. Lily marveled at their ability to sense those who needed them most.

Lily threw in another load of laundry and stationed herself at the computer to get caught up on emails and take a look at her booking calendar. Her last weekend of the season would be the one before Halloween and she needed as many bookings as possible before then. She scanned the calendar and found several new reservations, bringing her to full capacity for this month and most weekends in October.

Fall was a beautiful time in Driftwood Bay, but crowds naturally declined as it got closer to the winter months. Lily had to make money while she could and stash it away for the lean season. As she looked at all the blank spaces stretching across December and into February, a shiver of doubt rippled through her. She'd never faced having that much time on her hands. She was frugal and knew she could stretch her funds, but had to find something to do once Kevin went back to school in January.

The sound of a mug scraping against the counter jarred her from her thoughts. Mel was brewing tea. Lily finished up her notes she kept on a paper calendar and joined her in the kitchen.

"How's studying going?"

Mel shrugged as she poured water over the tea bags. "Not bad." As she waited for the tea to brew, she added, "I think I'd like to go see that doctor on Friday."

6

Between chores and homework on Wednesday, Lily broached the prospect of going to Mac's on Sunday. Mel's eyes brightened at the mention of dinner and a visit with Mac's llamas, Margo and Coco. "He tells me he's considering adding some alpacas soon."

That bit of news brought a grin to Mel's face. "They are so cute. I don't know much about them, but will research them next week when I get back to the library." Lily let out a breath at the enthusiasm in Mel's voice and her eagerness to learn. She was happiest with her nose in a book or immersed in research at the library. It was a good sign.

After lunch, Lily gathered Bodie's leash and hollered out to Mel that she was on her way out to the training facility. Minutes later, Mel came bounding up the stairs with her new backpack they had picked up in town. "Uh, I thought I'd go with you, if that's okay?"

Surprised, but remembering Mel's obsession with locking the door yesterday, she said, "Sure, you'll have to sit in the waiting room or outside, since they don't like any distractions for the pups at this point, but you're welcome to come with us. Everything locked up downstairs?"

Mel smiled and nodded her head. "Can Fritz come? I hate to leave him on his own. I can walk him and wait outside with him."

Lily could swear Fritz winked at the girl. "Why not? We'll all go. Let's get a move on."

There was a large fenced exercise area behind the training building and Lily left Mel in Fritz's capable hands, while she and Bodie attended their session. The training went well, with Bodie having mastered the commands and they were given some new homework. As Lily gathered Bodie's sweet face in her hands, she wasn't sure how she would ever be able to let him go next year, when he would have to move on to more advanced training. The silver lining was she would be able to see him all the time once he graduated, since he was being paired with Andy.

She had first met him when she had called the handyman in her uncle's notebook and Andy and his dad, Wade, showed up. They had been doing work around the cottages for years and meeting Andy and learning he had lost his hearing as a teenager opened her heart to the idea of helping train Bodie to be a hearing assistant dog. Andy loved Bodie and Fritz and Lily knew when Bodie was fully trained, he would change Andy's life.

Soon after they got home, Mel returned to her homework, and the dogs stretched out on the deck for a nap. Lily had just finished brewing a pitcher of iced tea when the doorbell rang. Andy had been on her mind and now he stood at her front door. She welcomed him inside, motioning him to the deck.

She put some leftover pastries on a plate and delivered them along with glasses of iced tea, to the table outside, where Andy leaned over his chair, giving both dogs thorough belly rubs. The sheer joy on his face when he interacted with Bodie was all she needed to see to know she was doing the right thing in being a puppy trainer for the hearing dog program.

She hadn't seen Andy in a few weeks and her minimal signing skills were rusty. Andy knew she had made a trip back east and asked her about it and Kevin. She highlighted a few things and made a point of not mentioning Mel's ordeal. "Kevin likes his classes and is looking forward to coming here for Thanksgiving and then he'll be here almost a month for the holiday break."

He signed back to her indicating her happy smile when she spoke of her son. "How is Mel doing?" he asked, in his quiet voice.

"She's busy with her homework, with classes starting. She's an eager student and I'm sure she'll do well." Lily took a sip of tea. "How about you? What have you been up to?" She tried to sign as she asked.

He chuckled as he corrected her mistakes. "Lots of jobs now, so Dad and I are working extra." He glanced at the clock. "I need to go. I'm supposed to be at the hardware store, but wanted to stop and say hi to Bodie and Fritz."

He cuddled Bodie once more before waving goodbye and hurrying to his truck. He drove away, ignoring Lily's wave, his focus intent on the street traffic and his mirrors. Andy was a cautious driver and took extra care, worried that he may not hear a siren, so paid close attention to his surroundings.

Mel was never talkative, but she was even more quiet than usual on the drive to the community college. Lily made sure she had her new cell phone and smiled when Mel reached in the back to pet Bodie and Fritz before getting out of the car. Lily waited as she watched Mel stand, staring wide-eyed at the campus. It was a gorgeous setting not far from the water, and while larger than a typical high school, not overwhelming. They catered to locals for two-year degree programs, career education, and vocational classes.

Donna had helped Mel decide on her class choices and urged her to try things and use this time to figure out what she enjoyed studying most. Mel had settled on creative writing, history, and an art class. She stood rooted to the sidewalk and Lily climbed from behind the wheel and leaned against the car, next to her.

She risked putting arm around her shoulder. "You're going to have a great adventure here. I'm very proud of you. You've studied the layout of the campus and know where you're going and I know you're dying to spend some time in that gorgeous library. Donna will be here just after five to pick you up and then I want to hear all about your day. Call me on your lunch break if you need to."

Mel turned to face Lily, nodded, and set off on the concrete pathway to find her first class. Lily let out a breath, hoping her pep talk proved to be true. Mel looked more like a scared girl on her first day of junior high than an almost twenty-year old woman going to college.

She waited until Mel disappeared around a corner and then got back in the car. Part of Bodie's puppy training involved taking him to new places and getting him used to commotion and distractions. This morning, since they were already out and about, she drove them to the ferry terminal, where there was always a bit of action and noise. Driftwood Bay didn't have a bustling metro area, so the dock would have to do. Bodie would need to learn to be comfortable on a ferry and today would be his maiden voyage.

Lily parked and attached leashes to both dogs, making sure Bodie's training vest was secured before slipping on her back-pack. The crossing to Coupeville was just over thirty minutes, so it was an easy adventure. Puppies are inquisitive, which meant Lily had to keep reminding Bodie to focus and keep his head up, instead of sniffing at every new thing he encountered. There weren't many people boarding, but enough to intrigue Bodie. He hadn't yet met anyone he didn't think was a fan.

Fritz was also a friendly dog, but being older and wiser, he had mastered sticking close to Lily and not darting or tugging on his leash to reach every new visitor. She got her ticket and followed the walkway for passengers and made her way to the outdoor deck. Bodie's head darted from side to side as he took in all the new smells and sounds. The weather was perfect, with clear skies and the sun warming her through the lightweight jacket she wore.

Bodie quivered with nervousness or excitement, she wasn't sure which. He took in all the activity and squirmed near her feet. She gave him the command for down and it took a few tries, but he finally settled next to Fritz. As the ferry pulled away, Bodie stood, disturbed by the motion and noise below deck.

Running her hands over him, Lily did her best to reassure him and urge him into his down position. She gazed out at the water, which looked like panes of rippled blue stained glass, and inhaled the fresh air. She hadn't traveled by ferry much, but living in Driftwood Bay she would have many opportunities to use her new favorite mode of transportation.

As she looked across at the lighthouse near Fort Warden, her mind drifted to Mel and what she would be doing. Lily hoped she was beginning to relax and had met some new friends. Along with the excitement of a new adventure for Mel and an opportunity for her to use her sharp mind, worry niggled at the back of Lily's mind. She feared Mel was the type to throw in the towel if she met resistance. Kids, even those in college, could be mean and unwelcoming, especially to someone who was different. Lily hoped with everything she had that Mel would be enthusiastic when she came home tonight, and that she wouldn't have to work to convince her to return next week.

The seven-mile journey didn't last long and before she knew it, the captain was announcing their arrival at the Coupeville landing. Lily collected the leashes and led the dogs off the ferry, keeping a firm grip on Bodie's leash, correcting him along the pathway.

Fort Casey State Park was less than a ten-minute walk from the ferry landing and Lily guided the dogs in that direction. They had over an hour to explore the park, take a break, and get back to the terminal in time for the next ferry. Swishing tails from side to side revealed how happy the dogs were on their excursion. Lily stopped at a shaded bench and placed the dogs on the thick grass next to her. She unearthed bottles of water and a travel bowl and let them take a long drink, while she drank from her own bottle.

They made a short loop around one area of the park, with Bodie tempted by every bush and shrub along their way. They didn't encounter any other people on their walk, until they got closer to the ferry dock and the surrounding traffic. Bodie stopped in his tracks at the blare of a horn, but calmed as soon as Lily reassured him. Her job, as the trainer explained, was to expose him to different things and build his confidence.

As they settled in for the return trip, Lily's cell phone pinged. She dug it out of her pocket and smiled at the message from Mel. She was eating the lunch Lily had helped her pack and then heading to the library. Lily tapped in a quick reply with a happy emoji and breathed a sigh of relief.

While Mel hadn't been effusive in her brief message, Lily was confident if Mel had been unhappy, the message would have had a negative tone. She patted both dogs on their heads and said, "How about that, boys? I think Mel is having a good day. She deserves that much, at least."

They were back in Driftwood Bay before noon and Lily

stopped by Muffins and More, treated herself to a late breakfast, alfresco style, and took a fresh loaf of bread with her when she left.

The dogs were tired, with their eyes closing as she drove home. Once she got them inside, they sprawled out on the deck and slept in the shade. She checked the slow cooker she had started before leaving and gave it a stir. Mel loved the potato soup at the café by the library and Lily wanted to surprise her with her version of it for dinner.

Today's guests were due to arrive in just over an hour, giving her time to decompress with a cup of tea and a few chapters of her book.

Lily had the guests checked in and orientated and had just added the cream to the soup when the front door opened and the dogs hurried to greet Mel. Her cheeks were flushed when she came into the kitchen and set her backpack near the top of the stairs.

Lily looked up from the sink and arched her brows. "Well, how was the first day?"

Mel shrugged as she opened the fridge. "Not bad. My classes are okay so far and the library is *so* nice." She went on, more animated than Lily had ever seen her, describing the furnishings and the walls of windows that let in all the natural light. She had perused the shelves and spent her break at one of the wooden tables, reading ahead in her textbook.

Mel finished pouring her glass of iced tea and slid into one of the chairs at the counter. "The library is modern and sleek, and quite beautiful, but I like the Driftwood Bay Library better. It's cozier and comfortable. All those stacks of fiction books feel like old friends." Her brows rose as she glanced at the slow cooker. "Something smells good."

"Potato soup. It's done so we can eat whenever you're ready."

"I'm starving." Mel grinned and headed for the cabinet to retrieve plates and bowls.

Friday, after their jaunt to the beach, Lily loaded Mel and Bodie in the car. This time, she left Fritz home, so Bodie could get in some field trip time while Mel was at her appointment.

Mel's leg bobbed up and down and she rubbed her thumb over the top of her finger while Lily drove downtown and parked in front of an old Victorian home that served as Dr. Clay's office. "Do you want me to go in with you?"

Mel stared at the house not answering. Lily tapped her shoulder. "Are you okay on your own or shall I go in with you?"

"I'll be okay." She nodded, grabbed her backpack, and plodded up the steps. Lily kept an eye on her while she unloaded Bodie. Mel was standing at the door, staring at it. She reached out for the doorknob and then pulled away, as if it was too hot to touch. Lily tucked her head behind the seat, pretending to look for something, willing Mel to go inside.

Finally, she opened the door and disappeared behind it. Lily let out the breath she had been holding and led Bodie down the sidewalk in search of activity and distractions.

As she and Bodie strolled down the street, she saw flyers drawing attention to the last few Saturday Farmer's Markets and made a mental note to stop by tomorrow. Her cottage guests were all part of a wedding party and would not be around tonight or tomorrow for her normal social hour, so she was free in the afternoon and evenings. There was live music tomorrow night and that would be a great place to take Bodie and introduce him to a crowd.

Fifty minutes went by quickly and she and Bodie were back at the car waiting when Mel emerged from the office. Lily loaded Bodie into the backseat, while Mel settled into the passenger seat. "Did you like her?" Lily slid behind the wheel.

"She was nice. Better than I expected. She wants to see me twice a week. Tuesdays, which I set up to coincide with Bodie's training time, and Fridays."

"That's perfect. I'm glad you liked her." Lily checked her rearview mirror and smiled at Bodie's sweet face. "Bodie and I are going to come down to the Farmer's Market and stay for the music tomorrow night. Do you want to join us?"

"Don't we have to do the snacks for the guests?"

"They're going to a wedding, so we've got two nights off." She winked and pulled out into traffic. "I was thinking a movie and popcorn tonight and the market, pizza, and music tomorrow. Mac wants us to come to his place on Sunday, so we have a full weekend."

Lily turned into her driveway, surprised to see Jeff leaning against an old patrol car. Stripped of its decals and emblems, shiny silver paint patches stood out against the otherwise faded body of the four-door Crown Victoria. She pulled to a stop and waved.

She unloaded Bodie and walked over to Jeff. "What are you doing here and when did you get demoted to this old battleax?

He grinned. "This isn't mine. It's actually a gift. For Mel."

Lily waved her arm over the car. "Mel, Jeff has a surprise for you."

When Mel reached them, Jeff tapped the hood of the car and explained the department was auctioning off some of their old equipment. He was able to get the organization that supports victims of crime to put up the costs for it, the registration, and the first year of insurance.. "

Mel's mouth hung open as she took in the huge car. "I've never driven before."

"We've got a retired officer that teaches driver's education," Jeff continued. "He can get you trained and ready for your driving test. Donna and I thought this would give you some freedom to go wherever you need to, plus it's big and safe." He opened the door. "Get in and see how it feels. I can show you the basics and get your seat and mirrors adjusted for you. We can take it down to the DMV and get it registered."

Lily smiled at Mel, who despite her nervousness, grinned as she climbed into the driver's seat. She looked so small behind the wheel. The land yacht wasn't pretty, but would provide solid transportation. Between it and her cell phone, Mel would have more security and freedom.

Jeff showed her how all the controls in the car worked and convinced her to let him take her to register the car and get it insured. Lily waved as she watched them leave. She led Bodie up the steps, where Fritz, who was trustworthy enough to be left in the house alone, greeted them at the door.

"Mel's got herself a new set of wheels, boys. We'll have to see if she'll give all of us a ride once she gets a few lessons under her belt."

Sunday, the guests checked out, and Mel helped Lily clean and ready the cottages before they set out for lunch and an afternoon at Mac's. Lily let Mel drive and helped her tuck an old blanket around the backseat, to keep the seats as free of dog hair as possible. Bodie and Fritz happily loaded into the spacious area, ready for a new adventure.

Mel's stiff posture and the many adjustments to her mirrors and seat revealed her unease. Lily remembered teaching Kevin to drive, her hands gripping the dash in front of her and always telling him to slow down or watch out. Kevin had been much more confident and relaxed, not taking it as seriously as she would have liked.

Lily willed herself to relax and do better with Mel. The

young woman didn't need more pressure; she was applying enough of it herself. Before starting the car, Mel looked over to make sure Lily had her seatbelt fastened. She didn't turn on the radio and glanced in the rearview mirror before putting the car in gear.

She eased onto the street like a ninety-year old grandma on her way to church. Lily kept her eyes focused straight ahead, giving her directions on where to turn, not certain that Mel would remember. Quick moves weren't in Mel's comfort zone, so Lily gave her plenty of notice. Speeding would never be a problem for Mel. Several cars whizzed by them on the way to Mac's, while Mel continued to travel about five miles under the speed limit.

As they made the turn into Mac's property, Lily knew Mel would be a driving examiner's dream pupil. She did everything by the book. With more experience, she would become more confident and hopefully speed up a bit.

Mel parked the car and turned to Lily. "How did I do?"

"Great job following all the rules of the road. This was your first time out in the country, so you'll just need more practice where the speed limit is higher, so you get used to it. I'm sure your instructor will have you out on the highway to practice."

Mel nodded as she got out and opened the rear door to let Bodie and Fritz out. Mac and Sherlock stood at the edge of the driveway, waiting for them. The two goldens took off like rockets and Sherlock bolted from his spot. Golden fur and feathered tails flowed in the wind, like a commercial for hair-care products or long-lost loves reuniting. Lily laughed as she watched the dogs meet and touch noses, with Bodie pawing at Sherlock and Fritz.

Mac herded the golden bundle, wiggling and rolling with each other, into the fenced yard, where toys and fresh water awaited them. "You'd think they hadn't seen each other in months, instead of a few days."

Lily chuckled as she watched the threesome play.

Mac glanced at Mel. "It looks like you're doing great on your driving. Getting in lots of practice?"

With a shy nod, Mel pointed at the pasture. "I'm going to go say hi to Margo and Coco."

"I thought you might want to treat them," Mac said, and pointed at a container on the deck. "I cut up some apples and carrots for you to give them."

A smile filled Mel's face, lifting Lily's heart in the process. Such unfettered joy was rare to see in the serious young woman she found herself becoming more attached to each day. Mel quickened her pace and retrieved the plastic container.

"How about a nice glass of iced tea or lemonade?" Mac offered Lily his arm and led her toward the house. "I invited Cyndy to join us, so she should be here soon."

Lily glanced over at the dogs, still full of energy as they pounded on one another and chased through the thick grass. "They're going to sleep like babies tonight."

Mac opened the door off the deck and a spicy aroma greeted them. "With the chill in the air, I opted to make a pot of chili. Cyndy is bringing some side dishes."

No sooner had he uttered her name, than Cyndy appeared at the side door, smiling and carrying a huge flowered tote bag. He hurried to the door and took the bag. "I could have come and carried that for you."

Her sweet laugh filled the kitchen. "I'll let you go and get the dessert off the seat of my car."

Lily finished pouring iced tea for herself, and turned toward Cyndy. "Lemonade, iced tea, or?" She raised her brows at the woman she had come to consider a friend and chuckled at the rhetorical question she had asked her. Cyndy loved wine and never missed an opportunity to enjoy a glass or two.

Mac set a warm pie on the counter. "This smells delicious, Cynd." The inviting aroma of cinnamon and apples wafted from the deep-dish plate. "I'm going to run out and check on the dogs."

Cyndy put a huge bowl into the refrigerator, then took the glass Lily had poured. "Perfect. Wine sounds lovely, thank you." She giggled and raised her brows as she took a healthy sip.

Lily chuckled as she unearthed another bottle from Cyndy's tote. Her hand brushed against something warm inside under a heavy quilted covering. "Does this need to go in the oven?"

"It's cornbread, so yeah, let's put it in to keep it warm."

Lily slid the pan into the oven, as Cyndy took a quick look around the kitchen and whispered, "How's Mel doing?"

"I think better." Lily pointed outside. "She's visiting the llamas. It seems the therapist is helping and while she isn't eager to go, she hasn't skipped her appointments. It's hard to know because she is so quiet and I hate to pry. I can tell the sessions are hard on her, sometimes after her appointment, she goes downstairs and stays in her room for hours. It's difficult to know what to do and say, but overall she spends more time with me instead of always in her room like when she first came."

"Everybody is being extra vigilant after what happened to her. The whole town is watching out for her." Cyndy put another bowl in the refrigerator and reached for her glass of wine. "By the way, I gave your name and number to a friend of mine from San Juan Island. Kate is her name and she's planning a trip to go to the huge gift shop tradeshow and wants to book a cottage."

"Wonderful, I'll be sure to get right back to her."

"She and her friend are coming next Monday, and leaving on Saturday, so I hope you have room."

Lily pulled her cell phone from her pocket and tapped it a few times. "Yes, I've got room. I'll block out a cottage right now."

Before dinner, Cyndy spread out newspapers on the picnic table and Mac covered the table with pumpkins. Cyndy had a supply of stencils and tools in her tote bag and proceeded to give them a designer pumpkin carving class. Mac handled the slimy mess of scooping out the pumpkins and saved the flesh for treats for the llamas, while Cyndy offered her expert advice on designs.

As Mel traced a pattern, she confessed that she had never actually carved a pumpkin. "I have random memories of watching my dad do it when I was a kid, but I've never done it on my own." She smiled as she worked. "And never anything like these artistic stencils, just the plain old triangle eyes, nose, and mouth."

The adults exchanged a sorrowful glance as they watched Mel delight in her project. She was a perfectionist and took her time carving the intricate design. Cyndy added a battery-operated candle to each of them. "When it gets dark, they'll be fabulous."

"Mel and Lily can take mine and decorate with it. That way you'll have one for each of the cottages," offered Mac. "I don't do much decorating out here."

They enjoyed a perfect fall meal, after which Mac offered the ladies a choice of board games or fun at his horseshoe pit. After a heated horseshoe competition, where they had to teach Mel the techniques, and she paired up with Mac to beat the two women in a tight match, they enjoyed their pie and warm drinks by the firepit, with the artistic inspired pumpkins on display.

While Mac and Lily gathered the dogs, Mel offered to help Cyndy tidy the kitchen and load her car with the serving dishes.

Evening was settling in and the chill of the air once Lily was away from the warmth of the fire, caused her to shiver. Mac slipped an arm around her and hugged her closer to him. "This has been the best day. Just perfect."

She slid her arm around his waist. "I agree."

7

Kate, Cyndy's friend, and Izzy arrived on Monday. They were warm and friendly; the kind of women that made Lily feel as if she had known them forever. Cyndy invited them to dinner and included Lily and Mac in the invitation. With Mel working late at the library and Donna and Jeff looking after her, Lily felt comfortable going. Part of her still hated the idea of leaving Mel on her own, but she would have to get over it.

Knowing Mac was bringing Sherlock and Sunny, a beautiful golden he had taken in from a patient who was ill and could no longer care for her, Lily loaded her dogs into the car for the short drive to Cyndy's. The dogs played and romped in the yard, and Mac whispered that he was certain Sunny had chosen Izzy as her person. Mac did his best to sell Izzy on the idea over his sister's scrumptious meal. Sunny was such a sweet dog and missed her owner terribly. Lily kept her fingers crossed, hoping Izzy would decide to adopt the good-natured dog.

They had a fun evening visiting and getting to know Kate and Izzy. As they left, Lily could tell Sunny had made an impact on Izzy and that she was giving the idea serious consideration.

The next morning, Lily's heart warmed at the new ripple of excitement in Mel when she talked about her driving lessons and added them to the calendar Lily had on her office wall. Jeff had helped her get her instruction permit and secure insurance for the car and she had taken a couple of driving lessons with Bob, the driving instructor and retired officer.

Knowing she would have her own transportation, eased Lily's mind. Mel was a quick study and had been immersed in the driver's handbook ever since Jeff brought her home. Lily had no doubt she would master the written test, but would have to build her confidence behind the wheel.

Driftwood Bay was by no means a crime riddled town, so the idea of Mel meeting danger again was slim, especially with Sally out of the picture. A shiver ran over Lily's arms as she thought of Mel scared and stuck in a storage shed. She didn't press her to talk about it and left it up to Dr. Clay and her expertise to help Mel recover.

Tuesdays and Fridays, therapy days, were always a toss-up, with Lily not sure what sort of mood Mel would be in after her session. Some days she was cheerful and a bit more talkative, smiling when she told Lily about a writing project for school or a new book at the library. Other days, she was even more withdrawn than usual and holed up in her bedroom for hours. Giving Mel space and letting her know she was available was all Lily knew to do. She also made sure to have some of her favorite cookies on hand. Cookies were the answer to many of life's problems.

Mel wouldn't be able to drive on her own until she completed her driving classes and passed the test, so Lily dropped her off at her appointments. Dogs sensed when people needed them most and on Tuesday when they picked up Mel, Bodie crawled over the console to be closer to her. Lily had been working to get him comfortable with his harness in the backseat, but couldn't resist the love and acceptance in his eyes and the way Mel looked at him. Mel's eyes were puffy and she held a rumpled tissue in her fist, but the corners of her mouth lifted when she petted Bodie. He nosed higher and licked her chin.

Lily, of all people, knew the power of a furry friend. The unconditional love and support they offered. The comfort of their warm body next to yours when you were scared and alone. Their patience and understanding when you rambled on and on, or cried into their soft neck. The paw on top of your hand, providing the reassurance you needed. The swish of their tail that vibrated with excitement, letting you know you were the most important person in their world.

Fritz had helped her through Gary's death and moving here. She wouldn't have made it without him. She made a mental note to bring Fritz and Bodie with her when she picked Mel up on Friday. They were exactly what she needed.

Along with helping with the cleaning and laundry, Mel was settling into her new routine of therapy, work at the library, and college classes. She spent most of her spare time doing homework, reading, or driving in preparation for her exam. This week, with only Kate and Izzy as guests, Lily invited Cyndy and Mac to join them for appetizers, along with Nora, whom she had first met as a guest at the cottage. She had stayed during her interview for a police officer and had been hired by Jeff. She and her daughter Bree, were still settling in as new residents of Driftwood Bay.

By the time Friday rolled around, Izzy had decided to adopt Sunny and give her a forever home. Mac was thrilled and outfitted Izzy with all Sunny's toys and bedding. Izzy spent most of the afternoon playing in the backyard with all three dogs and they were tuckered out by the time Cyndy and Kate arrived from their last day of shopping at the tradeshow.

Lily had prepared one of her epic charcuterie boards for the evening. There was a guest lecture and reception at the library, and both Bree and Mel were interested in it. Despite Mel being about four years older, the young women got along well, and with both of them being new to town, they served as support for each other. Nora insisted on treating them both to dinner and dropped them at the café before the lecture, and Donna offered to make sure they got home when it was over, leaving Nora and Lily free for the evening.

The selection of snacks Lily had prepared was more than enough for dinner, and the group gathered around the fire pit in her lovely yard while they visited and nibbled. Lily longed for friends like those seated next to her. She hadn't had a close circle of girlfriends back in Virginia. She had used her work friends as her social circle, but it wasn't the same as listening to Kate and Izzy share some of their heartbreaking experiences. Even Mac chimed in and talked about the loss of his wife and his rocky relationship with his daughter, Missy.

People, no matter how put together they appeared on the outside, were often struggling with something deep inside. Sometimes, the ones who seemed the most polished, like Kate, were fighting the hardest battles.

So much had changed in Lily's life over the past couple of years. Looking through the fluttering flames from the fire, she knew Cyndy was a loyal friend, someone who would be in her life forever.

Nora was struggling with her teenaged daughter, who made it clear she would rather be living with her father, and Nora's heartbreak was evident in the glint in her eyes and the crack in her voice. Mac commiserated with her on that point, as did Izzy.

That same sense of understanding and acceptance was evident in the way Kate and Izzy spoke with such openness and feeling, making it easy for everyone to share their fears and struggles. Lily's worries lightened, buoyed by their understanding and acceptance. If only they lived closer.

Some days it was hard not to focus on what she had lost. The pain, both physical and emotional that came when she thought of Gary, could bring her to her knees. Some mornings she didn't have the energy or desire to get out of bed. Some nights she held Gary's urn in her arms to get to sleep. Had it not been for Fritz, and now the responsibility for Bodie and Mel, she would have sunk into a deep despair. She wondered how her uncle had been able to go on without her aunt, living here with all these reminders.

Maybe it felt like she was still here. Maybe he took comfort in the life and legacy they had built, and her mosaics and sea glass creations soothed him. Maybe like her memories of Glass Beach Cottage, he savored all the happy times and years they spent together, admiring the view and sitting, like she was tonight, enjoying the lush yard and the sky filled with millions of twinkling lights.

Having a pity party was easy, looking for positive signs took more effort. Only now was she beginning to believe, truly believe, not just pretend, that she would be okay.

The blanket of stars across the sky, the soft glow from the almost full moon shining down upon them, and the crispness of the air, made for a wonderful fall evening. The dogs were piled next to each other a few feet away. Sitting here in the yard where she had spent so many fun summers, both made her smile and filled her with regret.

She wished she had spent more time with her aunt and uncle. She had been so wrapped up in her own life and kept thinking next year, always next year. It was easy to do. Everyone did it. The losses in her life had been sudden and tragic and now with Gary gone, it only served to drive home what she knew. She should not waste time, not prioritize work. It was a hard habit to break, but part of the reason she had moved was to have a clean slate, a do over.

She would not make those same mistakes. She would always

be responsible and hard-working, that was ingrained in her, but she would make time for joy and fun. Most of all, she would make time for the people who were important to her and live her life focused on doing what made her happy. She wouldn't save every dime and would spend money to make a trip to see Kevin or fly him out to see her. Instead of regarding time spent lingering over coffee to visit or chatting with Cyndy in her shop, admiring all the beautiful things, as a waste of time, she would reframe it as living a full life.

Thanks to her uncle and her pension, plus Gary's, she didn't need to worry about making ends meet. Her competitive nature and the challenge of making the cottages profitable spurred her forward, but she knew that wasn't why her uncle had left her this property. He knew she loved it here and she had been happy here. He bestowed upon her much more than a valuable piece of land—he had given her a second chance at joy, at life.

She glanced over at Mac and her heart fluttered with a tingle of excitement. His handsome features and gorgeous eyes were only overshadowed by his kindness and gentle spirit. Being with him brought her joy and comfort. He must have sensed her gaze and winked at her, rewarding her with a slow grin.

Deep inside she knew Gary would like him and approve. She was a lucky woman and sensed she and Mac were on the brink of something special. Exactly what, she wasn't sure, but the flutter in her chest told her it was deeper than friendship.

8

Lily welcomed Mac and Sherlock through the house and to the deck. Ignoring the enticing aroma from the takeout bags in Mac's hands, the dog made a beeline for the other two, who were down the stairs lounging in the grassy yard. Lily gestured to the table she had set. "I think it's warm enough to eat out here, don't you?"

"Fine by me." He set the bags on the table and began unpacking them. Mel was working late at the library and wouldn't be home for hours, giving them time to discuss the prospect of them taking a trip to San Juan Island. Together.

Over tender crab cakes and a delicious chicken pasta dish loaded with basil, tomatoes, and zesty lemon, they chatted about their day. When they couldn't eat another bite or find another topic, Lily slid the email from Izzy across the table. "So, what do you think?"

"I'd love to go, but I don't want to rush things between us or make you feel uncomfortable. Taking a trip together, that's sort of a big step."

She nodded. "I know. I wouldn't feel right going unless I told

Kevin about you. I wouldn't want him to find out and be upset, thinking I was hiding things from him."

"How do you think he will react?"

Her voice wobbled. "I don't know." A tear slid from her eye. "I never expected to face this, you know, situation. After Gary, I just assumed I'd be alone forever. It's hard to explain what it is we have. I just know I love spending time with you and miss you when I don't get the chance to see you or talk to you. It's been so long since I dated anyone, everything has changed."

He chuckled, reaching for his glass of iced tea. "You're telling me. Unlike you, I don't feel a need to explain things to Missy. Her reaction would not be positive and we talk so infrequently, it wouldn't come up in conversation. Like you, I don't know exactly what we have, but I know it's good. I don't want it to end and I don't want to jeopardize it in any way."

She nodded. "I feel the same way. Izzy has room enough at her place that we can each have our own room. It's not like we're going away on some fantasy singles sex holiday."

He choked and sprayed iced tea across the table. Chuckling, he tried to mop up the mess with a napkin. They both laughed so hard tears rolled down their cheeks. The dogs stopped playing and Fritz hurried up the stairs, worried at the commotion and determined to check on Lily. Sherlock and Bodie followed him and the three dogs stood staring at their humans.

A new round of giggling ensued at the cocked heads and confused looks on the dogs' faces. Finally, Lily took a deep breath to compose herself. She gathered up the dishes and carried them inside, while Mac disposed of the carryout containers and cleaned off the table.

She returned with a beer for Mac and a rare glass of wine for her. "That must have been our collective nervous energy spilling out, right?"

He clinked his beer bottle against the edge of her glass.

"Probably. This was all easier when I was younger. There was no thought at all, just hormones."

The giddiness that had taken over was gone. Lily took a sip from her glass and set it down, twirling the stem between her fingers. "I don't think I could handle losing anything else in my life right now. You. Kevin. Mel. I finally feel like I can do this and I can't risk the thought of anything upsetting the precarious footing I'm on. I'm not saying no to a more intimate relationship, just saying not right now. I'm not ready."

He reached across the table and took her hand. "There is no rush. I'm not here for that. Those days are long behind me. If, and like you, it's a big if, I embark on a serious relationship, it will be for much more than the physical side."

Lily sighed. "Then, let's go and visit Izzy and Kate. I think we'll have a great time and we can just take it slow and enjoy ourselves without any pressure hanging over us. I'll call Kevin to let him know tomorrow."

"Sounds great." He winked and added, "I already marked myself out of the clinic just in case we decided to go. Are you okay to leave the cottages and Mel?"

She smiled. "My season technically ends the weekend before, so I'm set. Mel is scheduled to take her driving test Wednesday and I predict she will pass, so she'll be driving herself and can stay with Jeff and Donna, unless she's comfortable here alone."

"Without the dogs, I think she'd be better off with Jeff and Donna."

Lily nodded and finished her wine. "I agree. She's still skittish and I don't want any worries while we're away." She reached down and ruffled the top of Fritz's head.

Mac took a long pull from the bottle. "Just to be clear, I wouldn't say no to a fantasy sex holiday with you in the future."

That did it. They both started laughing again.

~

Lily had arranged a small get-together at the pizza place by the waterfront to celebrate Mel's successful driving test. If it didn't go well, she was prepared to call it off, but was certain Mel would pass. While she waited for her, she reflected on the video chat she had with Kevin early yesterday morning.

She had worked herself into a knot, her stomach roiling and her head aching, anticipating how she would present Mac and their trip to her son. Then once connected, her nervousness had become overwhelming, and she'd spewed out all the information, not doing a great job of any of the things she had learned in all the various communications classes she had taken over the years. She explained that she didn't want him to think she was replacing Gary or had forgotten his beloved father and the man she would always love, then let him know that she wasn't sure where her relationship with Mac would go. She felt comfortable with him and although they had initially bonded over their love of goldens and their shared grief, she felt there was more to their friendship.

Without getting into the details she couldn't imagine a young man wanting to discuss with his mother, she assured him their trip was just a chance to sightsee and spend time with each other and they were both committed to taking things slowly and would be staying in separate rooms.

She had watched Kevin's reactions, looking for any sign of angst or concern, and by the time she took a breath, the stress had her sweating through her shirt and her throat was bone dry.

To her surprise, Kevin was thrilled for her. He assured her he was happy that she'd found someone to spend time with and trusted her completely. "Dad would never want you to be sad and alone, and neither do I." Those words still echoed in her heart. She was beyond lucky to have such a wonderful son.

Talking to Kevin and having his support had lifted a heavy weight from her heart. If she was honest with herself, Kevin was one of the main reasons she wanted to put off any kind of intimacy with Mac. The thought of her son disapproving or thinking less of her was something that scared her to her core.

With that task behind her and a happy outcome, Lily was walking on air. If Mel passed her test, it would make it an even better week. A few minutes later, Mel emerged from the office, a smile filling her face as she waved her new, shiny license at Lily. "I passed. I got a perfect score."

Lily couldn't help herself and reached out to hug Mel. "I knew you would. I'm thrilled for you. How about we celebrate with pizza tonight?"

"Sure, that sounds great." She was still admiring her license.

"Before that, let's run by the Mercantile and you can pick out a new coat. They just got in their new selection and I want you to have a good one for fall and winter." She sensed an objection coming from Mel and held up her hand. "I'm not taking no for an answer. It's in celebration of you getting your license. A gift. Let's go." She pointed to the driver's door.

Mel took the same care she always did, as she prepared to drive them the few blocks down the road. After perusing the racks, she selected a stylish three-in-one jacket in a pretty raspberry color that could keep the rain away and also add extra warmth. They were having a special sale and with the purchase she also got a free cozy vest that would be perfect for fall. She tried on several colors and agreed with Lily that the deep plum was gorgeous. Lily couldn't resist adding on a pair of cute ankle boots and Mel's love of them won over her reluctance to accept anything for free.

"I'll do some extra chores to pay you back for the boots," she said, admiring them in the full-length mirror.

Lily added them to their shopping cart. "Deal. They're so cute, you're going to love them."

Lily dragged out the visit, taking her time looking through all the racks and trying on a few pairs of boots, before adding another pair like Mel's, for herself. She glanced at her watch. The others should be at the restaurant by now.

When Lily led the way to the alcove in the back of the pizza place and Mel noticed everyone, her eyes widened and her mouth hung open in utter astonishment. Instead of happy, she looked scared, like she might bolt. Lily stuck close to her and put an arm around her shoulder, amid the shouts of congratulations.

Jeff and Donna, Mac and Cyndy, Andy, Wade, and Barb all held balloons and noisemakers, showering Mel with hoots and whistles. Her cheeks flushed and she turned toward Lily, her eyes wide and shiny. "You did all this for me?"

"Of course. You deserve a celebration. It's not every day you get your driver's license." For the first time, Mel turned and hugged Lily. An actual hug from the girl who liked to keep her distance.

"Thank you," she whispered, her eyes brimming with tears. Lily suggested she go pick up the pitchers of drinks from the counter, to give her a few minutes to compose herself, and Mel hurried from the room. Lily signed to Andy that he could go help Mel, and he nodded and followed her to the counter.

She knew Mel didn't like to be the center of attention, but wanted to do something special to commemorate her accomplishment. So much of the young woman's childhood had been stolen from her, and she deserved every drop of happiness she could squeeze out of the little things in life. Most of all, Lily didn't want Mel to feel like a boarder. She wanted her to feel safe and secure, as if she belonged.

Soon after they returned with the drinks, the wait staff delivered three huge pizzas and everybody dug into their favorites. While they ate and visited, Lily pointed out Mel's perfect score and Jeff beamed with pride. When they were finished with the pizza, they all presented Mel with small gifts.

Before opening each one, she read the card, and held it close to her chest, offering thanks to the giver.

She took her time, untying the ribbons on her bags and packages and peeling away the paper, taking great care not to tear it. Her face lit up when she unveiled each gift, a flashlight, umbrella, car organizer, and gas cards, and then again when she passed them around the table. She admired them once more before placing them all in one of the colorful giftbags, then neatly folded all the paper and added them and the ribbon to the same bag.

Donna had picked up a cake from the bakery and once the pizza pans and plates had been collected, unveiled it. The bakery had decorated the round cake with a set of car keys and a glittery, personalized license plate with Mel's name. Road signs had been crafted and placed along the outer sides of the cake. Donna let Mel cut the first slice and then served everyone. Mel liked chocolate and was thrilled with the delicious cake and fudge filling.

It was a perfect evening and one that Lily would not soon forget. Mel smiled more than she had in the last few months. The thoughtful gifts, though small in nature, had an impact that was far greater. The fog she had been under since her ordeal in the city seemed to lift, at least for tonight. Maybe for the first time in a very long time, just maybe, Mel truly understood that people cared about her. It may even be her first taste at what being part of a supportive family was like, albeit an unconventional one.

9

It was the last weekend of the season, although like her uncle, Lily was willing to accept off-season reservations from previous guests and referrals, but wouldn't be tied down like she had been all summer. The three cottages were booked by five women who took a trip together each year and had chosen Driftwood Bay as their destination.

Lily had listened to them giggling and visiting with each other late into the evening last night, but would be getting to know them better at her appetizer social tonight. Mel was becoming more involved at school and had signed up for a weekend art experience workshop. Since getting her driver's license, she had become more confident and was beginning to blossom. She was still quite serious, but smiled more easily and was open to new ideas. She thanked Lily more than once for getting her a cell phone. That's how students communicated with each other, so she would have been left out of activities and study groups, had she not had one.

There wouldn't be much work at the cottages for Mel during the off-season. Lily had suggested she think about getting a part-time job. Mel had already started checking out the local help wanted ads and had taken the big step of opening a social media account, which gave her access to some of the local groups and businesses. She was intent on finding something and assured Lily she would pull her own weight.

Lily had no concern about Mel staying with her or anything else, but understood and admired Mel's work ethic and desire to be self-sufficient. It was a respectable character trait in a young person and Lily intended to nurture it.

Bodie had been working on staying and being calm around people. With five guests in the yard, he would be put to the test tonight. He had a tendency to get over-excited and wanted to be near people so much, that he often whined, while sitting in place. He knew what he was supposed to do, but let Lily know he didn't like it much. Fritz was a good sport and sat with him, which seemed to make it easier for Bodie to relax.

Lily was busy organizing the appetizers and wine for the evening when Mel called out that she was heading to the college and would be home when the event was over at ten o'clock. Lily noticed she was wearing her new furry vest and boots. She looked so grown-up and stylish. Both dogs were stretched out napping and at the last minute, Lily elected to leave them in the house, not certain the women were as excited about dogs as Bodie and Fritz would be about them.

When Lily had checked with Cecilia, the woman who had made the reservations for the group, to inquire if the women drank wine or preferred something else, Cecilia had assured her they loved wine and were looking forward to the evening. She let Lily know they referred to themselves as the Winey Widows. Lily checked over what she had planned and grabbed two more bottles to take outside.

The ladies, most of them in their seventies, had spent some time shopping and sightseeing downtown, but were already gathering around the fire pit while Lily was getting organized.

Lily chuckled to herself, picturing them lined up for the early bird specials.

They complimented Lily on her array of snacks and Cecilia offered to handle pouring the wine. Lily helped the ladies fill their plates and draped some throws and blankets over the backs of their chairs, so they'd have them within easy reach if they got chilly. She knew a few of their names, but couldn't actually place names with faces yet, as she hadn't been formally introduced to all of them.

Cecilia knew how to fill a glass. They held far more wine than Lily would have poured, but the cheerful woman didn't bat an eye and was a seasoned master, balancing the liquid without spilling a drop. Lily eased into her own chair and took a drink from her glass of iced tea.

"Don't you want some wine, dear?" Cecilia twirled around from the side table clutching a bottle and taking a step toward Lily, the colorful ruana she wore over her black pants and sparkly top flowing in the breeze. The slim woman had an engaging smile and gorgeous steely gray hair, expertly styled, and her jewelry matched the colorful tones in her wrap.

Lily held up her hand, feeling underdressed in her jeans and sweater. "No, thank you, though. You ladies drink all you want, I have plenty, but don't often drink."

The shortest one, who Lily guessed was barely five feet tall, with hair dyed a shocking dark brown, giggled. She wore chunky heels with her black and white print dress and black jacket. "I think there's a story there, ladies. What kind of woman has all this wine at her fingertips and doesn't drink it? You must tell us Lily." She held up her glass of pink rosé and took a long sip.

"Oh, Agnes." Cecilia wagged a finger at her friend. "Leave the poor woman alone. You watch way too many detective shows." She handed a glass filled with a beautiful golden white to the tall, almost bird-like woman. "Here you go, Norma."

Norma thanked her and turned her attention to Lily. "Cecilia and I are the oldest of friends. We both started working the same year at the local high school. I was the librarian and she taught math. We worked there together for thirty years." Lily took in her short, mousy brown hair, the ankle length denim skirt and rather frumpy cardigan she wore, and agreed librarian fit her.

Cecilia poured another glass, this one the color of rubies. "We had such fun in those days, but I think we've had even more fun these last, what, almost twenty years now since we retired?" She put the bottle down, lost in thought.

She glanced at Lily, "Time goes by so quickly, it's hard to keep track. We're all widows, and while Norma and I have been friends forever, the rest of us met at a grief support group, over the last ten years. We're all from the same area of Vermont and we take at least one trip together each year, more if we can make our schedules work."

She delivered the red wine to a plump woman with gorgeous skin and auburn hair. "Here you go, Jean."

Jean cradled her glass, her nail polish matching the wine, and smiled at Lily. "I just love the décor and elements you used in the cottages. They are utter perfection."

"Thank you, but I can't take the credit. My friend owns Bayside Gifts and I gave her free rein to design and decorate them. She did a fabulous job. Have you seen her shop?"

Jean nodded. "Yes, it was lovely. I hope to go back tomorrow. I had an interior design business for years, so I'm prone to admiring and window shopping." Her flair for design was reflected in her classy tailored pants and blouse, with a long cashmere sweater in burgundy and a scarf with gold metallic threads that added a bit of panache to her monochromatic outfit.

"And giving her opinions about everything that is wrong with a room," said the woman Lily remembered was Margot.

Her voice was so gravelly, it was easy to distinguish. "She's always wanting to feng shui my bookstore or add more chairs."

Jean chuckled as Cecilia splashed deep red merlot into two glasses. She delivered one to Margot and set the other one in front of her own chair. Margot and Norma were dressed more casually than the others, who looked like they were ready for a party or a board meeting, at least.

Margot wore jeans with a thin gray turtleneck, topped by a gray waterfall cardigan and cute suede ankle boots the color of her wine. The gray tones and the long silver necklace she wore picked up the threads of silver in her dark hair. She raised her glass and thanked Cecilia. "I'm the only one of the bunch who still works for a living. I own a bookstore."

With the wine poured, Cecilia took her chair and began nibbling at the food on her plate. As they chatted, Lily learned Agnes had been married to a successful endodontist and had never worked outside her home. Cecilia and Norma lived off their pensions and Jean's husband had been a realtor who had left her with no financial worries.

Margot sat closest to Lily. "I read the notes in the binder in the cottage and learned these cottages have been here for decades. Have you always lived in the area?"

Lily shook her head and explained that she too, was a widow and how the tragedy of losing her husband, coupled with the loss of her parents years before, and then her uncle passing away and leaving her this property, prompted her to move. The five women sat, rapt with attention, as she explained her circumstances and she had only moved to Driftwood Bay in May.

They gasped when Lily told them she had also been a police officer, albeit in a gentler and calmer venue than Gary. Agnes was particularly curious about any interesting cases or stories. Lily smiled, but couldn't think of anything noteworthy off the top of her head.

"Oh, my dear," said Jean, "that is just heartbreaking. Suffice it to say we all understand how hard it is to lose a husband, but not at your young age and in such a tragic way. I'm so very sorry."

Lily swallowed the lump in her throat. "Seeing you all enjoying life, gives me hope. I'm just now starting to think things will be okay. The hardest thing was leaving my son, Kevin, behind. He's in college in Virginia."

Lily's comment shifted the conversation to children and grandchildren. Their spirits lifted when they mentioned their grown sons and daughters and bragged about their grandkids. Except for Margot, who was a dog lover, none of them had pets. Lily excused herself to check on the dogs, who she decided would be staying in the house until the ladies retired to their cottages.

They were still talking about the pros and cons of pet ownership when she returned. "Fritz has been my constant companion since losing Gary. He's like a faithful friend and helped me through the worst of it, so I can't imagine not having a dog. Now, I'm training a puppy to be a hearing assistant dog, so with the two of them, it's more work, but they bring me so much joy."

"Pets just complicate travel. I like to be able to take a spontaneous trip without worrying about finding someone to take care of a pet." Agnes refilled her wine and added, "I live in a community where I don't have to take care of the yard or anything, it's all done through the HOA fees. It simplifies things."

Norma and Cecilia often traveled together and enjoyed taking trips with women's groups. Jean had family in Florida and most years spent the winter months there, with Margot being the only one who spent the majority of her time at home and at work.

Jean sighed. "With you being young and more independent,

you will probably come to terms with it easier than any of us. In our generation, our identities were largely wrapped up in our husbands'. Norma and Cecilia had their own careers, but for all of us, our husbands were the primary income earners and decision makers. Margot has had her bookstore for years, but her husband Tom ran the local hardware business that had been in his family for generations. He bought the bookstore for her to enjoy as a hobby. It's different, better, for women now."

"How long did it take you, or did you ever feel comfortable dating after losing your husbands?" Lily asked the question in a quiet voice.

Cecilia gazed around the circle of women. "I think it has varied for all of us. Norma hasn't dated at all, Agnes never seems to see the same guy twice, I've got a wonderful male friend who lost his wife, and we do things together, more for companionship than romance."

Jean nodded. "I dated a few men, but I've lost interest in the idea of being married again. I'm not opposed to it, but haven't found anyone I'd like to be around that much. I spend time with a man who is kind and we have fun and enjoy each other, but it's not serious. It took me about two years to even consider the possibility." She took another generous sip from her glass. "But, we're much older dear, and times are different. You're young and stunning and deserve a second chance at happiness."

Agnes put an end to the quiet moment. "I, for one, don't like being alone, so while I'm sure I was judged for it, I began dating just within a month of losing Bernie. I am dreadful alone, and much happier having others in my life and although I haven't found one that merits a forever, I am happier having had them in my life."

Margot took a sip of wine and Cecilia disappeared to refill their glasses. "I live in a tiny town, so the prospect of finding an eligible man is about the same as avoiding snow in March in Vermont." The five women giggled. "My son still lives in the same small town and has taken over the hardware store. He's recently divorced, so he and I spend more time together now and especially when his children come to visit. I have a full life with my bookstore and friends, plus family, and my sweet dog, Gladys. My daughter lives outside of Albany, about two hours away, so she often comes to visit."

Margot's eyes lit up when she spoke about her family. "With all that, I don't have the time or interest in finding a new man. I just live vicariously through Jean and Agnes." She winked and laughed.

Lily sucked in a deep breath. If only she could be as strong as these women. "I've missed my mom horribly and Gary helped ease that loss. My sister and I aren't close and even less so after Mom and Dad passed away. Gary became my everything. His death, so unexpected and awful, left me reeling. It seemed to reopen all the old wounds from Mom's death. I realized how truly alone I was."

Her throat tightened with emotion. "Listening to all of you, being around you, well any of you could have been my mom. It's lovely and comforting and makes me sad at the same time. I miss her wisdom, her calming way. I long to be able to chat with her and have her help me figure things out. I took all of that for granted and without her, it's been so hard."

Margot reached for Lily's hand. "I understand what you're saying. I felt my world slip away when I lost my mom. I was much older than you were and still couldn't imagine not being able to call her or chat with her. We talked about everything." With a far-away look in her eyes and a slight smile, she added, "And nothing."

The chatter had ceased as they all listened to Margot and bobbed their heads.

She squeezed Lily's hand. "If you're lucky enough to find love twice in your life, don't let it slip through your fingers." The others nodded and murmured assurances.

. . .

Jean dipped her head in Lily's direction. "Have you met someone you have feelings for, dear?"

Lily's lips curved into a smile. "I think so. His name is Mac." She went on to tell them how they had met when she took Fritz to the vet clinic and he convinced her to take Bodie for training. "He lost his wife several years ago and we're not sure where it will lead, but we both feel something for each other. We're actually going on a trip together to visit the San Juan Islands next weekend."

As she stammered to make sure they understood it wasn't a romantic getaway, only a visit to see a friend she met during her stay at the cottages and that they were taking all three dogs, the heat rose in Lily's cheeks. She was thankful for the dim light of the evening as she braced herself for their thoughts. She often wondered what her mother would think.

Jean's smile widened. "That's terrific. He sounds like a wonderful man and friend."

Margot nodded. "I agree. It sounds like you have so much in common and that you're both being sensible." She waved her hand around the circle of women. "As you can tell by listening to all of us old crows ramble on, there is not a one-size-fits-all answer. You must do what feels right to you, what makes you happy. I have a feeling your mother would only want you to be happy, dear."

Cecilia got up again to refill glasses and as she made the circle, she stopped in front of Lily. "You're far too young to be alone for the rest of your days. I would suspect your husband would want you to seize upon the chance for a happy life, but I agree you're smart to take it slow." Her eyes darted toward Agnes, as if her friend's choices could be used as a cautionary tale. "It's wise to be sure, but don't let the need for perfection paralyze you."

Jean raised her glass. "Hear, hear. I'll never replace my sweet Phillip and I don't want to. He will also have a piece of my heart and always be with me. It took me some time to feel confident enough to go out with another man. I was worried my kids wouldn't approve. I was worried I'd be frowned upon by the gossiping crowd, but I'm much happier having taken the chance, taken the risk. My life is fuller and much less lonely because of it."

Although their internal clocks were three hours ahead, the vibrant group of women didn't have any trouble keeping Lily up late into the night. The more wine they drank, the more they laughed and giggled. Their energy and zest for life and laughter was contagious and calming. Their wisdom helped ease Lily's concerns about Mac, about dating, and all that it meant.

10

The ladies from Vermont left on Monday morning, promising to return again and showering Lily with hugs and well wishes as she helped them load their rental car. They had been the perfect group to wrap up the season, and caused Lily to chuckle as she added more wine bottles than she could remember having ever collected to the recycling bin in the garage.

She and Mel got started on the laundry while the housekeeping service gave each cottage a thorough cleaning to button them up for the winter. As Lily went through the cottages, making sure the ladies hadn't left anything behind, she found they had each left her a lovely card with a personal note inside.

Margot had added her business card from Town Square Books, telling Lily she was welcome to visit anytime. Tears blurred in her eyes as she read their encouraging words. They all offered their phone numbers and addresses and invited Lily to visit and call anytime she needed to talk. She clutched the cards to her chest. The sweet women would probably never know how much they meant to her, but they would all be getting a Christmas card at the holidays.

By the afternoon, with their chores done and a light rain coming down, Lily suggested they reward themselves by binge-watching her latest obsession, *Vera*. She had become addicted to the frumpy older character who headed up a homicide squad in the northernmost part of England. It didn't take long for Mel to become captivated by the twisty stories and the gruff main character.

Over tomato soup and grilled cheese sandwiches for dinner, Lily reminded Mel she would be leaving early Friday morning. "Donna and Jeff are expecting you after school for dinner on Thursday. You can take your suitcase with you or I can drop it by while you're at school. You'll be okay staying there until I get home Monday?"

Mel dunked her sandwich into the soup and nodded. "Yep, I've got a tough writing project, so will be working on that most of the weekend."

"You've got your key, so if you forget anything, you can always come back and get it. Just make sure you lock up."

Mel rolled her eyes. "Like you have to remind me. Dr. Clay tells me I'm overcompensating in an effort to guarantee safety after the whole kidnapping thing. She says I have OCD tendencies anyway and now they're more pronounced." She shrugged and grinned. "News flash, right?"

It was her first mention of her therapy and it lifted Lily's heart to hear the bit of humor Mel used when she mentioned it. That had to be a good sign. "Well, that's understandable. I'm sure it's similar to PTSD. I always felt I had a touch of that after losing Gary. When something traumatic happens, it's hard to get it out of your mind."

Mel chewed on her bottom lip. "I didn't think it would help to talk about it, but Dr. Clay is super nice and she makes it easy to discuss everything. She explained that the trauma of losing my parents and not having had a support system, makes it difficult for me to trust and form close relationships. Add on the kidnapping and betrayal by Sally and it makes things worse. She suggested a few books and I requested them at the library."

Lily placed a hand on her arm. "I admire your bravery, Mel. I can only imagine the fear you felt and marvel at how smart you were to seek help and find a way to get a message through the library. I know your experience was awful, but I'm thankful it brought you to Dr. Clay."

"I know I'm, uh, different now. Books, the library, all of that is my way of coping. It's a way for me to escape. It's where I've always felt safe." She looked down at her empty plate and whispered, "Until now."

Lily wanted to swoop Mel into a giant hug, but held herself back and opted to squeeze her shoulder instead. The last thing she wanted to do was push Mel harder than she should. As she collected their dishes from the table, Lily bent closer to Mel. "I'm just happy we found each other."

Lily's stomach fluttered as she double-checked the house and made sure she had everything she needed, plus all the supplies for the dogs. She gave herself a final pep talk and promised not to overthink this time away with Mac or let the guilt that nagged at the back of her mind, like a tiny hangnail you didn't notice until you snagged it on something, dominate her thoughts.

She didn't have much time to contemplate it, as she looked out to see Mac heading toward the front door. "Good morning," he said with a smile, as he took the leashes from her hand and grabbed a suitcase. "I'll get these two loaded with Sherlock and we'll be off. I stopped by and picked us up some coffee and snacks."

"Sounds wonderful. Hopefully, I haven't forgotten anything."

He winked at her, shutting the rear cargo door. "I'm sure

they have stores on the island." He hurried to open the passenger door for her and after she slid into the seat, bent down. "We're going to have a great time, a relaxing time, so don't worry about anything."

His enthusiasm and carefree attitude were contagious and once they were on the road and headed across the water on their first ferry ride, the worry that had clung to her disappeared in the crisp breeze. Although less than sixty miles from San Juan Island, the trip from Driftwood Bay involved ferry schedules and it would take the better part of the day to reach Friday Harbor.

On the first ferry, they unloaded the dogs and went to sit near the rail. It was a short ride, so they didn't bother getting a drink, but wanted to let the dogs stretch their legs. After walking them around the edge of the deck, the ferry inched forward toward Whidbey Island and Mac settled in next to her.

Since losing Gary, Lily hadn't had anyone to look after details or handle things as simple as the logistics for a trip. Realizing she didn't have to figure everything out on her own or worry about handling the dogs by herself, allowed Lily to lean back and soak in the rare beauty of the scenic ride among the islands. She didn't have to stress about the cottages, Mel was safe with Donna and Jeff, her sweet furry kids were with her, and last night, Kevin seemed excited she was doing something fun for herself.

This may have been the first real moment since Gary's death that she hadn't been thinking. Thinking of what she would do, how would she live without him, what it would mean to leave Virginia, and leave her son? Could she tackle being an innkeeper with zero experience, could she handle training a puppy, did she have what it took to take in Mel, how would she make it all work? Constant questions, constant planning—it was all she did.

Her only quiet time was spent on her morning sojourns to

the beach. Starting her day there, immersed in the beauty of nature, the sounds, the smells, it was the best part of her day. She believed that ritual had helped heal her heart. Not that it would ever be completely healed, but she felt more at ease there. More calm and less fearful. She would always believe Gary had been there with her, those first months, helping her, easing her into her new life. He always told her she was stronger than she gave herself credit for, but she didn't feel strong.

Now that she didn't feel him there in a physical sense, she could only deduce that he knew she didn't need him any longer. She only hoped he was right. She wasn't quite convinced. She had always trusted him and like Margot and Jean had said, he would always be with her, deep inside. She longed to get to the point those women had, where she could laugh and enjoy herself and not get teary when she mentioned him. They were right in that Gary would want her to live a full life, be happy, even find love again.

A wet nose against the back of her hand and Mac's voice talking to the dogs jarred her from her thoughts. A tear leaked from beneath her sunglasses and she swiped it away with her finger, taking another breath of cool air into her lungs. The warmth of Mac's body next to hers comforted her and bolstered her spirits. She imagined this was weird for him as well, but he'd had more time to adjust.

The ferry churned through the water, the sluggish pace helping to slow Lily's thoughts and heartrate. The gentle journey sure beat a crowded airport or freeway, and was the perfect way to start a relaxing vacation. The dogs had settled at their feet and Lily pushed her warm scarf over her mouth. With the breeze coming off the water, her neck and cheeks were cold.

Mac sighed and bumped his shoulder against hers. "This is gorgeous. I haven't had a fun getaway for a very long time. Too long."

She turned to face him. "When does it get easier?"

He slipped an arm around her shoulder. "Ah, I don't have a good answer for you. It's like an old injury, that may look healed, may look normal to the outside world, but certain activities, specific thoughts, those special occasions and holidays, they can cause the pain to flare. The flareups become less frequent, only with time, but I'm not sure they'll ever disappear."

She leaned her head on his shoulder, letting him support her. She reached for his other hand and wound her fingers between his. Thankful she wasn't alone, she shut her eyes and let the drone of the ferry lull her to sleep.

11

Izzy's house wasn't far from the ferry landing and easy to find. They had promised to treat Izzy to meals in return for her kind hospitality, but when they arrived and she had already picked up lunch from the deli, relief flooded through Lily. She was tired from the trip and wanted to make sure the dogs got acclimated before leaving them on their own.

Mac toted in all their belongings and took the dogs outside to let them romp with Sunny in the back yard. Izzy's home was welcoming and inviting, with the accent colors and touches from pieces Lily recognized from Cyndy's shop. Izzy gave her a tour and showed her upstairs.

"My office is up here, but I don't anticipate having to work this weekend, so you and Mac can have the run of the upstairs. You should have everything you need in the two guest rooms and I've set out extra towels in the bathroom."

Izzy motioned her to the office and a chair in front of her desk. Lily nodded as she took in the space. "Your home is quite lovely. We'll be fine and there's no need to afford us much privacy." She glanced out the window and sighed. "Mac and I are taking things slowly. We talked about things before we came, since a trip away together, just the two of us, is a big step." The color rose in her cheeks. "Suffice it to say, two bedrooms are perfect."

Izzy smiled. "I know what you mean. Relationships at our age are a bit different than when I met John, my ex-husband. I haven't dated much in all these years. I recently met a neighbor, Colin, and for the first time feel something different. I'm not certain it's serious or even close, but it's nice to have that little tingle of excitement coursing through me when I talk to him or see him." She shook her head and grinned. "Honestly, I never thought it would happen. I've just buried myself in work for so long and sort of relegated that part of me to the dusty corners of my mind. You'll meet him tomorrow at brunch. Colin is the manager here at Sunset Bay Golf and Tennis and lives just a few houses down from me. He's the one who organized the tickets for the Halloween party this weekend."

Lily noticed Izzy was more relaxed and happier than when she had come to visit the cottages and suspected Colin might be the reason. "From the twinkle in your eye when you mention him, I'd say he's something special." Lily walked over to the doors on the balcony and checked on the dogs and Mac. "I keep thinking it seems too soon after losing Gary, but know exactly what you mean about those feelings. I've felt a strong bond with Mac, with the dogs and both of us losing our spouses, but there is more to it. I look forward to seeing him, chatting with him, just having him there. I realized that even more when I went back to DC in September. I missed him."

Behind her in-charge demeanor that Lily was sure came in handy in her legal work, Izzy's eyes softened. "I don't think you can let anyone dictate a timetable to you or tell you when it's appropriate to date another man. If you're lucky enough to find someone who is kind, who makes you happy, and you do the same for him, that sounds ideal. Are you worried about what your son thinks?"

Lily gnawed on her bottom lip. "I was, but I talked to Kevin about Mac. I didn't feel right coming on this trip without Kevin knowing I was seeing someone. He's never met Mac, but he was terrific and told me I deserve to be happy and find someone to share my life with. That made me feel better."

Izzy smiled and sighed, her shoulders slumping. "You're lucky. Kevin sounds like a wonderful young man. As I told you when we visited in Driftwood Bay, Mia is a challenge and seems to do everything in her power to sabotage any of my attempts at happiness. I haven't mentioned Colin and probably won't. I just can't deal with any more negativity and drama from her."

Despite seeming to have everything under control, Lily detected the regret in Izzy's voice. "I'm sorry about your daughter. You're right about Kevin. I consider myself lucky to have a close relationship with him, even with him so far away. I often feel guilty about moving out here, but he's immersed in his own life and is enjoying school."

A few barks from down below interrupted them. Izzy stood and made her way to join Lily at the balcony. "We better get lunch organized and give Mac a break from the dogs. After lunch, you two should take a drive and explore some of the island or go into town and check out the shops along the harbor. I'll stay here and mind the dogs."

With a tourist map and directions from Izzy, it didn't take long for Mac to drive them to their first destination at the lavender farm. Although they had missed the peak blooming season, it was still gorgeous and Lily couldn't get enough of the scent. After she loaded up on all sorts of products and they sampled cookies and lemonade made with lavender, they headed down the road to the park and beach Izzy told them about where she loved to walk and view the lighthouse.

The gorgeous fall day provided the opportunity for some fabulous photos of the lighthouse and surrounding coastline. Driftwood Bay was beautiful, but this view was jaw-dropping. As the surf crashed into the rocky shore, it made for a fantastic spray of water. Mac captured some stunning photos and took several shots of them standing with the lighthouse in the background.

They sat on a nearby bench, staring out at the water, mesmerized by the rhythm of the tide and the waves slamming into the rocks. She squeezed Mac's hand. "The sea is so powerful, but yet relaxing and peaceful, isn't it?"

He nodded and turned his attention to her. "I agree. It's comforting. I think it's the ebb and flow, the way it can churn and storm, and then settle into a soothing presence. It's a bit like life, the ups and downs."

Lily moved her gaze from him to the dark rocks along the shore, imagined them being honed over thousands of years, thinking of the generations before her who sat in this same spot and witnessed the power of the sea, the security of the lighthouse, the beauty of it all. "There is definitely something to the healing power of the sea. Perhaps it's as simple as reminding us of the strength and resilience inside each of us."

Mac slipped his arm around her shoulder and drew her closer. "I like that idea. Nature is full of signs of resilience. The promise of spring after winter, the beauty in each season, the trust an animal places in me, even if he's come from an abusive situation. People, like nature, can be such inspiration. So many, after suffering unimaginable losses or illnesses, recover and bloom again."

She leaned her head against his shoulder and shuddered as the breeze carried the sea spray to them, darkening her jacket with tiny splotches. "They say the only constant in life is change, right? In a way the ocean is like that, it changes and can be angry and tumultuous and then calm and unruffled, but it's always there."

He smiled as he bobbed his head. "It's definitely beautiful, when it's calm and even when it's roiling." They sat for a few minutes longer, without speaking, listening to the crash of the waves as they admired the powerful force—capable of delivering calming beauty and powerful enough to erode the edges of rocks at the same time.

They walked hand-in-hand back to the car and made one more stop, at the alpaca farm Izzy had circled on the map. Mac's love for animals was evident in the way he hurried to the fence line to look at the alpacas and they warmed to him, letting him pet them without reservation. Lily had never seen so many of the cute animals, in a variety of colors.

They were smaller than Mac's llamas and as Lily watched him talking to them, she had a hunch Mac could be persuaded to add a couple of alpacas to his pasture with Margo and Coco. He explained the difference between the two species, and how the alpacas on the farm were Huacaya, the most popular of the two types of alpacas. He touted the strength and warmth of their fur, compared to wool.

After they spent time admiring the creatures, they tore themselves away from the gorgeous eyes and sweet faces, and wandered to the gift shop. Lily ran her hands over the soft sweaters and scarves, trying to decide what to take home. She selected a plain men's scarf for Kevin and two fur trimmed black ones, one for Mel and one for herself. She couldn't resist the cute alpaca stuffed toy for Mel. Even though she was in college, Lily was certain she'd love it and it would keep her company in her bedroom.

They made one more stop to visit the herd of alpacas before leaving. Lily was partial to the babies, one black and one a chocolate brown. "I think you need a couple of these at your house." She raised her brows at Mac.

"They are irresistible." He smirked and added, "I'll have to keep my eye out for some, although I don't really need to add more animals to my mini-zoo."

"They're just so sweet and adorable." Lily blew them a kiss goodbye as they turned to walk to the car.

They backtracked along the same route they had taken from Izzy's, having run out of time to make a loop around the other side of the island. As it was, they'd be pushing it to get back in time to get ready for dinner. There was no time to stop and admire the sunset on the water by the lighthouse, so they decided to save that for another time.

When they walked in, they found Izzy dressed for dinner and all four dogs, lounging at her feet. They hurried upstairs to change clothes and joined Izzy in the kitchen. "Colin is joining us for dinner and offered to pick us up." She checked her watch. "He should be here in about ten minutes."

Mac nodded at the dogs, who were lying together in a furry heap. "How'd the dogs do?"

"They were great. I think they're a bit worn out. Colin is going to add Jethro, his golden retriever, to the mix tomorrow. He's a sweetie, and he and Sunny are good buddies."

The doorbell rang and the dogs all rushed to greet Colin. After a few licks and belly rubs, they settled back down and Mac coerced them to calm down by giving them a few cookies and promising they'd be right back.

Over a wonderful meal and then drinks and coffee on the patio around the fire pit, Lily understood what Izzy saw in Colin. He was charming and his accent captivated her attention. She caught the knowing looks between them, the tiny gestures of them touching hands and it was easy to see they were both smitten with each other.

Since she wasn't driving and wasn't responsible for anyone, Lily indulged in a couple of glasses of wine, and a fabulous dessert. She couldn't remember such an enjoyable evening. The couple friends she and Gary had socialized with were all connected through work. Fellow officers, civilian coworkers, and others in the justice system comprised their social circle and usually their conversations were filled with war stories. Lots of them were funny and related to humorous events and they always enjoyed their time spent with friends, but this was different. Good different.

Much like her conversations with guests at the cottages, the idea of spending time and learning about people with varied interests appealed to Lily. Stories from work, like Mac's escapades with some animal patients and Colin's funny account of having to rescue a group stranded after their golfing buddy made an angry exit with the cart, dominated the conversation, but there was room for more.

They talked about how much dogs enriched their lives, their favorite foods and places to visit, books and movies, things they admired in others. It was new and refreshing and felt more substantial, more sincere than the conversations Lily recalled from going out with friends from work.

It brought her back to her conversation with Mac earlier in the day about change. Until recently all the changes in her life had included loss and were negative. She feared change but feared being chained to old memories more. Starting with the decision to leave Virginia, she had embraced change and although fearful, had persevered and started what felt like a new life. As she mulled things, she realized each time she had taken a risk and accepted a new change—be it remodeling the cottages, taking Bodie, or welcoming Mel—they had all enhanced her life.

Helping others, like Mel and Andy, did more good than any therapist she could imagine. It drove home how fortunate she was, even with the tragic losses she had suffered. Seeing the excitement in Andy and knowing how much Bodie would mean to him, filled her heart with joy. Watching Mel, who was truly alone in the world, begin to blossom, even after all the hardship, renewed Lily's faith in humanity. That satisfaction that came from being part of easing someone's burdens, helped to cure her heartbreak.

She had toyed with continuing therapy after her initial visits with the shrink the department provided, but despite the assurance that she wouldn't be judged for seeing a therapist, she knew there was a stigma associated with it. She didn't want to bare her soul to anyone within the department's system. The thought of finding a private doctor was overwhelming, so she had given up on the whole idea.

Looking back, she often wondered if it would have made a difference. Maybe she wouldn't have felt she had to leave Virginia. Maybe she could have come to terms with living with all of the memories. She would never know. She had made a choice and moved forward. Right now, as she glanced at Mac's smiling face, his eyes shimmering in the light of the fire, her doubts about moving to Driftwood Bay faded.

As the evening grew later, Lily struggled to keep her eyes open. She wasn't used to drinking wine and it had worked its magic, delivering the fruity blend through her veins, relaxing her as the night wore on. The Winey Widows would be proud.

Colin drove them home and while he and Izzy lingered at the door, she and Mac made their way upstairs. When they reached the landing, Mac turned to her and took both of her hands in his. "I had the best evening I can remember. I'm so happy we decided to take this trip together."

As he rubbed his thumbs over hers, she flinched at the tiny spark of electricity that traveled all the way to her toes. "I was thinking the same thing."

He bent and brushed his lips over hers, gently at first, and then with a bit more force. She tasted the caramel flavor of the beer he had drunk. That sensation, the tingle that she hadn't felt since she had last kissed Gary, stirred something inside her.

When they finally parted, it took all her willpower to pull herself away. She stretched to keep hold of his hand as she moved toward her bedroom door. "Sweet dreams, Mac."

He chuckled and blew her a kiss. "I can assure you they'll be sweet. I'll be dreaming of you."

12

By the time Lily got downstairs Saturday morning, Izzy had already left to pick up the food for her party. Mac was still sleeping, which was unusual. He was always up early and started work at the clinic at seven, to make it convenient for pet parents who worked. Lily brewed a cup of tea and made herself comfortable in Izzy's oversized chaise chair. The four dogs surrounded her and after they all received pets and ear scratches, settled in at her side.

The kiss dominated her thoughts. She blamed it on the wine, but knew it was more than that. She liked Mac. More than liked him. What was the proper label? He was a kind-hearted man, one she admired, and although it surprised her, she found herself reliving the kiss, like a schoolgirl with a crush.

As she sipped, she smiled when she thought of the Winey Widows. Their steadiness and the surefooted way they navigated their lives, gave Lily hope. A tear rolled down her cheek as she thought of her mom and dad and knew they would love Mac. As Margot and Jean had told her, she shouldn't squander a chance at finding love again.

Last night, Izzy had said she wasn't sure what she and Colin had, but watching them it was apparent there was a romantic connection between them. They were good together and made each other laugh and smile. She and Mac were the same. It was so easy to see in others, but she struggled to admit her own feelings. This trip had cemented her affection for him. He checked all the boxes and stirred something inside her she didn't expect. She suspected her heart was already his, but her mind kept holding her back, making her feel guilty. Deep down she knew Gary would like Mac and there was no reason to be ashamed of finding happiness again. Alerted to Mac's footsteps on the stairs, the dogs rushed to greet him and cut short Lily's musings.

He bent over to greet each of the dogs. "Wow, I can't believe I slept so late. I was hoping to take the dogs for a walk before we head off to golf."

"I'm sure they'll get in lots of exercise today. Izzy said Sam and her husband, Jeff have a large property and the dogs will have a ball."

"Well, we won't forget his name," said Mac. "Our Jeff and Izzy's Jeff."

"We can call our Jeff 'Chief' while we're here," said Lily and smiled. "He's the Chief of Police in Driftwood Bay."

Mac chuckled. "Good plan."

She pointed at her cup. "Coffee's brewed and the kettle is full."

He poured a cup of coffee. "How'd you sleep?" The dogs surrounded him as he slid into a chair at the counter.

"Like a baby. I think I overdid the wine." She chuckled as she petted the top of Sunny's head, who had returned to her after greeting Mac.

"I know. I never sleep in this late. It's been nice not having to worry about work or messages from patients or anything. I guess I needed a break."

"I'm sure you did. I tend to use work as an escape, maybe a substitute for...life, I guess. I'm worried I'm not going to know what to do with myself over these next few months with the cottages closed down for the season."

His brows rose over the rim of his cup. "Maybe we'll have to squeeze in a few more trips and do some exploring. I've been wanting to cut back at work, but never had a good reason." His eyes twinkled with mischief.

Lily smiled and rose, carrying her empty cup into the kitchen. She stopped in front of Mac and bent down, pressing her lips to his. "I like the sound of that."

The dogs scurried to the garage door, alerted to the sound of Izzy's arrival. Soon after Mac helped her cart in the food, Max arrived. The two of them left, immersed in a conversation of medicine and golf, promising to be back in plenty of time for brunch. Minutes later, Colin arrived to transport the dogs to Jeff and Sam's house. Lily couldn't help but worry about Bodie and Fritz, but relaxed when she saw how happy they were running around with Jethro and Sunny. Izzy assured her Jeff and Sam would take excellent care of the dogs and they would have a great time. Between the three of them, they bundled the dogs and their supplies into Colin's SUV. With five fluffy tails wagging in the back window, Lily and Izzy watched as he drove out of sight.

Izzy tucked an arm through Lily's. "They'll be fine. Come help me get the rest of the brunch ready."

Lily vacuumed and helped organize the buffet area. Once Izzy was happy with everything, she suggested they take a cup of tea and split one of the yummy pastries she had picked up. On the patio, the weather was gorgeous and they chatted as they nibbled and watched the golfers.

"Mac and I were saying this morning how lovely it is here. You've found the perfect place."

Izzy smiled. "I fell in love with the island, the people, just all of it. I had intended to go back to Richland at the end of summer, but there was something tugging at me to stay and for once, I decided to be spontaneous."

"I've been trying to think of how to keep busy over the next few months. I've closed the cabins for the season. We don't get many tourists during the winter months."

"Feel free to come back and visit. I've decided I'm spending Christmas right here. After that I don't have any plans, but things are up in the air with my daughter, so who knows how that will work out. The only plan I have is to go back to Richland in February for the big anniversary celebration at the winery. I'd love to have you if you're able to make another trip."

"That's so kind of you." She glanced across the greens. "It's very tempting. We had such fun checking out the spots you told us about, but need more time to see all the things on the island, not to mention the other islands."

"I haven't seen all of what I want to see either, especially the other islands. That would be a fun trip. Maybe we can plan a getaway over to Orcas Island before you reopen for the season. The guys could golf or fish while we pamper ourselves at the spa. Would that work?"

"That sounds fantastic."

"You'll get to meet everyone today. You're going to love them as much as I do, I'm sure. I hate January, so that might be something fun to look forward to in an otherwise dreary month. I'll see what we can organize with everyone. Most, even the ones that still work, can manage a few days off."

"That sounds perfect. I'll most likely open again in mid-March. I'm sort of feeling my way as I go this first year, but taking cues from how my uncle ran the business and following in his footsteps."

They finished the pastry and Izzy collected the plate. "I'm going to get changed. Feel free to relax out here as long as you like."

Lily took another sip. "I'll finish my tea and then go and get changed. See you in a few." She settled back into her chair and closed her eyes. Moments later, she heard her name and saw Mac and Max, along with their golfing partners waving at her from the fairway.

She watched them take their swings, listening to them laugh and joke, and smiled. It felt good to be happy.

Max delivered Mac in time for him to shower and change clothes. Lily offered to handle the door duties and welcomed Izzy's friends as they arrived. Kate hugged her and after introducing her to Spence, he set off to find Max, who was visiting with Mac and would make sure Spence got to know him. All of the couples greeted Lily with smiles and warmth, like she was an old friend.

She held Mac's hand as they watched Linda, the local florist and Max's wife, lead Izzy to the front porch. Huge pots of mums in stunning fall colors decorated the space and Linda pointed out the mini solar lights in each of the pots. Linda let Izzy admire them for a few minutes before tugging on her arm and motioning her to the back of the house.

Mac and Lily followed and watched as Izzy gasped when she saw a new glider bench. Jeff explained it had been taking up space at the hardware store and everyone had chipped in to treat Izzy to it and the pretty stone fountain they had placed in the shrubbery. They wanted her to have a special place to relax and enjoy her new view.

Mac and Lily presented Izzy with a custom house number plaque, complete with her surname. She gushed over it and Jeff offered to install it for her. The group enjoyed the delicious food as they visited and laughed. Lily used all her old tricks from her years at work to keep the couples straight. Kate and Spence were easy, because she had already met her and he definitely gave off the vibe of a police detective. Sam, who owned the coffee shop and Jeff, her husband who ran the hardware store, were always smiling and holding hands every chance they got. Max, the doctor and golfer, was the perfect match for soft-spoken and creative Linda. Nate and Regi, doted on sweet little Emma, who Lily learned they had adopted. Izzy's brother, Blake was funny and loud, full of life, and made his sweet wife Ellie laugh. Feeling the obvious love the group of friends had for each other, it was easy to see what drew Izzy to make this her new home.

At one point, Mac winked at her and reached for her hand. He leaned close and whispered, "I feel like I've known them forever, don't you? Max is already talking about me coming again to play more golf and maybe do a bit of fishing."

She chuckled. "Izzy and I were plotting along the same lines, thinking it would be fun to visit Orcas Island next time and have a spa day while you guys golf and fish. Great minds, huh?"

In answer, he grazed her cheek with his lips. She smiled, his touch reminding her how much she missed being part of a couple. Having someone close, someone to make plans with, someone to share joys with—she had missed that.

Daylight woke Lily on Sunday. She had slept far longer than usual, but after all the dancing and fun at the Halloween party, she had fallen into bed exhausted. Dressed as Ginger and Skipper from *Gilligan's Island*, she and Mac had enjoyed themselves. Izzy had gathered the perfect items of clothing from the thrift shop, including a feather boa, to outfit both of them.

Colin's staff had done a superb job with the entertainment and the buffet. Mac even convinced her to join him in karaoke and they had danced for what seemed like hours. There was a scavenger hunt and both she and Mac won some prizes, including a free round of golf and a meal at a local restaurant. They insisted the others take their gifts and put them to good use and finally convinced Blake and Ellie to accept them.

After enjoying coffee with Izzy, they offered to take Sunny with them, so she could play with the other dogs and romp along the beach later in the day. Once they had the dogs loaded, Mac and Lily set off for more exploring. Their first stop was for breakfast along the harbor. They were able to park right in front and Mac got the dogs to settle down in the back of his SUV, while Lily secured an outdoor table where they could keep an eye on them.

There were some quaint boutiques lining the blocks surrounding the waterfront, but with it being Sunday, most of the shops were closed and the sidewalks were quiet. As soon as they finished breakfast, Mac winked at Lily. "I have a surprise for you."

"What kind of surprise? Should I be worried?"

He chuckled. "It's a bit of an adventure." He glanced at his watch. "Come on, we don't want to be late."

Mac drove along the scenic route on the eastern side of the island and turned at the sign for Harbor Resort, situated on the northwest point. Lily frowned, having not been able to get him to divulge his secret adventure. "Well, this is certainly gorgeous. What are we doing here?"

Mac grinned and as he opened his door, Jeff walked up to greet them. "You're all set and I can take charge of the hooligans while you're out there." He pointed to the water.

Mac shook his hand in thanks and turned back to Lily. "We're going kayaking. This is Jeff's family's place and he helped me arrange a kayak excursion."

Sweat began to form at the back of her neck. "I can't remember the last time I kayaked." It had to have been decades ago and she didn't remember much about how to do it. She had always been athletic, but hadn't put herself to the test in the last year.

"Ah, not to worry. It's been years for me. Jeff hooked us up with a guide, Tim. He'll be taking us out and helping us learn the ropes."

Jeff went on to explain his brother lived at the resort and between the two of them, they'd keep the dogs occupied. He pointed across the parking area. "Here's Tim now." Lily's fears eased as a young man with a Harbor Resort cap rushed to greet them.

Jeff made the introductions before gathering the dogs. "We'll see you two when you get back."

Tim offered each of them a dry jacket to wear and some gloves, then led them over to the dock where two kayaks waited. He went over all the safety instructions and showed them how to get into the kayak, suggesting Mac take the rear seat of the two-seater. Once Lily was seated, he helped her attach the spray skirt to keep any water from entering the compartment.

"It's a calm day, so it'll be an easy trip. We'll just hug the coastline and most likely run into some seals and otters and keep watch for any whales." Once he had them situated, he jumped in his kayak and led them out of the sheltered harbor, pointing out different landmarks as they made their way along the shore.

The tiny splash as their oars slipped into the glassy water was the only sound on the pristine bay. The view was nothing less than majestic. Lily was amazed at the mansions that hugged the rugged coastline, tucked into the trees, visible only from the water. She concentrated on rowing in unison with Mac, who was tasked with steering the kayak.

Every so often, Tim stopped rowing and they sat atop the water, motionless as he scanned the shoreline. He pointed out wildlife along the shore, including a bald eagle sitting in a tree.

They remained stationary, waiting and hoping for a glimpse of the imposing bird in flight. It only took a few minutes for him to leave his perch in pursuit of a fish. Lily gasped as the bird flew overhead and scooped up his lunch.

She hadn't seen a bald eagle in the wild and never in flight. As he rose in the air again, she turned to Tim. "I can't get over the wingspan. That had to be at least six feet."

He grinned and started rowing again. "That's about the average, but there are some larger ones than that guy."

They continued to the area Tim had in mind for viewing seals and otters, among the kelp beds. As they rowed, he talked about the island, where he'd lived all of his life, and his love of nature. He had worked for Jeff's family his entire career, starting out working summers in high school. "The Coopers have been here forever and are beloved by the community. Working here is like a dream come true." During their high season Tim often led up to three excursions each day and enjoyed doing the all-day tours as well as overnight camping and kayaking trips.

He led them a bit further from shore and Lily noticed the ribbons of kelp as she dipped her oar into the water. She and Mac snapped photos of the playful otters and seals that were congregated together. Tim reached into the water and pulled on one of the thick tubes of bull kelp. He cut off a couple of chunks, took a bite from one and offered the other to them to try.

Mac didn't need much persuasion and bit off a piece, raising his brows and nodding. "Not bad. Have a bite, Lily."

She wasn't too sure, but took a small bite and was surprised that it wasn't slimy, like she expected. It was a bit briny and quite crunchy. Tim explained the kelp forests around the islands provided a habitat for the marine life in the area and that many marine biology students come to the island to do research on it.

She and Mac were amazed to learn that the kelp can grow up to ten inches in a day.

They continued watching the cute otters, who seemed content to float on their backs amid the kelp. Tim explained that otters eat sea urchins, which help the kelp forests to flourish, since too many urchins can decimate the kelp. Lily loved the otters, their cute faces and cuddly personalities making them seem like pets.

As they turned to go back to the harbor, Tim continued to educate them about the marine life when they came across some seals. Lily still favored the otters and asked more about them. She learned that they rely on their dense fur, which is sixteen times as dense as the fur of a dog, for warmth and don't have a layer of blubber to help keep them warm. Tim pointed at one chewing on something. "They have to eat a ton of calories, like seven thousand, each day and spend most of their time doing just that or lounging in the water." No wonder she liked them.

Not used to the exertion, Lily's arms were tired and she was glad to see the dock come into view. They disembarked and after sitting for so long, her legs were shaky and she felt every bit her age. At Tim's suggestion, they sat on the dock, letting their bodies adjust before they walked back toward the cabins at the resort.

As they rested, they chatted about how they'd worked up an appetite and were looking forward to treating Izzy and Colin to dinner. Feeling less shaky, she took Mac's offer of a hand up, they thanked Tim for the tour, and set out to find Jeff. Mac slipped his arm around Lily's shoulders. "Did you have fun?"

She smiled and leaned into him. "It was wonderful." Despite feeling a bit worn out, it had been a glorious day and the highlight of the trip. "I wasn't sure about the idea at first, but am so glad we did this."

"We'll have to add a kayak trip to our calendar when we get

home. I know they rent them out, but only during the summer. Luckily, Jeff was able to arrange an off-season tour for us. I'm hooked, I enjoyed it."

She loved the idea that he was making plans for next year. Plans with her. This trip had helped her understand she didn't need to relegate herself to a life alone. For the first time since losing Gary, she imagined a future, a full one with another chance at love.

13

As the ferry lumbered forward, leaving the dock at Friday Harbor behind, Lily plucked the gloves from her pocket and put them on. There was a noticeable chill in the air, and them moving across the water only added to the nip she felt in her fingers. Mac went to the snack counter and returned with steaming cups of tea for both of them, then they and the dogs settled in for the voyage.

Lily took a sip and sighed. "It makes me sad to leave all this behind. Not that Driftwood Bay isn't beautiful, but the island seems like another world."

"It's definitely stunning and a relaxing place to visit. I think it's just getting away from real life for a few days that does it for me. I'm serious about coming back again. I'd love to get in some fishing. All the guys are up for it, but Blake, Jeff, and Nate are really into it."

"I say we plan for something. Izzy and I were thinking January, after all the holidays. You and I both know, life's too short, so I say we mark it on our calendars when we get home and make it happen."

He slipped an arm around her shoulder and she rested her

head against him. After she had lost Gary, she wasn't sure that she would ever feel safe again. Not that she was scared or worried she couldn't take care of herself, but she missed that sense of belonging with someone, having him next to her no matter what. Leaning against Mac provided that sense of security she feared she'd lost forever. She emptied her mind, letting the peaceful beauty of the ocean wash over her.

The dogs snoozed for most of the trip, only waking when the ferry engine noise deepened as they docked in Anacortes. After driving from the landing, Mac took the road for Whidbey Island and they traveled across the majestic bridge at Deception Pass. They stopped at the park and let the dogs out to run, while they admired the tree covered islands and water beneath the bridge.

The last wisps of fog were burning off and blue skies framed the stunning water and islands connected by the iconic bridge. On their trip over, it had been so early and they had been in a hurry to make their ferry connections, they had driven by without stopping to take in the scenic views. Lily hadn't been to this park since she was a teenager and memories of her aunt and uncle came rushing back.

Whenever she came for the summer, they made a special point of "taking a ride," as Uncle Leo would say. They'd pack a picnic and spend a lazy day hiking and enjoying the view. It was always a highlight of her summer and made for wonderful memories.

As if reading her mind, Mac suggested they take their time. "We're in no rush to get home. How about we find a place to get some takeout lunch and find a park along the waterfront in Coupeville while we're here? We could spend the day as tourists and take the six o'clock ferry."

Lily nodded and dug her phone out of her pocket. I'll just text Mel so she knows. She'll be working late at the library tonight."

"Tell her we'll take her to dinner when she gets off. My treat."

Lily smiled as she tapped in a message and received a quick reply with a promise from Mel to meet them at Tides, a popular tavern on the waterfront. With that sorted, they hiked down to the water and took a few photos. They even managed to corral all the dogs for a selfie, with Mac stretching his arm out to capture them all.

Once back at his SUV, they toweled off the dogs as best they could, and made the short, but gorgeous drive into Coupeville. As they passed by Oak Harbor, Lily thought of Mel's aunt, who had lived there years ago. She wondered if Mel would ever want to make the trip or if it would stir up too many sad memories.

With it being a Monday and tourist season over, finding a parking spot was easy. Mac pointed toward a red building across the street. "I'm friends with the veterinarian here and he always recommends The Point. It's never disappointed. The park is just down the block. I'll take the dogs and get them settled and watered and you pick out lunch."

Lily made her way to the café and while she studied the menu, Sheri, the woman behind the counter made small talk. The aroma of potato soup tempted Lily, but she knew trying to eat it in the park would be cumbersome. When Sheri learned they were traveling with their dogs and planning to eat in the park, she insisted they eat on the side deck of the café. "I've got one of those fancy heaters out there to keep you warm and you'll be more comfortable there. We have lots of pet parents and I cater to dog owners. I'll make sure and bring out some water bowls and special dog treats for them." She smiled as she wrote down Lily's selections. "If it were up to me, you could eat inside, but the health department frowns on it."

Lily paid and thanked her, promising to return in a few minutes. She found Mac, pitching balls and a frisbee to the dogs, who ran like the wind to chase and retrieve the items. Their happy faces and long tongues telegraphed their delight in the game. Bodie was the only one still due lunch, but Mac made sure the others received a nibble after their exercise.

He was delighted with the news that they could eat at an actual table and take advantage of plates and silverware. They made their way back across the street and took their chairs at the table that had been prepared for them, with the patio heater on and water bowls nestled next to a couple of dog beds nearby. Sheri had added a pot of tea and a cellophane bag tied with ribbon that held an array of doggy cookies.

Within a few minutes, she emerged from the café and delivered two platters with oversized cups of soup and half sandwiches, along with a cookie. She refilled their water glasses and made sure they had plenty of tea. "You enjoy your lunch and I'll be back to check on you in a few minutes." She bent and petted each of the dogs, talking to them in a soft and high voice.

Their tails thumped against the wooden deck and she asked if she could give them each a cookie. Mac and Lily nodded and smiled as she made each of them sit before rewarding them with a crunchy treat. "They are gorgeous dogs. My sweet Bart is home at the moment, otherwise, he'd be wanting to play with these two."

A ringing phone called her back inside and Lily and Mac dug into their tasty lunch. Lily moaned as she swallowed her first spoonful of soup. "Your veterinarian friend is a genius. This place is beyond good."

Mac grinned as he prepared to take a bite of his thick sandwich. "We could come over here for a fun outing anytime. It's such a quick ride on the ferry."

"I'd love to. There are so many cute shops to see along the waterfront. It would be a bit easier to enjoy without the dogs."

"Agreed. They aren't the best shoppers."

Although there was a chilly breeze, between the soup and the patio heater, they were more than comfortable. The dogs settled down and dozed while Mac and Lily took their time savoring their lunch and watching the activity on the water.

When Sheri had cleared their plates and brought them a second pot of tea, Mac reached for Lily's hand. "I'm happy to stay here with the dogs and you can go peruse some of those shops that caught your eye."

It didn't take much arm twisting to get her to stroll along the waterfront and peek in a few windows. She had always enjoyed buying herself a small gift from trips she had taken and while admiring the array of items in a gift shop, a bracelet caught her eye. She already had the alpaca scarf, but couldn't resist slipping the strands of silver and beads that reminded her of Aunt Maggie's sea glass on her wrist. It was the perfect keepsake for a wonderful getaway.

She had time to duck into the chocolate shop and selected a few boxes, along with some individual pieces for a treat for Mac.

When she returned to the café, they took the dogs to the park, made several laps with them and played a few more games of fetch. Before getting in line for the ferry, they stopped at a coffee place and picked up some warm drinks for the ride home. It had been a perfect day, a perfect trip. As they pulled into the dock at Driftwood Bay, a hint of sadness crept over her. She hated to see the long weekend come to an end.

He pulled into her driveway, unloading and toting in everything while she let the dogs into the backyard. He didn't have time to drive home, so Sherlock would have to stay at Lily's while they met Mel for dinner. After making sure the dogs had their dinner, they left them downstairs so they could come and go through the doggy door as they pleased and headed to the restaurant.

They had just slid into the booth when Mel walked through the door. She was wearing her new vest and boots and Lily noticed a touch of lip gloss. "How was the library today?"

Mel's eyes brightened. "It was great. We got in a new shipment of books and Donna let me take one of them home first. I told her I'd have it back in a couple of days. I also have some exciting news."

"Oh, do tell," said Lily, smiling at Mac and then returning her gaze across the table.

"I found a part-time job. They have a job outreach office at the college and I stopped by Friday and said I was looking for something part-time and the lady printed me out a list. The job at Sunrise Coffee had just been posted, so she called and got me an interview. They called this afternoon and said the job was mine."

"Wow, that is terrific news," said Lily. "I'm so proud of you and excited for you."

"I was nervous, but didn't have time to be too nervous."

Mac chuckled. "That's probably a good thing. The anticipation of stuff is often worse than the actual event. Like Lily says, that is wonderful news."

Mel took a sip from her glass and frowned. "The only bad thing is, I may have to cut back on my volunteer hours with Donna. She said it's not a problem, but I feel bad letting her down."

Lily marveled at her dedication to the library. "You've been a devoted volunteer. I'm sure Donna means it when she says she understands. That's the nature of volunteer work. I'm just excited you'll have some spending money and I'm sure that's a fun place to work."

Excitement replaced the concern in Mel's eyes. "We can drink whatever we want while we're there and can have a free pastry on our break, and we get an employee discount at other times."

Mac grinned at her. "You had me at free coffee and pastries. I don't get any perks at my own clinic. When's your first day? I'll make sure I stop by and give you a healthy tip."

"I start training on Wednesday and then my first actual shift is on Monday."

Mac's phone rang and he excused himself, answering with his doctor greeting.

Mel and Lily chatted more about the coffee shop with Mel telling her she had been studying the menu and trying to learn all the coffee drinks. Mac slid back into his seat moments before the waiter arrived.

After they ordered, Mac showed her the photos he took at the alpaca farm. "Aww, I love them. You need to get some. They would love playing with Coco and Margo."

He grinned and laughed. "That's exactly what Lily recommended."

Lily reached in her tote. "I bought you a souvenir." She handed her the box wrapped with a raffia bow. Mel's surprise at getting a gift almost broke her heart. Much like when they had celebrated her driver's license, Mel was overcome with emotion.

She unwrapped the strands of purple raffia and dug through the tissue. She pulled out the cute stuffed alpaca first and ran her hands over it. "Oh, it's such a cutie." Then she unearthed the beautiful scarf and her mouth fell open. She put it to her cheek. "I think it's the softest thing I've ever felt." Tears glistened in her eyes and she wrapped it around her neck.

A lump formed in Lily's throat as she took in the joy reflected in Mel's face. "I bought myself one, too. I just love them." The waiter interrupted with their plates and Lily helped Mel repackage her gifts and get them out of the way.

As they ate, they told Mel about kayaking and showed her photos of the otters and the shoreline. "Wasn't it scary to be on the water?"

Lily laughed and glanced at Mac. "I wasn't totally sure, but we had an experienced guide and the water was totally calm. I wouldn't want to do it in a fast-moving river, like those white-water adventures."

Mac nodded. "It was relaxing. We thought we might try it here, in Driftwood Bay, next summer."

After their plates were cleared the waiter appeared with a fudge brownie sundae and three spoons and placed it in the middle of the table. Lily frowned and started to say he must have the wrong table, but then saw the flicker in Mac's eye.

He shrugged and said, "I thought we needed to celebrate Mel's new job."

Lily ate a few bites, but left the bulk of it to Mel, who couldn't quit raving about the dessert. She and Mac polished it off, both looking pleased with themselves as they scraped the plate to get the last bit of fudge.

When they had finished their meal and were waiting for the check, Lily passed her phone to Mel with the shots she had taken at Deception Pass. "I thought you might want to take a trip one day and visit Oak Harbor. I know you mentioned that's where you remember your aunt living."

Mel scanned through the photos and bobbed her head, but didn't say anything. Mac took the check and said he'd meet them at the door. His sensitivity and thoughtfulness weren't lost on Lily.

She took the phone back from Mel. "You don't have to decide right now. It's just an idea. Like we talked about going to Seaside this spring."

Mel gathered her gift and stood next to Lily. "I think I would like to visit there again. I remember it being a nice place."

Lily slipped an arm around Mel as they walked through the restaurant. "We'll figure out a day and make the trip while the cottages are closed for the season." She squeezed Mel's shoulder in reassurance. "Did you stay busy with homework this weekend or squeeze in some time for anything fun?"

Mel's eyes sparkled as she told them about driving Donna

and Jeff to the ice cream shop, Jeff making dinner for them, and Donna giving her a bag of makeup samples she thought Mel could use.

Seeing Mel smile and chat instead of shrugging lifted Lily's spirits. A tinge of worry had nagged at her while she had been away, hoping Mel wouldn't regress. Mel thrived on routine, and Lily didn't want to be the one that toppled her progress. Her appointments with Dr. Clay, and perhaps her newfound excitement about school and driving, boosted Mel's frame of mind. She even stood taller.

When they got home, Mac came in for a few minutes to retrieve Sherlock. Upon seeing Mel, the dogs mobbed her, almost knocking her down in an effort to greet her. She laughed and giggled as she let them maul her and cover her in doggy kisses.

Mac leaned close enough to Lily she felt the stubble against her cheek. He whispered, "That is the magic of dogs. If you ever doubt what you are doing by helping train Bodie, that is a glimpse into the why. That joy and acceptance on Mel's face says it all."

14

The week began a new routine, one with Mel embarking on a new job at the coffee shop and Lily without any guests to serve. The freedom to linger at the beach each morning and take the dogs on more excursions was lovely, but by Friday, Lily began to wonder what she was going to do with all her free time. After the dogs ate their breakfast they lounged on the deck, soaking up the warmth and napping after their exercise.

Mac had invited her to the annual lantern festival at the waterfront that night and she could hardly wait. The monotony of the week was getting old. He also included Mel in the invitation, but she had made plans with Bree. Over the Saturday breakfast they were sharing, Lily suggested that the girls could have a sleepover downstairs, if they wanted.

Mel's eyes widened as she bit into her toast. "I've never been to a sleepover. I've only read about them in books."

That revelation broke Lily's heart. "There's not much to them. Usually, they involve stories, maybe painting your nails, watching movies, lots of eating, and staying up way too late." Lily took a sip of tea. "Bree can come over this afternoon and you girls could have the run of the downstairs with the television and I've got plenty of snack food that needs to be eaten since we won't be doing our weekend social hours."

Mel grinned and her eyes widened. "That sounds fun. I'll call Bree and ask her." She shoveled in the rest of her breakfast and hurried downstairs.

Mel never came right out and said staying alone still bothered her, but Lily suspected it might. Having Bree and the dogs there would reassure her and let her take one more step toward being at the house alone. Before Lily had the breakfast dishes done, Mel bounded up the stairs, smiling. "Bree checked with her mom and she said yes. She's going to drop her off around noon."

"That's great. Go to the freezer and take out whatever cookies or brownies look good." Lily went downstairs and made sure Mel knew how to work the device that allowed her to use the streaming services Lily subscribed to on the downstairs television. Mel spent most of her time reading and watched television only with Lily upstairs.

Mel's room was neat and tidy, as was the bathroom. Lily never had to worry about Mel shirking her responsibilities. "Do you want to use the firepit tonight? I can show you how to turn it on."

A hint of doubt crept into Mel's eyes. "Nah, I think we'll just stay inside."

"I want you to feel safe here, Mel. How about we install my security camera monitor system on your phone? That way you'll get a notification to any motion and won't have to worry while you're here."

Mel plucked her phone from her pocket and they went back upstairs where Lily showed her how to use the app and view the video the system stored. "I'm sure you'll be fine and the dogs are great at letting you know if anything is amiss. If you have an emergency just call nine-one-one, but even if you get worried, call my cell and we'll come right back, deal?"

Mel nodded as she concentrated on the screen. "Thanks, Lily."

"Okay, let's make you girls a bunch of snacks." By the time they finished the fridge was loaded with enough food to get them through a harsh winter. Minutes before noon, the doorbell rang and Mel rushed to let Bree inside, helping her carry a tote bag and a pizza box. Nora beeped her horn as she pulled away.

"Mom treated us to pizza for lunch," said Bree, beaming as she followed Mel into the kitchen. "Hi, Lily. Mom said to tell you she's off tomorrow, so can come and pick me up whenever it's convenient."

Lily pulled some plates from the cupboard. "Stay as long as you like." When she had first met Bree, as a guest when Nora came for her job interview, she had been full of snark and could have been the poster child for a difficult teenager, but she had settled in and seemed to have adjusted to life in Driftwood Bay.

Lily joined them for a piece of pizza and having not had teenaged girls around her household much, marveled at the incessant chatter coming from Bree. Mel was quieter, but the more Bree babbled on, the looser Mel's tongue became. Bree held up the tote bag and explained she brought all of her makeup and nail polish supplies.

Lily put her plate in the dishwasher. "Just make sure to put down some old towels when you use the polish and remover. There's a stack downstairs in the utility room."

Mel nodded. "We'll be extra careful, don't worry." If Lily hadn't known Mel was in college, she would have pegged her for a high school girl, with the giddiness she displayed. They finished lunch and the dogs followed their mad dash downstairs.

Lily laughed and went to the computer in the office off the

kitchen. She emailed Izzy with some dates in late January that would work for a visit to the island. She and Mac had compared calendars and found a few long weekends they could spare. She also booked a bed and breakfast in Seaside, Oregon for mid-March, before spring break, early in the week, hoping to avoid crowds, but still with the hope of good weather. They needed to squeeze in the trip before her high season kicked into gear.

She updated the reservation calendar and sent Kevin a text to check in. With all of that done, she spent some time looking up the local arts community center at Fort Warden Park. When Lily had voiced her concerns about having too much time on her hands, Donna had mentioned they were always looking for volunteers.

Lily hadn't attended any of their events, but they offered art shows, performances, readings and lectures, music festivals, tons of art and music classes, and several annual outdoor events during the summer. It looked promising. As she was scrolling, she saw a class on making sea glass mosaics. It made her think of Aunt Maggie and the containers of sea glass stashed in the cupboards. It was a one-day workshop on a Friday the week after Thanksgiving. Before she could think too long, she registered.

While the girls were occupied, she decided to take Bodie on a walk, hoping to expose him to some different sounds and distractions. She put on her fanny pack filled with the soft treats Bodie loved and attached his leash to the harness that let people know he was in training and not to pet him. She left Fritz to watch over the girls and set out toward town.

As she turned the corner to follow one of the busier streets, a loud siren rang out and flashing lights announced a fire engine heading their way. This was a perfect experience for Bodie. She had been working with him to make sure he stopped and sat whenever she stopped walking and he was sitting on the sidewalk now, alert to the shrill noise.

As the engine approached the intersection the blare from its horn startled her, but Bodie remained resolute. He watched the truck, but didn't flinch. "Good boy, Bodie." Lily started walking and he followed, moving to her left side like she had trained him. She led him to the waterfront where things were bustling. They were setting up for the lantern festival with vendors putting up their booths and a few food trucks rolling in to augment the restaurants in the area.

Bodie loved people and that was proving to be difficult for training purposes. He was friendly to a fault, thinking anyone who made eye contact was looking for a greeting. Lily knew she would have her work cut out for her as she surveyed the busy sidewalks surrounding the waterfront.

After practicing with the trainer, Lily had mastered keeping a handful of the soft treats in the palm of her hand and using their scent to capture Bodie's attention. She made sure she had a fistful ready and set out with Bodie. She must have said "leave it" more than a hundred times as they navigated the streets. The trainer had reminded her last week about the importance of rewarding Bodie within a second or two of his good behavior. Each time he ignored the distractions, she slipped him a tasty treat and praised him.

The aroma of grilled meat and sugary fried dough wafted through the air. Several local vendors were setting up booths, and a favorite area donut truck already had a line forming in front of it. She was distracted by the array of smells and could only imagine what it was doing to Bodie, who when he wasn't honing in on a person, had his nose in the air, sniffing at the breeze.

Lily was mentally exhausted from trying to keep up with dispensing praise and treats, while offering corrections as they circled the area. When they reached the outskirts of the activity, she gave Bodie his last treat and bent down to ruffle his ears and tell him what a good boy he was. He pushed his head into her hand and leaned against her, offering her a few licks of appreciation.

"Let's get you home and I'll make the girls help me give you and Fritz a bath." He looked up at her, eyes wide, as if understanding. She laughed and detoured through the park, one of his favorite places to visit, on the way to the house.

When they arrived home, she found the girls downstairs glued to the television, with Fritz lounging at their feet. Lily organized the bath supplies outside and the girls paused their show to help get both of the dogs into the oversized plastic container she used for a bathtub. Fritz loved the pampering that came with a bath and stretched as they lathered him, massaging as they went.

Bodie, on the other hand, was not as relaxed. Despite the adhesive ducks Lily had applied to the slick plastic bottom of the container, Bodie's paw slipped out from under him. She tried to reposition his feet so they were on top of the non-slip stickers, but made a note to find an anti-slip mat. His legs shook as she continued working the soap into his fur. "It's okay, sweet boy. I won't let you fall." She let the girls finish Fritz and had them hold onto Bodie while she used the hose to rinse him.

Unlike Fritz, with never ending patience, who waited for Lily to release him with a command, Bodie bolted from the tub the moment Lily finished spraying him. He shook, releasing a shower of water that drenched Lily, while the girls watched, giggling. Fritz, obedient as ever, sprawled on the grass waiting to be toweled dry.

Lily tasked Bree with drying Fritz while she and Mel tackled Bodie, using the towel to get his attention. Like a red cape to a bull, the towel did the trick and he came rushing toward them. Both dogs liked to skid across the grass when they were wet, but Bodie also used the tactic as a way to escape. He calmed when Lily covered him, including his head with a towel, and they hurried to rub his fur dry.

With the bulk of the drying done, Lily added paw pad cream into each paw. Fritz loved this part of the spa treatment and Bodie quieted down, except for trying to lick at Lily's hands as she made sure each pad was coated. She checked each of their ears and made sure they were clean and then asked Mel to get the toothbrushes.

Fritz was an old pro, but it helped having an extra set of hands to keep Bodie occupied, while Lily brushed his teeth. At this stage, she was still trying to get him used to the process. He loved the doggy toothpaste, but it was a bit of struggle to actually get each tooth brushed.

Mel and Bree cleaned up the tub and put everything away while she let the dogs run in circles, their fur drying a bit more as they played. "Now I need a shower," said Lily, after thanking the girls for helping. "Those two should be tuckered out and take a nap now." She left them outside and made her way upstairs.

As she showered, the aroma of the lavender soap she had brought home from their trip reminded her of Mac. Though everything seemed perfect between them, Lily still felt a hint of guilt, deep inside. She had enjoyed their trip and loved spending time with him. He was easy to be around and so thoughtful. His kindness was clear in how he treated animals and how much he did for others. Watching him interact with Mel and take special care to make sure she felt comfortable and valued, along with the obvious love he had for his sister, cemented Lily's high opinion of him.

Gary would have liked him. Tears fell from Lily's eyes and mixed with the hot spray from the showerhead. She knew he wouldn't want her to be unhappy, mourning him for the rest of her life, but why did it still feel like she was cheating on him? She longed for Kevin to meet Mac at Thanksgiving. She hoped he would like him, genuinely like him, not just be polite and want her to be happy.

She gasped when she thought of Mac's daughter, Missy. With his rocky relationship with her, Lily wondered how she would react if their relationship became more serious, more permanent. He hadn't even mentioned her to Missy. She pushed the doubt about what that meant far from her thoughts. She didn't want to be the cause of a further rift between them. Finding love in mid-life was turning out to be complicated. It was difficult to leave out how their decisions would impact their larger families.

She rinsed her hair again, letting the hot water cascade over her shoulders. If she had made a list of what she was looking for in a man, Mac would have ticked every box. The thing was, she hadn't been looking. That made her think of the Winey Widows and what they had said about living and moving forward after loss. She knew finding love wasn't something you could plan. It wasn't a quest, where if you did everything right, you were guaranteed the prize at the end. It was one of those things left up to fate.

She couldn't deny her feelings for Mac or the fact that she was happier on the days she saw him or talked to him. It was hard to imagine her life without him. If only she could be rid of the guilt.

15

Mac arrived with Sherlock in tow, at Lily's request. She thought Sherlock shouldn't have to be alone and the girls could watch three dogs as easily as two. Lily made sure the dogs were indoors and locked the downstairs exterior doors and the doggy door.

"Okay, you're all set. Plenty of food and you both have our cell numbers, so just call us if you need anything. The doors are locked and we should be home by eleven, at the latest."

They were in a hurry to get downstairs and back to their binging on television and snacks. The dogs bounded after them and Mac and Lily were left to lock the door behind them. She made sure she had her cell phone in her jacket pocket and tucked some cash in her jeans, opting to leave her purse at home. Like the gentleman he was, Mac opened the passenger door for her and waited until she was settled before closing it.

There was a definite nip in the air and Lily was glad to have her warm alpaca scarf around her neck. She was used to seeing Mac in scrubs or one of his casual polo shirts, but he had upped his game tonight. He added a button-down shirt and blazer to his normal jeans. The shirt had a narrow blue stripe that matched the color of his eyes and the gray toned jacket accentuated the silver threads in his hair. Her pulse quickened when he smiled at her.

She had taken a bit of extra care choosing her own outfit, not knowing exactly what to expect. She wore her new boots and jeans, plus a deep blue sweater over a white shirt and topped it with her black leather jacket. It and the new scarf would ward off the cool breeze.

Mac drove the few blocks to the waterfront, where parking was scarce. He pulled into a driveway just a block from the marina. He grinned at Lily's questioning look. "A long-time client lives here and said I could park in the driveway."

"It pays to be the beloved town vet." She chuckled and before she could release the handle, he was out of the car and at the door.

"I made reservations at Bayside Grille. Have you been there?"

"No, but I'm up for anything." He took her hand and they made their way through the already crowded sidewalks to the restaurant.

Driftwood Bay wasn't large enough to attract any of the popular chain restaurants, but had several small, locally-owned dining spots. Lily hadn't gone anywhere more exotic than for pizza and the pub-style restaurant Mel liked, but knew the reputation of Bayside Grille was upscale and excellent.

The hostess led them to a cozy table with an impeccable view over the harbor. The sun was just setting and the golden glow over the water was breathtaking. The restaurant made ample use of white twinkly lights, draping them across the window ledges and tucking them in plants. Candles burned atop each table and a fire glowed in the hearth near the bar and lounge.

The menu offered many tempting dishes, but Lily settled on the potato leek soup and a salmon entrée. Mac went with prime rib and a salad. Lily gazed outside, taking in the stunning sunset over the water and the activity below. "The view here is incredible."

Mac nodded, his eyes fixed on her. "I couldn't agree more. You look lovely tonight."

She covered her embarrassment with a laugh. "It's the magic of candlelight. That's kind of you, but I was talking about the sunset."

"Bayside Grille is known for its waterfront views and great food. I haven't been here for years."

As they ate their first course, they chatted about the week, with Mac telling her about a surgery on a dog, where he found multiple pairs of kids' underwear and socks the dog had ingested. "This is not the first time Brewster has raided the laundry. You'd think the owners would learn and make sure their kids picked up their belongings. It's not a cheap surgery and can be quite dangerous for the dog." He shook his head as he put his fork on the empty salad plate.

"That would scare me to death. I'd hate to have anything happen to Fritz or Bodie."

"These people are nice, but haven't been successful at training their kids or their dogs. Did you do anything fun this week?"

"I did my qualification with my gun at the range, so that's out of the way for another year. I also signed up for a workshop at the arts center. I'm thinking I might volunteer there and thought it would be a good way to check it out."

He chuckled at her revelation. "A sharp shooter and an art class are quite the juxtaposition. You are like no other woman I've ever met." He smiled and added, "That's a good thing."

The waiter delivered their entrees and each of them admired the other's plate. "Do you want to split them?" Lily raised her brows. "I'm happy to cut this in half."

Mac grinned. "Great idea. I couldn't decide and almost

ordered that." He cut the prime rib in half and they made the transfer across the table. "The arts center puts on a ton of events and performances. People come from all over for their festivals. I've been to a few, but Cyndy is a season ticket holder, so she could give you more insight."

"I realized this week, I need something to do. I can't just sit around the house for the next few months."

"I know what you mean. Whenever I think about cutting back or even retiring, I worry that I won't know what to do with myself. I've been a veterinarian for the majority of my life and I love it." He took his first bite of salmon. "Oh, this is delicious. Thanks for sharing."

"The cottages have been a good transition for me, from working full time. It's given me a bit of freedom, which I love. Bodie, and now Mel, keep me busy, but without the hubbub of guests coming and going, I think I'll be bored."

"Our little getaway did teach me that I need to do a better job of scheduling time off and actually go away instead of just doing chores at home. I'm looking forward to our trip in January."

"Izzy should be getting back to us this week to finalize the dates." She let out a long breath. "Kevin will be here for Thanksgiving and I'm anxious and a little nervous for him to meet you. Actually, from what you've said about Missy, I'm more worried about meeting her. Is she coming home for Thanksgiving or Christmas?"

Sadness flashed in Mac's eyes, followed by a quick smile. "Honestly, I don't know, but I doubt it. She hasn't been home for the holidays in years. Last I knew, she was all the way across the country in Georgia. Do you have any plans for what you'll do with Kevin here?"

Lily frowned. "No, I need to come up with something fun. Back to Missy, I don't want to stress you about her, but have you told her about me?"

He shook his head and reached across the table for her hand. "It's nothing to do with you. I know it sounds horrible, but I don't talk to her often. I tried, really tried for a long time, calling her a few times a week, trying to build some type of relationship, but never made much progress. After getting the cold shoulder and worse, my calls dwindled to once every couple of weeks, once a month, then a few times a year. Cyndy always invites her to Thanksgiving and she always says no. This year is no different."

"I just don't want to be the reason for more angst between the two of you."

"If it will make you feel better, I'll make a point of calling her this weekend and telling her about you and offer her a ticket home for the holidays." He looked up at the ceiling. "Just understand, whatever she says, and I anticipate it will be nothing good, it's not to do with you. She's made it clear she doesn't want to be around me or even care about me, so all the ugliness that will come out will be about me. I can't do anything right, trust me."

Tears filled Lily's eyes and she let go of Mac's hand to dab at them with her napkin. "That is so heartbreaking. I'm sorry, Mac. I wish there was something I could do to help."

"I'd be lying if I said it didn't bother me. It used to torment me. I know that played a big part in me leading a solitary life, other than my animals." He grinned, but she noticed the anguish in his eyes and the forced smile. "I thought I could wait her out and she'd come home and we'd be a family again, albeit just the two of us. I spent years doing that and nothing changed. Thank goodness Cyndy still maintains a relationship with her. That's the only way I have of knowing the little I do about her life."

The waiter cleared their empty plates and offered dessert. Lily shook her head and opted for hot tea instead. "I'm sorry, Mac. I didn't mean to dredge up bad memories. I have no doubt you've tried your best to forge a relationship. I just feel so awful for you, for both of you."

He sighed. "Honestly, if I think about it too much, I get depressed. I've been down that dark hole and I don't want to go back. That's part of the reason I work so much. It's easier than facing my own thoughts."

"I understand that coping method. I've used it myself. Wendy, my sister, and I have a non-existent relationship. Like you, it hurt me, especially after losing our parents and I struggled with it. I reached out to her in every way I knew how. She rebuffed me and I finally gave up." She took a sip from her cup and wrapped her hands around the warm ceramic. "I totally get the futility of constantly reaching out, only to have your hand bitten each time."

"I remember you mentioning her before. She lives far away, right?"

Lily nodded. "Texas. She and her bazilliionaire husband live the life of luxury. Huge house, travel, toys, all of it. We're about as opposite as can be. She doesn't work and he's in investment banking, has his own company. No children, so she's the center of the universe. She came to Gary's funeral, but didn't stick around. More like a duty to make an appearance."

"That's tough," he said, pouring the last of the tea into his cup. "I never would have made it without Cyndy. She's the best sister a guy could ask for. She's like my mom was. I'm grateful she's here and such an important part of my life."

"When I think about Wendy, it makes me sad. Our parents would be so disappointed. Growing up, we were close. She was younger, so could be a royal pain, but I never imagined we'd grow up to be virtual strangers. Families are complicated."

The waiter brought the check and Mac slipped his credit card into the portfolio. "That is an understatement."

While they waited for the receipt, Lily tapped in a text to

check on Mel. Moments later, she received a reply that all was well. Relieved, she smiled and put her phone back in her pocket.

As he helped her slip into her jacket, Mac winked. "Are the girls okay?"

She smiled and nodded. "They're fine."

He took her hand and they made their way to the tent where they collected their lantern kits. As they navigated through the crowd to one of the tables set up with markers and other supplies, people greeted Mac with warm smiles and claps on the shoulder. She recognized many of them and those that she didn't, Mac introduced to her, always letting them know she was Leo's niece and was now the innkeeper at Glass Beach Cottage.

With all the greetings and well wishes from the townspeople, it was clear Mac was a cherished member of the community. As soon as they sat down, Cyndy slid into the chair next to Mac. "Isn't this a lovely evening?" The soft glow coming from the strings of globe lights above them, accentuated the excitement in her eyes.

They got to work assembling the paper lanterns, with Cyndy producing a designer quality one, while Lily's looked more like a child's effort. Some people were writing complete poems on all four sides of their lanterns, or like Cyndy drawing intricate designs. Lily chose to write only four words—love, hope, faith, and strength. They summed up her thoughts about the past, present, and future.

When she finished assembling hers and making sure it was square, she looked up to see Mac still staring at the blank paper. He shook his head. "I can't think of anything to put on it and I'm no artist." He gestured to Cyndy's.

"I kept it simple. I couldn't think of a poem or anything spectacular." She showed him hers.

He nodded. "Those are good ones." He thought for a few minutes and added four words to his. "I stole two of yours." She smiled and saw that he had added wishes and believe to hope and love.

"Perfect." She helped him finish assembling his. "This was more pressure than I thought it would be. Cyndy was smart to draw hers." She was still busy coloring in one side, opting for black and white designs on all four sides.

When she finished it, she explained the designs were known as Zentangle, a form of drawing patterns that was meant to be relaxing and creative. Mac and Lily were impressed. In the time they had written four words, she had decorated all four sides of her lantern. "They have classes at the arts center, if you're interested."

"Oh, speaking of the arts center, I wanted to ask you about it." Lily explained she was taking a class and thinking about volunteering.

"You'd love it there. They're a nice group of people and are happy to have help, plus you get some free tickets and access to classes at a discount. By the way, I'm making Sunday dinner tomorrow and would love for you to join us."

"You won't have to twist my arm to enjoy your cooking." Lily chuckled as she checked her lantern again.

A group of three women descended upon them and all started chatting at once, asking Cyndy where she'd been. They'd been looking for her for the last hour. She smiled and was off to find the wine tent and await the launching of the lanterns.

Mac shook his head, laughing as he watched his sister leave. "She is always in demand and going a hundred miles an hour."

"I admire her easy, outgoing personality. That's just not me. Sometimes, I wish I was like that."

He brought her hand to his lips. "I think you're perfect, just the way you are."

Moments later, the speakers crackled as an announcer asked the participants to make their way to the path that led to the beach. Upbeat music played, and the lights along the dock plus the full moon provided plenty of light. There wasn't enough room on the beach for everyone to stand at the edge, so they launched their lanterns in groups.

Mac added the LED tea lights to their lanterns and he and Lily pushed their wooden bases across the water, letting them float with the hundreds of others, flickering on the ocean. They stood watching for a few minutes, fascinated by the number of lanterns and the beauty of them against the backdrop of the dark sea.

Finally, they made their way back to the dock. Standing at the railing, the effect of the lanterns was even more magnificent. Kids, wrapped with glow-in-the-dark necklaces, darted in and out of the crowd as everyone pointed and admired the view.

"The girls should have come. They would have enjoyed this," said Lily, squeezing closer to Mac as more people gathered around them. They watched as the current carried the lanterns further away.

Mac grabbed her hand. "I've got an idea. Come with me." He led her through the crowd and hurried back to the car. Once they were settled, he drove through the mostly empty streets and made it to their destination, only two miles from the waterfront.

Lily recognized the parking lot at Fort Warden State Park. After opening her door, he took her hand again and led her to the walkway atop the cliffs. There, they stood in awe of the mass of light moving toward them. The lanterns bobbed along, riding the current to where the organizers would ultimately pick them up and recycle them, but until then, the two of them, wrapped in each other's arms delighted in the warm glow of the magical lights. As Mac kissed her, Lily wanted to believe in the words she and Mac had written on their lanterns. She wanted to believe in the hope of love.

It wasn't even ten o'clock when Mac started to make the turn toward Lily's house. He caught himself and went one more block. "How about we pick up a hot chocolate and take a walk on the beach? There's nothing better than a beach, a full moon, and a beautiful woman."

"I can't refuse any offer that includes chocolate and the beach." Lily linked her arm through his as they entered the café by the library.

It was far enough from the bustle of the waterfront, that they were the only two people there. The young woman behind the counter made their hot chocolates, adding whipped cream, and a drizzle of chocolate sauce, plus a dusting of cinnamon to one and shavings from peppermint bark to the other. After one sip, Lily knew she could never go back to the instant packets in her cupboard.

Not wanting to disturb the girls or trigger an alert of the security cameras, they drove to the park near Lily's house. It was empty, with well-lit pathways. They walked through, following the trail below the park that connected to the beach Lily visited every morning.

The full moon made for easy navigation, plus Mac held her hand and led the way. They stayed away from the shoreline, so as not to get their shoes soaked and he gestured to a large piece of driftwood. "Care to sit?"

They eased onto the thick trunk of a log that had settled into the beach long ago. The top of the log was worn smooth by the sea, with shallow indentations making perfect seats by those who had come before them and sat at the same spot to gaze across the water at the beauty before them.

Although devoid of the stunning colors at sunrise, the moonlight atop the water was enchanting. The huge moon hung in the dark sky, as if mere feet above the water. Lily could see the battered and scarred surface, where patches were significantly darker than others. Like the beam of a powerful flashlight, its light painted a white stripe across the water, shimmering with the gentle waves and emphasizing the white froth as the waves ebbed and flowed along the shore.

The gentle lap of the water along the beach soothed her mind, similar to the mornings she spent at her spot farther down the beach, where she marveled at the sight of the sun rising. So beautiful, but in a different way, and perhaps even more relaxing. Without the promise of the sun to warm her face and shoulders, she snuggled closer to Mac, sipping the still warm chocolate.

Stars twinkled in the inky sky, but the moon played the lead tonight. Lily hadn't ventured out to the beach at night, staying in the yard and enjoying the fire pit and visiting with the guests or sitting on the deck with her tea. She had missed out on the beauty and tranquility of the dark beach. Next summer, she'd make a point of taking advantage of the warm evenings, especially when there was a full moon.

"It's magical," she whispered.

Mac turned toward her, grinning. "A night on a moonlit beach is something special." He bent his head closer to her. The cool sensation of peppermint pricked her lips as they met his. Thoughts of her reservations about a relationship and Mac's complicated situation with his daughter melted away with the chill she had felt. As his mouth wandered to the side of her neck, she gasped, thankful for the cover of darkness and the empty beach.

16

With the girls sleeping late, the house was quiet and Lily would have loved to languish in bed longer, but for the two wet noses resting against her arm and the four gentle brown eyes staring at her. The boys needed to go outside and would want breakfast.

She slipped her hooded cardigan over her pajamas decorated with teacups, then tiptoed out, so as not to wake anyone downstairs. After she let the dogs out, she filled their bowls and brewed a cup of tea. She glanced at the refrigerator where a copy of Mel's schedule hung. She had to work at the coffee shop from noon until closing.

Long ago, she and Gary had trained Fritz to rest after he ate and she had trained Bodie to do the same. With them lounging outside on the deck, she took her tea and climbed back into bed, savoring the coziness.

She scrolled through her tablet, getting caught up on the news and email. Her phone pinged with a text from Nora asking if she could pick up the girls at ten o'clock and treat them to brunch. Lily promised to have them up and ready to go.

Giving up on the idea of spending the morning in bed, Lily

showered and got ready for the day before going downstairs to rustle the girls from their beds. She let them know about Nora's brunch plans and took the dogs to the beach, albeit late.

They forgave her tardiness and set out for the trail, tails wagging, their jaws set in the permanent smile that golden retrievers were blessed with, as they kept in step with Lily. They went further than usual, stopping at the same log from last night. The dogs sniffed at the bits of driftwood and seaweed along the shoreline, stepping into the water, but coming back to Lily when she hollered for them. She wasn't up for giving them another bath.

She tossed the balls she always made sure were in her pockets and threw them away from the water, so as to remove the temptation. The dogs ran and loped, enjoying the cool temperature and the deserted beach. Lily's thoughts wandered to the romantic hour she had spent here last night, wrapped in Mac's arms, enjoying his kisses like a hormone-driven teenager. She blushed at the memory.

Once the dogs had exercised, she led them back, keeping away from the water. At home, she wiped their feet and let them in the downstairs, which to her delight had been tidied.

She had checked on the girls when she got home last night and helped to extricate Sherlock from the puddle of pups stationed by the couch, but hadn't visited with them. The girls were waiting upstairs and showed her their nails. Each of them had added glitter to the polish, with Mel choosing a deep plum color and Bree going crazy with a vivid green.

They chattered on about the movies they had watched and the smile on Mel's face assured Lily she had enjoyed her first sleepover. Nora arrived and visited for a few minutes before packing Bree and her belongings into her car. Mel elected to drive herself, so she could go directly from brunch to work. She had dressed in the required black pants and shirt with the Sunrise Coffee logo.

Lily waved at her from the driveway, reminding her she'd be having dinner at Cyndy's, but would be home before Mel got off work. Back inside, she started a load of laundry, and checked her wine stash, pulling a couple of bottles to take to Cyndy's. She wouldn't need a supply until next season, and Cyndy would enjoy it.

She had no sooner gotten comfortable in her recliner, with the dogs nestled at her feet, and selected a new series to watch, when her doorbell rang. She opened it to a smiling young woman holding a bouquet of flowers.

She carried the gorgeous arrangement of dahlias and chrysanthemums into the kitchen. After admiring the pale pinks, beiges, and white flowers, she plucked the card from them. *Thanks for making me believe in hope again. With love, Mac.*

She clutched the card to her heart. The two dogs stood, looking at her, as if wondering who sent the flowers. "He's definitely a keeper, isn't he?"

In full agreement, they thumped their tails against the floor.

Dinner at Cyndy's was a treat. Not only was her meal fabulous, but she was such a wonderful hostess, making Lily feel right at home. Along with the crispy chicken thighs seasoned with fresh garlic and rosemary, she served a beautiful unconstructed Waldorf salad, and creamy butternut squash soup.

As Lily admired the gorgeous table, decorated with fall flowers and candles, and the dishes that looked more like artwork, she wished she could create such a masterpiece. She couldn't wait to see what Cyndy did for Thanksgiving later in the week. "I'd love to contribute something to your Thanksgiving table, but cooking is not my forte. I'm afraid anything I would make would pale in comparison to your dishes. Is there something I could do?"

Mac grinned. "I always bring the pies. Technically, I order the pies and pick them up from the bakery." He winked at Cyndy. "Already done, by the way."

Lily took another piece of the garlic bread. "With zero kitchen skills, all I can offer is wine or buying ingredients, but I'm happy to do both."

Cyndy reached for her wine glass. "You don't need to worry about it. I've got it under control." She eyed her glass, and added, "I never refuse good wine, though."

Mac and Lily laughed. "Izzy gave me quite a supply from her family's winery, so I'll bring several bottles."

Cyndy winked at her. "What day does Kevin arrive?"

"He gets in on Wednesday and is going to take the shuttle. He didn't want me to have to hassle with the holiday traffic. He goes back on Sunday." Her smile faded. "Such a short visit, but then he'll be here for almost a month for the holiday break in December and January." The sparkle returned to her eyes.

"Oh, that will be wonderful for you. I'm looking forward to having the two of you and Mel for dinner. The last couple of years without Mom and Dad, it's just not the same, so having guests will be so much fun."

"Kevin is even more excited than I am, knowing you're a fabulous cook and he won't have to suffer through my attempt. I think Mel is equally enthusiastic, not having had much in the way of Thanksgiving these last few years."

Cyndy glanced at her brother. "We were hoping Missy might join us this year, but we called her today and she can't come."

Mac cleared his throat and turned toward Lily. "I promised you I would reach out to her, invite her for the holidays, and tell her about you." He sighed. "Mission accomplished, but I'm afraid it went as I feared it would."

Cyndy shook her head. "I can usually get through to her, but she's difficult and delights in getting under her dad's skin."

Lily winced. "I'm so sorry, Mac. I just didn't want her to be taken by surprise if she did visit. I can't imagine how awful that is for you."

He shrugged, but she saw the sadness in his eyes. "I'm used to it."

Cyndy sighed. "I had hoped by now, as Missy got older, she would recognize the importance of family, staying connected, and quite frankly, treat her father better. I think we all gave her a pass when Jill died and made excuses for her. I know I did. Now, though, her behavior is out of control."

Lily couldn't imagine not having Kevin in her life, not talking to him and texting each week, not seeing him. Her heart broke for Mac. She reached for his hand. "I regret asking you to call her. I underestimated the whole situation."

He moved his hand and patted her arm. "It's not your fault, believe me. This has been ongoing. I agree, she needs to know about you, about us. I didn't intend to hide it from her. It's always just easier not to engage with her. She still knows how to hurt me, even from all the way across the country."

Cyndy's sorrowful gaze met her brother's. "There's no easy answer. If Mac ignores her, she plays the nobody cares about me card and if he engages with her all she does is hurl insults and hurtful words. I'm not sure what it will take to lead her back to us or if she will ever find her way."

"What's for dessert?" Mac scanned the kitchen counters. Lily didn't blame him for wanting to change the subject.

Cyndy hurried from the table and returned with an apple slab pie. She scooped out generous slices and passed them. Mac topped his with homemade whipped cream and took a forkful.

Lily couldn't bring herself to eat a bite. Rocks formed in her stomach as she thought more about the anguish Mac suffered with his daughter. Seeing how he and Cyndy supported each other also made her think of Wendy. Lily had to make more of an effort with her and try to recapture some type of relationship with her. Her parents would expect nothing less.

By the time she helped Cyndy with the dishes, while Mac worked on a small repair upstairs, it was almost seven o'clock. Cyndy had made two care packages, stuffing leftovers into containers Lily and Mac could take home.

Mac had an early morning and Lily wanted to get home before Mel, so they hugged Cyndy goodbye, thanking her for dinner and the leftovers, and waved as Mac drove them away from the house. He was quiet on the way to Lily's and left the car running when he pulled into the driveway.

"Come in just for a cup of tea or coffee," she said, taking the hand he offered her as he held the passenger door open.

He walked her to the door, carrying her leftovers. "I better not tonight. I'm beat and afraid I wouldn't be great company. I need to drop by the clinic and check on a patient anyway."

She opened the door to Fritz and Bodie, who made a beeline for Mac and then went about sniffing at the bag he set in the entryway. "Thanks again for the beautiful flowers."

He engulfed her in a tight embrace. "You're welcome and I meant what I said on the card." He released her and bent his forehead to touch hers. "The call with Missy rattled me and I just need to deal with it. I let myself get my hopes up. I'm not sure why I keep going back, just to get abused. It's like a kid touching a hot stove—you'd think I would learn."

She smiled and kissed him. "I understand. Don't be so hard on yourself."

He squeezed her hand. "I'll call you this week. I thought it might be nice to go to dinner with Kevin Wednesday night. Let me know if that works out and we could do pizza or something casual that he'd like. Mel, too, of course."

"That sounds perfect. Let's plan on it. He should be here in the early afternoon."

He kissed her again. "I'm looking forward to it."

She stood in the open doorway, watching as he walked back to the car, the usual bounce in his step subdued. There was nothing she could do to take away the pain he felt. The despair and disappointment of being alienated from his daughter and being powerless to change it would be enough to depress anyone.

She waved as he left the driveway. She hoped his heart would heal and suspected one reason he poured so much love into treating animals was because they were accepting and provided him with the unconditional love he craved.

17

Lily wiped the counters and checked Kevin's bedroom for the umpteenth time while she waited to pick him up from the shuttle drop downtown. The house was spotless and she had made his favorite brownies, loaded with walnuts, along with chocolate chunk cookies. She had the ingredients on hand to make the cinnamon and nut pastry she had always made for holidays. It had been a favorite of Gary's and Kevin's and she wasn't about to break with tradition. Outside of that, for Thanksgiving morning, she planned to go out to eat.

Having messaged Wendy to wish her a Happy Thanksgiving and open the door to having a longer conversation, she checked her phone to see if her sister had replied to the text. Nothing yet. It had been a long time since she had talked to her and she couldn't be sure Wendy still had the same phone number. She dashed to the office and sent off an email to her, letting her know she hoped to talk to her soon. That way, both bases were covered and Wendy was sure to get one of the messages.

She had splurged and had both the dogs groomed, and they were sporting their Thanksgiving-themed bandanas, looking and smelling like a million bucks. They had picked up on Lily's excitement and knew something was up. She checked her watch one more time. "It's almost time to pick up your brother," she said, bending down to ruffle both of their ears. She was sure Fritz knew what that meant, as he began to spin in circles.

They were set to meet Mac for pizza at six o'clock and Mel ended up having to work so she wouldn't be there. She also had to work all weekend, so wouldn't be joining them on their excursion over to Whidbey Island on Saturday. One of the small cities on the southern part of Whidbey kicked off their holiday celebration with a tree lighting and festival the weekend after Thanksgiving. Lily wanted to make sure Kevin enjoyed himself and made reservations on the ferry.

It was finally time to go, and she left the dogs with cookies, promising to be home soon. She, of course, was early and had to wait for the shuttle to arrive. The city workers were prepping the streets along the waterfront with holiday decorations. Their local tree lighting would take place during the first weekend in December in the square near the fountain.

For the first time since losing Gary, she was looking forward to the season. A large part of her excitement was having Kevin home, but she also loved the idea of a small-town Christmas and all the activities planned in the community, not to mention being able to spend time with Mac and Cyndy. She and Mac already had plans to attend the festivities and he had made a reservation for dinner after the tree lighting.

The shuttle pulled to the curb and Lily had to stop herself from rushing to the door. Instead, she stood on the sidewalk in front of her car, trying to look nonchalant. She didn't want to embarrass Kevin, but couldn't wait to hug him.

He was the last of a handful of people to step off the shuttle. She waved and he spotted her, as he extended the handle of his bag and wheeled it with him. "Hey, Mom." He wrapped his arms around her.

The worry that always nagged at her whenever one of them had to fly disappeared as she delighted in the long hug. "I'm so happy you're here." She took the handle of his suitcase and lugged it to the back of her car. "Long day, huh?"

He nodded and yawned. "Yeah and I'm starving. I know we've got dinner plans, but I can't wait until then."

"Oh, no problem. Let's just run over to the café and have something to tide you over." She clicked the key fob and led the way down the street.

Kevin opted for breakfast and Lily ordered a pot of tea. "You look great, Mom. So happy."

"That's sweet of you to say. Tell me about school and what you've been up to."

They visited and Lily's spirits rose as she listened to her son and his enthusiasm for school. It made her happy to see him smiling and relaxed. "Hopefully, you're up for a quick ferry ride over to Whidbey Island on Saturday. They start their holiday celebration and have a tree lighting, so I thought that would be fun."

He continued to eat and nodded. "Sounds good to me."

"I was going to arrange a trip over to Victoria when you're here for Christmas. They have a huge holiday celebration and decorations. I thought it would be fun to go over on the ferry and stay overnight. You'll have to remember to bring your passport."

"I'm up for anything."

"I just don't want you to get bored."

He laughed. "I won't be bored. I plan to sleep and lounge around and do as little as possible, but I'm happy to do a few things. I'm just so tired from being up early and studying late, I'm looking forward to vegging."

She smiled and sipped her tea. "I'm excited and nervous for you to meet Mac tonight."

"Don't be nervous. If you like him, I'll like him. I trust your judgment. Like I said, you seem happy and if he's responsible for that, I like him already."

Her nerves settled at his words. "Speaking of dating, have you met any nice girls?"

Kevin's cheeks reddened as he shrugged. Lily's brows rose, but she didn't press him. He added jam to his toast and said, "There's one girl that seems nice and she's super smart. Brooke. She's from a small town in New Hampshire."

"A group of ladies came to visit the cottages from Vermont. They made it sound lovely. I've always wanted to visit that area in the fall, for the colors."

He dug his phone out of his pocket and turned the screen to show her a photo. "Brooke sent me a couple photos." There was a gorgeous shot from the plane showcasing the beautiful fall trees along a river and another of a huge brick house surrounded by trees with brilliant red and orange leaves.

"Wow, those are stunning."

"She was anxious to get home and left a day early. Her grandfather is ill." Part of Lily was excited that Kevin had a friend, possibly a girlfriend, but a tiny part of her was sad at the realization that one day he would meet the woman who would become his wife and he would no longer be coming home for every holiday.

He finished his meal and they made their way home. Fritz couldn't contain himself and ran at Kevin the minute Lily opened the door. Bodie was enthusiastic, joining in the jumping and licking fest that served as a greeting.

"I guess Bodie isn't waiting for an introduction." Lily shook her head as she watched the crazy antics. Kevin laughed and finally sat on the floor so Fritz could get as close as possible. The dog sprawled across Kevin's lap with Bodie jumping onto the pile. Lily gave up trying to use her stern voice to get them to mind and took Kevin's bag downstairs.

By the time she returned, Kevin had migrated to the recliner and was doing his best to keep the dogs on the floor in front of him. As he petted them, he glanced over to her. "I was going to try to grab a couple of hours of sleep before we go to dinner. Is that okay?"

"Sure, your room's ready. I'll make sure and wake you."

He didn't have to call the dogs to follow; they were at his heels and bounded down the stairs with him. Lily shrugged and laughed. "I guess I'm second rate when Kev's around."

Lily woke Kevin in time for him to get changed and they arrived to find Mac already at a table. He shook hands with Kevin. "Your mom has been looking forward to your visit for weeks. I'm happy to finally meet you."

Kevin grinned. "Pleased to meet you, sir."

Mac shook his head. "No sir necessary. Mac will do fine. My name is actually Jack, but everyone has called me Mac for so long it stuck."

"Mac, then." Kevin slid into a chair, while Mac pulled out Lily's.

They let Kevin choose the pizza toppings and ordered one to go so they'd be able to take some home for Mel. Mac asked Kevin about college and his courses and talked about how much he had enjoyed going to school in Davis, California. "It wasn't too far from home, but far enough away that I could have my own life. Those were some of the best years of my life. It's important you enjoy that time."

Lily hadn't told Kevin much about Mac, just that he was Cyndy's brother, a widower for many years, a veterinarian, and had family ties to Driftwood Bay. "Do you have kids?" Kevin asked, taking his first slice of pizza from the extra-large pan in the middle of the table.

Lily may have mentioned Mac's daughter, but wasn't sure.

She held her breath as Mac explained about Missy and that she lived in Georgia, but that they had a strained and distant relationship. He did it without assigning any blame to her or becoming overly emotional. She admired that about him. Maybe it came from having to deliver difficult news to pet parents. She couldn't have held it together.

Kevin frowned as he listened. "I'm sorry about your daughter." He glanced at Lily. "I can't imagine not talking to my mom or not being a part of her life."

Lily smiled and took the opportunity to change the subject. "Mac is in charge of pies for tomorrow."

He held up his hand. "Not to worry, just ordering them, not making them."

"Cyndy is such a great cook, I can hardly wait for tomorrow." Lily went on to describe their meal Cyndy had made on Sunday. She smirked at Kevin and added, "I volunteered to bring wine."

He feigned shock and wiped his hand across his brow. "Whew. Saved from her boxed stuffing mix."

"You've never turned down my cookies or brownies, though."

Kevin nodded. "You're a good baker."

"I've got both of your favorites at home for dessert tonight. Mel should be home by eight, so we'll have dessert with her."

"That's right, you haven't met her." Mac reached for one more slice of pizza. "She's come out of her shell this last month, especially."

Kevin eyed the two pieces of pizza left and Mac spun the pan around so they were in front of him. "All yours."

Kevin grinned and scooped them onto his plate. "Did she ever say any more about being kidnapped? That had to be so scary."

Lily shook her head. "She hasn't said much about it and I

haven't asked her." Her eyes narrowed. "Don't you mention it, either."

Kevin rolled his eyes. "Gee, Mom, really? I wasn't going to. I just think she's brave."

"I agree, but she's not your typical college freshman. In some ways, she's old beyond her years, and in other ways, still child-like. I think she's settling into a routine and is much happier lately. She's excited about her new job and loves school."

Mac swallowed the last of his iced tea and nodded. "Having your mom care about her and knowing she's safe has done wonders for Mel. She's not nearly as withdrawn."

Lily smiled at Mac. "I think having a car and being able to have some control of her life, going to school and work, plus her therapy is all working. It makes me happy to see her beginning to flourish."

Mac insisted on treating them to dinner, and once the waiter delivered their takeout pizza, he followed Lily and Kevin back to the house. While Lily put some cookies and brownies on a tray, Kevin and Mac played with the dogs and Mac told Kevin about Sherlock and his other animals.

"When you're here for your break, we'll organize something out at the house and introduce you to all of them."

The dogs took off for the front door, which meant Mel was home. She greeted them with a soft caress before coming into the kitchen. Lily introduced her to Kevin and pointed at the oven. "I put your pizza in there to keep it warm, but you're home early, so it should be fine."

"The manager let us off, since it was so quiet."

"You're off tomorrow, right?" Kevin asked, as he helped himself to a brownie.

Mel opened the lid on the pizza box. "Yes, but then I work all weekend. I volunteered since I'm not real big on holidays."

"I was telling Kevin about planning a trip over to Victoria when he's here for Christmas. You're welcome to join us."

Mel wrinkled her nose. "I don't know. I'll think about it, but I'm planning to work as much as I can over the break, since I won't have to worry about school."

What she had said before about holidays echoed in Lily's mind. She could only imagine what holidays had been like for Mel over the last few years. She'd have to tamp down her enthusiasm and not overwhelm her. The holidays could be a grim reminder of what was missing, and the pressure to be happy when you didn't feel like celebrating pushed many people further into despair. Lily, of all people, understood. "Just know you're always welcome. You can decide later."

Mel finished her pizza and stored the rest in the fridge, helping herself to a cookie when she returned to the counter. "We did start decorating the coffee shop tonight with Christmas decorations. They're expecting to be busy this weekend. The campaign to get people to shop locally is working."

After they finished off the plate of cookies, Mac wished everyone a good evening. They couldn't convince him to stay to watch a movie, but he promised to see them at Cyndy's. Lily walked him to his car, where she was rewarded with a sweet kiss. "Kevin's a fine young man. I'm glad he's here to spend some time with you."

"I'm so happy he's here and got to meet you. I was sure he would like you, but wanted to see it for myself."

"Feel better now?" Mac hugged her close to him. "Go enjoy your movie and I'll see you tomorrow."

She waved as he pulled away and then hurried inside. Kevin had already loaded *Planes, Trains, and Automobiles*, a movie they enjoyed each holiday. The three of them snuggled together on the couch, with Lily in the middle and warm blankets covering them. With the dogs nestled at their feet and the comfort of Kevin next to her, Lily could think of nothing better.

18

Thanksgiving morning, Lily put the concoction of frozen rolls with cinnamon and nuts in the oven and hurried the dogs to the beach for a quick walk. They didn't have much time, but she didn't want to let a gorgeous morning pass without a stroll along the water. The beach was quiet, except for a few birds. As the sun brightened, Lily whispered, "Happy Thanksgiving," hoping Gary knew she was thinking of him.

It had always been one of his favorite holidays and she was glad to be going to Cyndy's today, making new memories, so as not to be surrounded by what had been, what she had lost. She shook her head, clearing away those recollections and forced her thoughts to the present. She'd have Mel and Kevin bring in all the boxes of Christmas decorations, so they could get to work on them tonight and tomorrow. The tree, a life-like artificial, would look perfect in the living room in front of the large windows.

She wondered if Mac put up a tree at his house. He had such high ceilings he could get a huge one. While she was thinking of it, she sent him a text wishing him a Happy Thanksgiving and asking if he would like to help her and Kevin decorate the tree on Friday.

She checked the text she had sent Wendy, just in case she had missed the reply, but there was none. Moments later, she received an answer from Mac telling her he was on call all weekend, but would be there provided he wasn't working.

She hurried the dogs home and upon opening the door, was greeted with the enticing aroma of baked sugar and cinnamon. There was less than a minute left on the timer and after taking the pan out of the oven, she set it on the cooktop to cool. The dogs ate their breakfast while she dashed to her bedroom for a shower.

When she returned, dressed and ready, she found Kevin in the living room with both dogs sprawled on top of him and a huge hunk missing from the sticky mass of breakfast goodness. As she cut a slice for herself, she plugged in the kettle.

"I was hoping you could get all my Christmas boxes out from the garage and bring them up here," she called from the kitchen. "I want to put up the tree tomorrow and invited Mac to come over for a decorating party when Mel gets off work."

He lumbered in, still in his pajamas, his hair sticking up like when he was a young boy. "One more piece of this and then I'll go get ready and do it."

Lily looked at her cell phone. "We should call your grandparents and see how they're doing, and wish them a Happy Thanksgiving." Kevin shoveled in the last of his breakfast and nodded.

Lily pressed the button and after saying hello, let Kevin do most of the talking. She had never been especially close to Gary's parents, or perhaps they weren't close to her. They had never been overly involved in their lives and rarely left Florida, so it wasn't unusual to be separated from them at the holidays. In their early years together, Gary had worked most holidays, and later they had made only a couple of holiday trips to Florida. When her parents died, she remembered thinking why did it have to be them. Losing Gary's parents would have been equally horrible, but easier in that they weren't a fixture in their lives. Now, she and Kevin spoke to them on holidays and birthdays, not that it was much different before Gary's death. They weren't a source of comfort for Lily and she struggled to think of what to say when she did chat with them.

With that obligation fulfilled, Kevin made his way downstairs to get ready. He and Mel passed each other, and the dogs rushed to the top of the stairs to greet Mel before she could get to the kitchen.

"Something smells delicious." She was dressed in a turtleneck that was a shade lighter than her new vest and wearing her new boots. She had come a long way from the young girl who had first visited Lily's doorstep this summer.

"I was hoping you'd help decorate the tree tomorrow when you get off work. I invited Mac to join us. I thought we'd have Chinese takeout and watch a movie while we decorate."

She bobbed her head as she took another forkful of the sweet pastry. "Sure, that sounds good." She scraped every bit of the sticky nuts from her plate. "That was so yummy."

Lily poured hot water into Mel's teacup and quizzed her about the hot chocolate mix they used at the coffee shop.

As soon as Kevin was dressed, he and Mel made quick work of retrieving the boxes and then they helped Lily rearrange the living room furniture to make space for the tree in front of the windows. Each box got a thorough inspection from each of the dogs, whose noses were working overtime.

With the chores done, Lily selected six bottles of wine and Kevin toted the box to the car. She loaded the dogs, who were happy to have Kevin with them in the backseat, and they set out for Cyndy's.

The meal, like everything Cyndy set her hand to, was marvelous. As much as Lily savored the outstanding homemade dishes and visiting, she found herself enjoying Mel's excitement more. It was like watching a child at the holidays, her eyes going wide as she took in the beautiful table and abundance of homecooked food. It had been a sunny day. Mac had a dartboard set up in the backyard, and he coached Mel and Kevin in playing. After dessert, Cyndy found a movie to watch with the kids while Mac and Lily took the dogs for a walk.

Lily extended an invitation to Cyndy to join them for tree decorating on Friday night, but she begged off, knowing she would be exhausted from her day at the store. It was one of the busiest shopping weekends of the year and she'd be slammed all weekend. Lily hugged her friend goodbye, promising to stop by the store and see her over the weekend.

All in all, it had been a perfect day, filled with laughter, friendship, and food. Cyndy sent them home with enough left-overs to get them through the long weekend and the dogs were more than ready to settle down for the evening after hours of romping and playing in the yard, plus a bit of turkey on top of their dinner.

Despite not doing anything all day, except eating, Lily was exhausted. Mel and Kevin opted to stay up and assemble the tree, but promised to leave the decorating for Friday. Lily took a cup of tea and padded to her bedroom.

She smiled as she listened to her son explain the best way to tackle the tree, sounding just like Gary when he had taught Kevin. She glanced at Gary's urn and her throat tightened. Oh, how she wished he was here to see Kevin growing into such a fine young man. She brushed her hand over the cool dark container and crawled into bed.

As she leaned back against her pillows it dawned on her. While she hadn't done much physically, all day she had been relegating her memories, her emotions, any comparisons from this year to others, to the dark recesses of her mind. She hadn't yet found that delicate balance of living her new life and embracing the past without letting it engulf her.

Friday had been a quiet day, with Lily making a trip downtown to pick up a few bargains, Mel working, and Kevin sleeping late. Mac had been called into work for a couple of patients with serious problems, but texted and promised to be at Lily's around five o'clock, when Mel was due to arrive with the order of Chinese food.

While Lily had been at the computer after lunch, Kevin's cell phone rang and he went out to the deck to take the call. Lily watched her son's smile light up as he chatted with Brooke via video. It didn't take long to understand Brooke was much more than just a nice girl from school. His laughter filled the air as he paced around the deck, his phone in front of him. He talked to her for almost an hour before returning to the kitchen. Her heart filled, knowing he had someone special, someone who made him so happy. She didn't want to make a big deal of it and embarrass him, so opted to keep quiet.

"You know," he said, leaning against her desk. "Earlier, Mel and I found a bunch of boxes of holiday decorations your uncle must have stored in the garage. They're labeled outdoor lights and decorations. What do you think about putting some lights on the deck and the front of the house?"

"I'm game. Just don't go too crazy so we have a bunch of work after Christmas, but the deck would be lovely."

He hurried to the garage and came back with two huge totes. They unearthed greenery with pre-strung white lights, ideal for draping across the railing, then tested each of the lengths to make sure the lights worked. Lily guessed they hadn't been used in several years. To her surprise, they were all in working order.

Once they attached those, they tackled the net of icicle lights across the roof of the deck. Lily assured Kevin she would not be opening the roof anytime soon and agreed the lights would be perfect. Kevin handled all the ladder work, while Lily untangled the lights. They found hooks along the roof line, which were perfect for attaching the lights.

"Uncle Leo must have done this a time or two," said Lily, handing Kevin the next section.

The doorbell rang and she hurried to answer it, finding Andy. His huge smile was contagious. "Come in, Andy. We're doing some decorating and the dogs are outside."

He greeted Kevin with a hearty handshake and the dogs smothered him with affection. "Did you have a nice Thanksgiving?" Lily asked, working to find the end of a section of lights.

He spoke and signed, assuring her their Thanksgiving had been terrific, and he was just stopping by since he had part of the day off and wanted to visit and snuggle with the dogs. He watched Kevin and held up a hand. "Be right back. Let me in the gate?"

Minutes later, he appeared with another ladder and his tool belt. Lily held the gate as he muscled it through and up to the deck. "You are too sweet, Andy. Thank you."

Between the two of them they were faster at attaching the lights than Lily was at unraveling them. Andy told them he and his dad had been busy with light installations for customers and they put up the lights for Uncle Leo every Christmas, so he was familiar with the process. It took no time for him to guide Kevin and Lily in transforming the deck and adding a few lights to the front of the house, lighting up the sign and entryway.

Andy had such a kind heart and brightened when he was with the dogs. The way the dogs stuck to him, following and watching him, it was clear their feelings were mutual. Lily made some tea and cocoa, reminding herself she had to find some better-quality mix like the cafe used so she'd have it as a winter treat. As they sat around the patio table, sipping and enjoying a few leftover cookies and brownies, Andy stroked Bodie. "I can hardly wait for the day Bodie will be certified and be my hearing dog."

Whenever Lily's heart hurt thinking about having to give Bodie up at the end of his puppy training period, she would imagine the twinkle in Andy's eyes and the love there for Bodie. He would be so much more to Andy than just a wonderful pet or companion. She had been in awe of learning how much the dogs did for their owners and although she would miss Bodie, she couldn't wait to see Andy's life change.

Lily cradled her warm cup in her hands. "Would you like to stay and have Chinese with us tonight? We're going to decorate the tree."

"Nah, I better get going. I promised Mom I'd help her and I've been gone longer than I said already. She'll be worried."

Lily made him call his mom, then Kevin helped him take the ladder back to his truck while Lily made him promise to come and visit during Kevin's break.

Mel and Mac, along with Sherlock, arrived within minutes of each other and were surprised to see the festive lights. "Wow, you guys have been busy today," said Mac, offering to carry some of the bags from Mel's car.

"Kevin and I started, but Andy stopped by and helped us finish." Lily motioned them inside. "Wait until you see the deck."

Lily organized plates for everyone and situated the dozens of oyster pails making a buffet atop the counter. Kevin scooted the dogs outside to the deck to let them run off some energy, since they were on overload at seeing Sherlock.

Once dinner had been eaten and the leftovers stored, Kevin opened the box of lights. He solicited Mel's help as he showed her the art of tucking in the lights so they filled the inner and outer branches. Lily and Mac tuned in the classic movie, *White Christmas*, and supervised the placement of the lights, letting them know when they needed to adjust.

The pair worked in tandem and put all ten strands of lights on the tree in the time it took to watch the entire movie. Kevin was particular about the lights and with Mel's inherent love of details, it made for a symmetrical display of white lights perfectly distributed across the green foliage. Next came the boxes of ornaments.

First, Lily gave Kevin a small bag. He unwrapped a cute ornament depicting Olympic National Park and smiled at her. "Each year, I give Kevin a special ornament with the promise that when he starts his own household, he can take them with him." She turned and plucked a small box, wrapped with glittery ribbon, and handed it to Mel. "Here's a little something for you."

Mel's eyes darted from Lily's to the box. "For me?"

"Yes, open it. I thought you should also have some of your own ornaments to start a collection."

Mel unwrapped four ornaments and smiled as she examined each one. Two of them were book themed, one was an artist's palette, and the other was a cute coffee cup to celebrate her first job as a barista. "I love these," she said, tears pooling in her eyes. She hugged Lily and whispered, "Thank you for making me feel like I belong."

Kevin helped Mel hang her new ornaments, while Lily turned her attention to the boxes and wiped a tear from her cheek. She unwrapped each one from the tissue she had used when she had taken down the tree last time. That had been before Gary had been killed. She hadn't been able to muster the strength to decorate or put up the tree until now. Her hands shook as she unwrapped an old-style police car ornament that Kevin had given Gary years ago. She swallowed the lump in her throat and kept going.

The tote of carefully stored novelties held more than cherished decorations. The box held pieces of her whole life and now the only connection to her parents and Gary. Seeing each ornament stirred memories. Some made Lily smile and others clouded her eyes with tears. She handed Kevin the crystal heart her parents had given them so many years ago, on their first Christmas as a married couple. Everyone, except her, that was connected to the beautifully engraved heart was gone.

She smiled at the sight of the golden retriever ornament and glanced at Fritz, who was sprawled out with the other two, sleeping. She would have to look for a golden puppy ornament so she would always remember Bodie. Through tears, she hung the two mercury glass ornaments she had from her mom's collection. She remembered decorating the entire tree with boxes of them when she and Wendy had been young.

Next came a satin ornament decorated with beads and sequins. She grinned, remembering the day her mom bought two of them, one for her and one for Wendy, from the craft fair at her school. Wendy's had been red and gold and Lily held the aqua and silver one in her hand. It was a similar color to the sea glass she was drawn to in Aunt Maggie's mosaics. She wondered if Wendy still had hers.

There were several theme-park characters from when Kevin was younger and they had trekked to Florida to spend Christmas with Gary's parents. She unwrapped another reminder of his parents in the set of palm tree ornaments. At least they didn't make her cry.

She gasped at the beautiful blown glass balls she and Kevin had bought at the local nursery one year. They were always a favorite of hers, especially when the lights reflected in them. She couldn't wait to see them on the tree. Next, came the set of iridescent glass snowflake ornaments Kevin had brought her. He had gone to a training class in New York City one year and paid a small fortune for the box of precious snowflakes. The lump in her throat grew and she excused herself to get a cup of tea.

Mel and Kevin continued hanging ornaments, but Mac and

the dogs followed her into the kitchen. He placed a hand on her shoulder. "Are you okay?"

She didn't trust her voice and nodded, pressing her lips into a tight line. She made a production of filling the kettle and turning it on and retrieving a selection of teabags. She did a double-take when she looked in the cupboard and noticed a canister of premium hot chocolate mix. A tiny Christmas tag on the top said it was a gift for Lily from Santa. The sweet gesture from Mel induced a flood of tears.

Lily buried her head in Mac's handy shoulder. Blubbering, she tried to reassure him she was fine. He patted her back and grabbed a few tissues, which he tucked between her face and his shirt, then eased her toward the door to the deck. In a loud voice, he hollered, "We're going to take the dogs outside. Do you kids want some tea or hot chocolate when we get back?"

Mel and Kevin both hollered out their orders for hot chocolate, and Mac ushered Lily out the door. "The deck is gorgeous," he said, as she turned her head to gaze at the light above.

She wiped at her eyes and blew her nose. "It really is. Andy was a lifesaver. He said Uncle Leo had him put up lights every year. They do make me happy, just looking at them."

He hugged her closer. "Holidays are tough. I'm sorry this is turning into a hard trip down memory lane for you."

She nodded. "I knew it would be, but didn't think I would melt into an inconsolable puddle." She shrugged. "I'll be okay. It's just the first time we've decorated since Gary."

"Believe me, I understand. Luckily, I had Cyndy and she made sure we always had the holidays covered, and then some." He chuckled, which made Lily smile. The dogs returned from their jaunt around the yard and stood by the door, ready to return to the action. "Ready to go back and have some hot chocolate?"

She nodded and whispered, "Thank you."

They got to work heating some milk and mixing in the dark

and sinful smelling chocolate. Lily found a can of whipping cream, which would have to suffice for homemade, and topped each cup. Mac sprinkled a bit of cinnamon on each one and Lily put them on a tray.

Kevin and Mel took a break and sipped from their cups. Kevin's eyes widened and he took another sip. "This is really good. Did you make this, Mom?"

She laughed and raised her brows at Mel. "Well, a sneaky elf brought me a gift of some high-end hot chocolate mix. It's so much better than those envelopes we're used to using." She met Mel's eyes with a conspiratorial wink.

The ornament boxes were empty and the huge tree shimmered in the window, lights dancing off the glittery ornaments. The only thing left was the tree topper. That had always been Gary's job, but Kevin found the Moravian star that they had always placed on top of the tree and climbed the ladder to install it. He plugged it into the outlet he had left vacant for it in the branches nearest the top, and then adjusted the position until Lily was happy. The warm white star was a magnificent focal point of the tree.

"That's stunning," said Mac, moving to turn off the overhead lights.

Mel and Lily gasped as the glow from the tree filled the room. Mel stepped closer to examine the glass snowflakes. "I've never seen a tree so beautiful."

Lily noticed the tears in Mel's eyes and risked putting an arm around her. "It's my favorite part of Christmas. I love sitting in the dark with only the lights from the tree. It's magical."

19

Saturday morning, Lily couldn't resist getting up early to sit by the tree and sip a cup of tea. Her usual buddies had turned into traitors. Fritz and Bodie had taken to sleeping in Kevin's room and she missed their sweet faces greeting her when she woke. She slipped into her cardigan and tiptoed into the living room.

She brought her hand to her mouth, stifling a scream when she noticed Mel bundled in blankets, sitting on the couch, staring at the tree. She winced at Lily. "Sorry, didn't mean to startle you."

Lily giggled. "It's okay. I didn't expect anyone to be here."

Mel grinned at her. "You were right. It's magical."

"I'm going to get a cup of tea. Do you want one?"

Mel nodded and snuggled deeper into the blanket. Seeing a smile on Mel's face and a bit of wonder in her eyes, filled Lily with happiness. As she waited for the kettle, she thought back to that day when Donna and Jeff suggested Mel stay with her. Lily had been so unsure, but a few short months later, she couldn't imagine not having Mel in the house. Being alone, especially now with no guests to keep her occupied, was not what she wanted. Mel had been placed in her path for a reason and in opening her home and part of her heart to the young woman, she had given Lily a purpose.

She delivered Mel's steaming cup to the living room and sank into her recliner, then pulled the soft throw blanket around herself. Mel sighed and put her cup on a coaster. "Thank you for giving me a place to stay, a real home, and all of this." She gestured to the tree and then reached for her cup and put it to her mouth.

"You're welcome, but I should really thank you."

Mel glanced at her with a frown.

"I have a home, but it was empty and you and Bodie helped me fill it. You've helped give me hope." A happy tear slid down Lily's cheek as Mel smiled.

Sunday brought gray skies and a drizzly rain. The gloomy weather matched Lily's mood as she drove home after dropping Kevin at the early shuttle. She hated goodbyes and wouldn't rest easy until she heard from him that he was safely on the ground in Virginia.

She tried to fill her mind with the fun she and Kevin had yesterday, taking the ferry to Whidbey Island and watching the tree lighting. Mac had been sweet enough to take charge of the dogs, letting them spend the day at his house, since he was still on call.

She and Kevin had done some Christmas shopping and he even solicited her help in choosing a lovely necklace for Brooke. She picked up a few varieties of hot chocolate mix from the chocolate shop, and they had enjoyed a delicious lunch with a waterfront view. The entire town was decked out in lights. Shop windows were painted with festive snowmen and reindeer, and cookies and cocoa stations were situated throughout the square.

It had been like stepping back in time. A perfect, fun, and relaxing day.

She thought of all that as the wiper blades whisked the rain from her window, but did nothing for the tears that clouded her vision before rolling down her cheeks. She hated feeling so weak and had put on a good front for Kevin, but once she turned her back on the van, she was done pretending. Thankful the streets were clear and the good people of Driftwood Bay were still sleeping, she pulled into the garage.

Her faithful dogs greeted her and followed her downstairs, where she knocked on Mel's door to make sure she was awake. She worked the early shift today, and had to be there before eight o'clock.

Mel opened her door, her hair a mess and her eyes groggy. She glanced at Lily and her eyes widened. "Are you okay?"

Lily nodded and held up her hand. Before she could turn to leave, Mel reached for her and hugged her. Lily couldn't stop the sobs that followed. "I'm sorry, Lily. I know you're sad to see Kevin leave, but he'll be back in just a few weeks."

Lily nodded as she listened to the young woman console her. Feeling like a fool for getting so weepy and emotional, she squeezed Mel tighter. "Thank you, sweet girl." Lily separated from Mel's embrace. "You go jump in the shower, so you aren't late for work."

Lily wiped her eyes and stripped Kevin's bed. The dogs watched her every move as she carried the bedding into the laundry room and started a load. "I'll get your breakfast, just a minute." Their ears perked at the mention of the meal they were awaiting.

She trudged upstairs and filled their bowls, then made some scrambled eggs and toast for Mel, dusted her own toast with cinnamon and sugar, and sat down with a cup of hot tea. The toast always made her think of her mom and of Kevin when he was young. She still thought her mom made the best cinnamon toast and craved that comfort today.

Mel came into the kitchen and eyed the plate with the steam rolling off the eggs. "Oh, that looks great. Thanks for making it. I wasn't sure I'd have time to eat this morning." She scarfed down her food, then gathered her things and headed for the door.

"Remember, Mac's coming for dinner tonight. I should say he's bringing dinner tonight."

"I'll be home by five. See you then." With that, the door slammed and Lily was left with the dogs. She wanted to crawl back into bed and sleep, but forced herself to tidy the kitchen and then take a shower. As the warm water worked its way into the muscles of her neck and shoulders, she relaxed. She had to snap out of this funk. Like Mel reminded her, Kevin would be back in just a few weeks. She couldn't even imagine what a wreck she would be when he left in January.

Once dressed, she went downstairs and gathered the dirty towels for another load of laundry and then curled up in the recliner to watch holiday movies. She checked her phone for any updates from Kevin and cradled it in her lap so she wouldn't miss a text or call. The tree lights twinkled as she began to nod off, lulled by the cheery program, the festive decorations, and the snoozing dogs at her feet.

Over an hour later, the doorbell startled her awake. The dogs were already at the front door, curious about the activity. Lily focused on her watch, confused from her nap, but knew it was too early for Mac.

She opened the door, frowning for a second, and then her mouth gaped as she stared at Wendy. "Aren't you going to invite me inside?" Wendy tugged on the handle of her large suitcase, a smaller one strapped to it, and another bag balanced across the top of it all. She handed Lily her tote bag and purse, causing Lily's arm to bend, surprised at the weight of them.

"What are you doing here? I had no idea you were coming." Lily's mind scrambled thinking she had missed a text or email, but was sure she hadn't.

The dogs scurried to get closer to Wendy and sniffed at her expensive French designer luggage. "Oh, oh, get them away from me." Wendy fanned her hand at them.

"They won't hurt you." Lily gave them the command for place and while Fritz darted for the cot that she had set up to train Bodie, she had to encourage Bodie to follow him and tear his attention away from Wendy.

After lugging her bags across the entryway, Wendy sighed. "I can't believe it's such an ordeal to get to this place. It's like literally in the middle of freaking nowhere."

"Did you take a shuttle or rent a car?"

"I took the disgusting shuttle. I've been travelling all day and am exhausted. And starving." She glanced around the living space. "This is, uh, cozy."

Lily motioned her toward the kitchen. "I've got some leftovers." She stared at the dogs, reminding them to stay while Wendy followed her. "I would have had something better had I known you were coming to visit."

Wendy huffed as she sat at the counter. "I didn't plan to come." Then she burst into tears. "I have nowhere else to go. I mean *nowhere*."

Lily didn't overreact, or even ask a question as she fixed a plate of food. The world revolved around Wendy and she could be melodramatic. She and her husband, Chad, lived in a huge house in Dallas, with a lavish lifestyle and all the best that money could buy. It was a world foreign to Lily, as she had only visited once and that had been more than enough. She only knew about Wendy's life through her photos she posted on social media. Lily tried to imagine what situation had driven her sister to her doorstep.

She filled the kettle, then put what consisted of a small Thanksgiving meal in front of her sister. Wendy turned up her nose. "What is this? I can't eat all these carbs."

Lily's neck tightened and her head began to throb. "I don't have anything else to offer you. You can go out to eat if you want." She glanced at the sound of the kettle turning off, raising her brows at her sister.

Wendy's bottom lip protruded, like it had since she was a young girl and didn't get her way. "I usually have a smoothie or a kale salad."

"I'm fresh out of smoothies and kale. Tea?" Lily added a teabag to her cup and at Wendy's nod did the same in a fresh cup. She poured the water over them and brought them to the counter.

Lily sipped her tea as she studied her sister. Instead of her usual perfectly applied makeup and styled hair, she noticed purple-tinted circles under her eyes and the rain hadn't done her hair any favors, plus her dark roots were showing in her usual weave of rich blonde. "So, what's going on, Wendy?"

In between bouts of crying and heavy sighs, she told Lily about federal agents coming to their house the day before Thanksgiving and arresting Chad and his business partner. He and his family had been celebrating the holiday with them. "It was awful. I can't even begin to tell you how humiliating it was and how awful we were treated. Like criminals."

As she kept talking, Lily asked a few questions, and concluded Chad and his partner were deeply involved in fraud and federal financial crimes. Through tears, Wendy went on to tell her that all their assets had been frozen and Chad's lawyer was trying to deal with it, but the holidays were making things difficult. He had advised her to leave town. "I can't believe they can take our house, our cars, everything. George, that's our lawyer, had to fight to get me to be able to get some clothes and personal things. He gave me some cash and bought me a plane ticket out here. Chad assured me it's a mistake and he'll get it straightened out."

"I'm sure that was stressful. I'm sorry you had to go through that. Kevin just left this morning, so his room is available downstairs, if you need to stay for a few days, until things are settled."

"I'm sure George will have it sorted this week. Thanks." She picked at the turkey, eating a few bites. She never once asked Lily how she had been or how Kevin was doing. Same old self-centered Wendy. Lily had a feeling Chad's troubles were just beginning and the chance of it being sorted this week was close to zero.

"Mel, a young woman I met earlier this year, stays downstairs. She helps me with the cottages and goes to the community college. She's working now but will be home this afternoon, so you'll meet her."

Wendy rolled her eyes. "How could you let a stranger move in here with you? Are you struggling that much that you needed to take in a boarder?"

Lily counted to ten before answering. "No, she's had a tough life and lost her parents. She was living in a shelter, so we worked out a deal where she can stay here in exchange for helping me, and in the off-season, she works downtown at a coffee shop. She's quiet and a bit fragile, so please be nice to her."

Wendy wrinkled her nose. "Eeeww, a shelter."

Lily's eyes narrowed. "Mel's a smart and lovely young woman, and she's also been through a lot, so keep that in mind." The phone in her pocket buzzed. She tugged it out and found a text from Kevin letting her know he had landed and that he loved her. She tapped in a quick reply as her heart lightened with the news.

Wendy pushed the plate of food away and stood, wandering

over to the door that led to the deck. She walked outside and pointed at the cottages. "The yard looks nice and at least you have a nice view here. Since that girl is staying downstairs, maybe I should just use one of the cottages. They look so cute."

Lily shook her head. She didn't need Wendy getting too comfortable. "No, they're all winterized and shut down for the season. It's downstairs or a hotel, if you'd rather."

Wendy put her hands on her hips. "I don't even have a credit card, so I can't stay in a hotel, or anywhere. My freedoms have been taken from me." Her whiny voice was grating on Lily. "I hope George sues the government." Her eyes sparkled. "Maybe we'll come out of this with a windfall."

Lily didn't want to break it to her, but she suspected whatever the feds had, Chad would most likely be going to prison and Wendy might have to get a job and learn to live like a normal person. She'd come to that realization soon enough. Lily hoped she wasn't around to witness it when Wendy got the news.

"If you want to get settled in, I'll show you around downstairs. You probably don't remember much since I think the last time you were here you were a young girl." The rain had let up, so she let the dogs outside, and then helped drag Wendy's bags downstairs.

If the upstairs wasn't up to Wendy's standards, she shuddered to think what her sister would have to say about the downstairs. It was clean and functional, but wouldn't be featured in any magazines. She showed her the common area, including the kitchenette. She pointed out Mel's bedroom on the opposite side of the main open room and led her into the other bedroom, near the utility room.

"It's so dark down here," said Wendy, shoving her bag through the door.

"Basements tend to be that way, but the main room gets a ton of light." She pointed out the bathroom and linens and showed her the washer and dryer. "You can get settled in. Mel will be home in an hour or so, and a friend of mine is bringing over dinner. We're watching a holiday movie. You're welcome to join us."

"Can you run me to the store? I want to pick up some food I can actually eat."

Lily almost bit through the inside of her cheek. "Sure, we just need to go now, so I'm home in time for dinner."

Wendy grabbed her designer handbag and followed Lily upstairs. After wiping off the dogs' feet, she got them settled inside and hurried Wendy to the garage. It only took a few minutes to get downtown, and she parked in front of the market. Wendy's eyes darted from side to side as she scanned the street. "This is it?" She then asked if there wasn't a certain snooty chain store known for its overpriced food.

Lily shook her head. "This is your best bet for fresh, local produce. There's another grocery store a few miles away, but this one has the best selection."

With an exaggerated huff, Wendy got out of the car and went inside the market. It had been such a short time since Wendy had arrived, and Lily was already wondering when she would leave. She didn't need her sister disrupting her routine or causing any grief for Mel. She could only image what Mac would think of her. She sent him a text to let him know her sister had shown up unexpectedly and warned him Wendy could be difficult. She grabbed her purse and took a basket from inside the door, scanning the aisles to pick up a few staples for the week ahead.

She hurried Wendy along, who was subjecting the manager to one of her snobbish tirades about stocking some sort of soy-based protein drink. As they checked out, Lily watched her sister spend over a hundred dollars on organic produce, soy milk, and fresh fish. She followed her to the car and loaded her bags in the back of the SUV. As she slid behind the wheel,

Wendy asked if Lily had a popular brand of an expensive power blender. She shook her head as she started the engine. "Just a regular old blender."

"I need to get one. Can you stop by a store?"

Lily grimaced. "You might have to order it online. I don't think Driftwood Bay Mercantile stocks those."

Wendy rolled her eyes again. "How can you stand living here?" She huffed and crossed her arms. "Since I no longer have a credit card, you'll have to order it for me and I'll pay you."

Lily didn't commit and drove them home, where they had only ten minutes before Mac was due to arrive with dinner. She hurried inside to give the dogs their dinner and put the groceries away while Wendy used her computer in the office off the kitchen to go online and look for her precious blender.

Lily didn't have time to change her clothes before the bell rang, announcing Mac and Sherlock. He greeted Lily with a kiss on the cheek and toted in the bags from Noni's.

She took one of the bags and leaned close to him. "Wendy is not a fan of dogs."

Mac frowned. "That could be a real problem for her." He chuckled as he followed Lily into the kitchen.

Lily noticed Wendy's shopping bags still full, strewn across the counter. She shook her head and emptied them into the refrigerator. "Mel should be here in a few minutes." She raised her voice and added, "Wendy, I'd like you to meet Jack MacMillan, who goes by Mac. He's the local veterinarian." Lily motioned to her. "This is my little sister, Wendy."

"Wonderful to meet you," said Mac, walking across the space to greet her. Wendy moved her hand from the keyboard just long enough to return his greeting with a limp handshake.

"I've never known a veterinarian. I can't imagine spending all day with sick and dirty dogs and cats." Her face looked like she'd just bit down on a sour lemon.

"Oh, not only dogs and cats. We treat horses, cows, goats,

pigs, sheep, even the occasional llama." Mel's arrival and the dogs rushing to greet her interrupted them. "Ah, here's the girl who never stops working."

Mel came into the kitchen, sniffing at the aroma wafting from the takeout bags. "I smell Noni's," she said, grinning. "I'm starving."

Mac moved to help get the plates and silverware organized while Lily slipped an arm around Mel. "I want you to meet my sister, Wendy. She surprised me with a visit and will be staying downstairs in Kevin's room."

Mel's eyes widened as Lily led her to the desk. Wendy glanced up. "I've got that blender I want picked out in the cart. You'll just need to put in your credit card information." She displayed a quick smile for Mel.

Mel returned the smile and extended her hand. "Nice to meet you, Wendy. You're so lucky to have Lily for a sister and what a wonderful surprise."

A surprise for sure, but Lily couldn't go so far as to say wonderful. Wendy tapped her finger on the screen, raising her brows at Lily.

Lily nodded at Wendy, trying not to gag at the five-hundred-dollar price tag. "I'll take a look after dinner. Come and eat and get to know Mel and Mac."

"Noni's has the best Italian food ever. You're going to love it." Mel waved Wendy to join them at the huge granite countertop where they ate so many of their meals. "You know you can get a zero-fee prepaid credit or debit card." Mel went on to explain the best deal she had found and where Wendy could obtain one.

Wendy made no effort to engage with Mel, acting as if she was invisible. Mel shrugged and wandered back to the kitchen. After several minutes, Wendy made a production of sliding the chair out and plodding over to join them. "I don't eat bread, pasta, or dairy, so I'll just make myself a smoothie. Where's your blender, Lily?"

While Mac and Mel tried to convince Wendy to try the chicken, Lily went to the cupboard and found the blender, setting it up on the counter near the sink. "There you go." She turned and loaded her plate with pasta and chicken piccata, adding two pieces of garlic bread and glaring at the back of her sister's head.

Mel chattered about her busy day at work with the locals out in force taking advantage of holiday shopping specials and keeping the baristas busy at the coffee shop. She asked Wendy a few questions about where she lived and then Lily took advantage of the loud whirring of the blender to whisper in Mel's ear. "She's having a crisis, so best to stay away from why she's here and where she lives. I'll explain it later."

Mel bobbed her head and reached for the garlic bread. Mac took over the conversation, telling them his emergency patient from Saturday was doing well and he would most likely go home tomorrow. Mel wanted to know every detail of the dog's problem and Mac patiently explained the surgery he performed on the German shepherd, Rebel, who had presented with bloat.

Wendy frowned and sneered, contorting her face each time Mac mentioned what was involved in rotating the dog's stomach. It didn't bother Mel at all, but Lily could see her sister was struggling to sip her pureed kale and spinach. Lily would have gagged on it without the medical descriptions. "How about we save the rest for later when we're done eating?" She caught Mac's eye and signaled toward Wendy.

"Oh, right. Sorry, I get so wrapped up, I tend to forget it's not the best dinner conversation." He changed the subject to asking Lily if she heard from Kevin.

She smiled and bobbed her head. "I was feeling so blue today when he left, but looking at the calendar, he'll be back here in just over two weeks. I'm looking forward to spending all that time with him, although I'm not sure what I'll do to entertain him."

Mac slid his empty plate toward the center of the counter. "How long are you able to stay, Wendy?"

She turned her eyes upward and with a look of pure contempt, groaned. "You mean how long do I *have* to stay? Hopefully, just a day or two."

Mac frowned and looked at Lily. She shook her head, begging him not to ask any more questions. His eyes flickered with understanding. "I think I'll take the dogs for a walk. Do you feel like coming with us, Mel?"

She sprang from her chair, nodding with enthusiasm. Once they were out the door, Lily took a deep breath and glared at her sister.

Wendy met her stare with a sigh. "Your life is so tragic. I guess losing Gary really wrecked everything. I know you guys didn't have much and worked all the time, but this is even worse. Now, you live in this backwoods place with that strange girl. Mac seems nice enough, but he certainly doesn't dress to impress, does he? I didn't realize how sad your life had become."

Rage surged in Lily and listening to Wendy reminded her why she hadn't seen her sister since Gary's funeral. She'd had enough of her pretentious and self-absorbed attitude to last a lifetime. Wendy's husband was under arrest, all her property had been seized, and she dared to judge Lily's life. She wanted to scream and toss her sister to the curb, but instead, kept her hands busy gathering dishes and storing the leftovers. She tried to channel her mom and knew how disappointed she would be to see the two of them at odds.

Focused on her tasks, she said nothing, ignoring Wendy and wishing with everything she had that the lawyer would bring good news that would allow her sister to return to Texas tomorrow. She couldn't survive much more of her.

20

Lily was up early Monday, anxious to get to the beach and the peace the gentle waves always delivered. Thankfully, last night Wendy had opted to go to bed instead of joining them for a movie. The tension had built in Lily's neck and shoulders all night as she waited for Wendy to say something hurtful to Mel or Mac. Once she had gone downstairs, the three of them had enjoyed a sweet holiday flick and more hot chocolate, along with fresh whipped cream and homemade marshmallows that Mel had brought home from work.

As she sat on her favorite piece of driftwood and let the dogs scamper along the shore, she breathed in the salty air and snuggled into her jacket and scarf. The feelings of guilt she had harbored about not trying harder to connect with Wendy had been replaced by the old resentment that always followed an encounter. How could two sisters raised in the same way be so different?

Her mom and dad had never had much, but had been comfortable in a middle-class neighborhood. The girls hadn't been raised with the finer things in life, but were never short-changed on time with their parents. They always had dinner together as a family, homework was a priority, and although Lily thought Wendy got off a bit easier than she did, being the baby of the family, both girls had chores and responsibilities. Like most of the kids, they had new coats, shoes, and clothes for school, but nothing extravagant in the way of material goods.

Their parents always saved for a trip during the summer, usually to somewhere educational as well as fun. They had all the books they ever wanted and tons of quality time with their parents during the summer. She closed her eyes at the memory of riding their bikes around the neighborhood all day and the smell of grilled burgers wafting from the backyard, signaling it was time for dinner. Their dad loved to barbecue and always planted a huge garden. She could almost taste the fresh tomatoes she loved to pluck right from the vine.

Only after they were both gone, did Lily realize and treasure those times. She ran a finger under her eye, dismayed at the tears. Holidays were the roughest and had her mind working overtime, pondering all the should haves. Brushing those memories aside, she focused on the dogs, wrestling with each other.

Today, Mel would be at the library, leaving Lily alone with Wendy. She shuddered at the thought of ten hours with her. She still hadn't ordered her blender for her. If she was set on returning home this week, what was the point? The dogs gave her a funny look when she laughed out loud at the memory of Mel giving Wendy advice about a debit card. Wendy had been so rude and dismissive, but it didn't deter Mel.

She took several deep breaths, concentrating on her posture and exhaling completely. After playing several rounds of fetch with the dogs, she felt better, looser, and mentally prepared to tackle a day with her sister. Maybe they could take a ride and do lunch. As she led the dogs back to the house, she held onto a tiny string of hope that Wendy would actually go back to Texas this week.

After getting their paws wiped, the dogs were anxious for breakfast and wolfed it down. She relegated them to the deck, while she hurried to take her shower. They could relax and not bother Wendy, if she appeared before Lily finished.

As she showered, she decided she'd take Wendy downtown and stop by Cyndy's store. She had to remember to work in some time with Bodie today for more exposure to new noises and places before his training tomorrow, but she could take him on a field trip of his own this morning.

She and Wendy could do some window shopping, go to lunch, and take in the view along the waterfront. Driftwood Bay didn't have much else to do, or at least much else that would pique Wendy's interest. This weekend, the season kicked off with the tree lighting and all the festivities, but with any luck Wendy would be home by then. She and Mac were looking forward to their evening and dinner after the tree lighting and Wendy tagging along with her unpleasantness, was not how Lily intended to spend the weekend.

Lily let Wendy choose the restaurant for lunch and after several specific instructions to the waiter, she was pleased with her salmon salad and even commented on the lovely view. Her grace was short-lived. As soon as they left and walked down the street, Wendy made several disparaging remarks about the lack of real shopping. However, she loved Cyndy's store. It was bustling with activity and fully decorated for the season with Christmas goodies and decorations tucked into every corner. The subtle scents of the homemade soaps she carried mingled with the inviting aroma of cinnamon and clove coming from the table set up with hot cider and cookies.

As Lily wandered through the space, admiring the unique and beautiful ornaments and housewares, she listened to the instrumental holiday songs playing in the background. It was like being inside a Christmas snow globe, a cozy space that made her want to spend the whole day in the glittery world.

Cyndy was her sweet self, visiting with customers, her infectious laugh bringing a smile to their faces. Wendy lingered over all the trees decorated with hundreds of different ornaments. When Cyndy finished with her customer, she made her way to Lily. "Wow, we've been so busy since Friday, which is great, but also tiring. How have you been? Did you and Kevin have fun on Whidbey Island?"

"It was great and I think Kevin had fun. We did some shopping and the tree lighting was fantastic. I made reservations to go over to Victoria right after Christmas, which I'm excited to do. Not sure how much Kevin will like it, but it will be something different."

Wendy wandered back near them and Lily introduced her. "Cyndy is Mac's sister and not only runs her gorgeous shop, but is the talented decorator who helped me with the cottages."

Wendy smiled and nodded. "Your store is exquisite. It's like finding a rare gem in...well, a pile of rubble. I was beginning to think my sister moved to a ghost town. There is just *nothing* here. I'm not sure how you all survive." Only Wendy could manage to wrap a compliment in an insult. Cyndy's smile faded and she excused herself to help a customer at the counter.

Wendy turned to Lily, holding a shopping basket filled with ornaments. "I'm trying to decide if I should even bother with new ornaments this year." She sighed and shook her head. "I still haven't heard from the lawyer. I haven't organized the designer who normally comes and puts up the tree and decorates. I'm afraid it's going to be too late if I don't get on his list soon."

Lily grimaced. "Since you've got a limited amount of cash, it might be wise to wait. I'm sure Cyndy would hold these for you for a few days, and let you decide if you want them."

Her eyes brightened. "Oh, that would be fabulous. That's a good idea." She turned to walk toward the counter. "You're so sensible, Lily. Whatever you lack in panache, you make up for in practicality."

Lily pasted a smile on her face. Another underhanded insult was no surprise. Why couldn't Wendy just dial it down and be nice? And did she actually buy new ornaments every year?

After Cyndy promised to keep the ornaments in the back room, Lily mouthed a silent thank you to her and followed her sister out the door. She was fresh out of suggestions on where they could go, since everything in Driftwood Bay was well beneath Wendy's standards.

The sunny sky had disappeared behind gray clouds, and the chilly breeze made Lily shudder. "Oh, my gosh, I'm freezing," Wendy hollered as she clutched at her stylish suede jacket.

Once they were in the car, Lily turned up the heat. "The weather is supposed to turn rainy for the next couple of days and clear out for the weekend."

"With any luck, I won't be here this weekend." She turned and glanced at Lily. "No offense, of course."

Lily kept her eyes on the road, hoping with all she had, that fate would grant her sister's wish to return to Texas. She had just made the turn for her street when Wendy's cell phone rang. "It's the lawyer," she shouted, before tapping the screen.

Lily pulled into the garage, trying not to eavesdrop, but catching the drift of the conversation from her sister's exasperated sighs and pleas. She left her in the car to finish her conversation and went inside, greeting the dogs and plugging in the kettle. Lily took her steaming cup and settled into her chair, under her warm blanket, staring at the beautiful tree, as she basked in the few moments of peace before Wendy and her drama returned.

She had only shut her eyes for a few minutes when the sound of the door slamming jolted her awake. A low growl came from Fritz as he hurried to investigate, and Bodie followed. When the dogs saw Wendy, they wagged their tails, doing their best to greet her.

She kicked at them. "Get away from me."

That did it. Lily sprang from the chair. She motioned the dogs to the door and out to the deck. "You have crossed a line," she said, her voice stern and clear. "You will never kick at or hit my dogs. Do you understand me?"

Wendy's eyes grew wide and she gasped. "I don't like dogs and they were coming at me."

Lily held her hand up. "Enough. I've had enough of your attitude. All you have done since arriving here is complain and belittle. I can take it, but I will not tolerate you mistreating my dogs or being disrespectful to Mel or Mac or anyone else. If you can't handle being polite and can't deal with the dogs, you need to get your stuff and get the hell out of here. I'm done with your selfishness and arrogance. This is my home and you will respect it and me."

Her sister said nothing, staring at her with her mouth open. Then, she burst into tears.

Lily shook her head and opened the door to let the dogs in. Tension filled the air and they moseyed past and went back into the living room, snuggling next to each other by Lily's chair.

"I'm not buying into your drama, Wendy. You're a grown woman and it's time you take responsibility." Lily lifted the lid on the slow cooker and stirred the soup she had put on to cook this morning. It was the potato one Mel favored. Lily ignored Wendy's tears, except for handing her a box of tissues. She retrieved the cream from the refrigerator.

The exaggerated sobs subsided, and Lily offered her sister a cup of tea. Wendy nodded and took it. "I'm just destroyed. You don't understand." She sniffed and wiped at her eyes. "The lawyer said it's hopeless. Chad's partner is blaming him for everything and made a statement. The FBI is involved and everything is gone. The house, the furniture, our cars were leased, our bank accounts, everything. I guess we had a ton of credit card debt." She shrugged. "Chad never said anything and he handled all of our finances. There's no money for bail."

Lily slipped the fresh bread she had picked up at the bakery out of the paper sleeve. "Did the lawyer have advice for you?"

Tears spilled down her cheeks. "Not really. He just said I couldn't have access to the house and I basically have nothing." She hiccupped. "Chad is sorry and doesn't know what to do. He's organizing a time when Chad can call me."

Knots formed in Lily's neck as she listened to her sister. She couldn't turn her out into the street, but she also wasn't going to let her destroy the calm haven she had built for herself. She didn't need the tension and angst and neither did the dogs or Mel. Until Wendy calmed down, talking would be futile.

"I've got potato soup made. You're welcome to some or you can make one of your smoothies. Mel works late tonight at the library, so she won't be home for at least an hour." Lily filled the bowls for the dogs and they devoured their food, then repositioned themselves across the floor. She brought her bowl of soup and a thick slice of bread slathered in butter to the counter.

After a few spoonfuls, she met Wendy's eyes. "I'm willing to let you stay here until you figure out what you're going to do, but I have some conditions."

Wendy slumped lower in her chair. "What choice do I have?" She frowned and took a sip from her cup.

"You could go back to Texas and stay with a friend."

Wendy shook her head. "I can't. I'd be mortified to see any of them. I'm sure we're already the topic of gossip among all of them." She slid off her chair and ladled soup into a bowl before returning to the counter.

Lily didn't say anything, happy that Wendy was eating. The stress of it all had to be weighing on her. Anyone who didn't know her would excuse her behavior because of the situation, but Wendy had acted like this for as long as she had been married. Lily wasn't sure if the gravity of what was happening had actually sunk in yet.

She reached for a notepad. "I tend to approach things logically and making a list of options can be helpful." She scribbled some notes and drew several lines across the paper. "You've established you can't go back to Dallas. Do you have any friends outside of the city where you could go?"

Wendy's eyes shifted in thought and then she hung her head. "No. Every friend I can think of is connected to Chad's work or him." She shoved her bowl away. "How pathetic is that? I don't even have friends of my own."

Chances are they weren't her friends in the true sense of the word, but Lily just made a mark on her paper. "Unless you've forged a relationship with our distant cousins?" Wendy shook her head. "I'm your only family option."

With a glance at her notes, Lily continued. "Like I said, you can stay here, but it's not going to be a vacation. You're going to have to contribute to helping around the house and you'll have to find a job."

Wendy's head snapped to attention. "I've never worked, except in high school. What could I possibly find here?"

Lily shrugged. "I don't know, but the wad of cash you arrived with isn't going to last forever. This time of year, places are looking for part-time holiday workers. Mel could probably help you. She's tuned into the online resources."

Wendy wrinkled her nose and then flopped her head down across her arms atop the counter. "This is the worst thing. How can I be homeless and have nothing? Part of me wants to wring Chad's neck and the other part is so worried about him being in jail. He must be scared to death."

"It sounds like it's out of your control. You weren't involved or privy to his business, and right now you're going to have to worry about yourself. I'm sure the lawyer will do all he can and keep you updated, right?"

She lifted her head and nodded, tears staining her cheeks. "You just have no idea how hard it is for me to be on my own. My whole world has imploded."

"Actually, I know exactly how it feels." Lily pushed the notepad away and took her dirty dishes to the sink.

The dogs hurried to their feet and raced to the front door. Moments later, Mel came into the kitchen. Her eyes darted from Wendy, still half slumped at the counter, to Lily. "You made my favorite soup." She helped herself to a bowl and took the seat Lily had vacated.

The poor girl attempted to fill the silence between the two sisters, chattering on about her day at the library. "They're having an open house in conjunction with the tree lighting this weekend, so we were busy decorating and organizing."

"Speaking of the library, I told Wendy you might be able to help her find some resources there or online. She's looking for a job here in Driftwood Bay."

Mel's eyebrows arched, but she didn't ask any questions, picking up on the almost imperceptible shake of Lily's head. "Oh, sure. There are a few sites online that post local jobs and I can check the boards at school."

Wendy sighed. "Thanks," she murmured, before slipping from her chair and heading down the stairs.

Lily tiptoed across the room and shut the door leading to the stairs. She leaned across the granite counter and in a hushed tone told Mel about Wendy's situation. Mel kept eating, but her eyes got bigger the longer Lily talked. "Bottom line, we're sort of stuck with her here. I honestly don't know how long she'll be here, or how long I can handle it." Lily collected Wendy's bowl and took it to the sink.

Mel finished her soup. "You're lucky you have a sister. I know she's a royal pain in the butt right now, but I'd give anything to have a family."

Lily stopped rinsing dishes. Mel's words tugged at her heart. Shame filled her when she realized how ungrateful she must seem to Mel. The poor girl had lost her parents in such tragic circumstances, then her aunt, and had been relegated to the foster system. She was truly alone and here Lily was, complaining about her sister, when she was fortunate enough to still have one. She needed to be a better person.

21

True to her word, Mel did some research online and showed Wendy how to navigate the job sites before she left on Tuesday morning. Lily didn't trust her sister alone with Fritz, so she bundled him into the car and took him to Bodie's training session.

Fritz was a good boy and the receptionist took pity on him, letting him stay behind the counter with her. Bodie did great with their trainer, Martha, following every command but then when Lily took over, it was a disaster. After struggling with even the simple task of keeping Bodie focused on her, Martha stepped in and took Bodie's leash.

"What's wrong, Lily? You're off today. Bodie's picking up on whatever it is."

Lily's cheeks reddened. "I'm sorry. It's been a stressful couple of days. My sister showed up, unexpectedly. We don't exactly have a close relationship and now she's going to have to stay with me for an indefinite amount of time."

"Dogs are very sensitive and pick up on your emotions, which is one reason they are such wonderful service animals.

With Bodie being young and not fully trained, his worry about you is overriding his ability to focus."

Lily nodded. "Understood. I'm not focused on him like I should be."

Martha glanced down at Bodie, sitting patiently. "Go out and take a walk, and I'll work with Bodie. We'll try again when you get back."

Lily apologized and collected Fritz, who was more than happy to accompany her on a jaunt around the property. Thick pasture grass covered most of the area, but there were gravel walking paths and even a few benches throughout the acreage. As Lily walked, she emptied her mind, trying to be more like Fritz and Bodie and live in the moment. It was harder than it sounded.

After Gary's death, her friend, the psychologist, had given her the advice of keeping herself in the present. The quickest way to do that, according to her, was to concentrate on the senses and what you could see, hear, taste, smell, and touch right now. It forced your mind to the moment.

Her entire career had trained her to expect the worst, plan several steps ahead, and be ready for any emergency or danger. That ingrained training, plus the tragic losses, often put her mind far in the past or worrying about the days in front of her. Today, she focused on the beauty around her. Despite the drizzle and gray clouds, Driftwood Bay was home to some of nature's most stunning work. Lily noticed the majestic trees surrounding the property, their branches slick with rain. She listened to the soft patter of new rain falling, spattering the hood she had pulled over her head.

Fritz didn't seem to mind the moisture, happy to be on an adventure. Rain was one of her favorite scents and she drew a long breath through her nose, taking her time to fill her lungs and then letting it out ever so slowly. The fresh aroma filled her nostrils. After twenty minutes, she was wet, but much more relaxed.

She led Fritz to the car, retrieved one of the towels she always carried and took him to the covered porch area to dry him. He flopped to the ground, loving the attention and stretching as she dried the feathers on his belly. For the most part, the water hadn't even penetrated his coat, the natural oils repelling the rain. She made sure his ears and head were dry and then led him back inside, where the receptionist rewarded him with a treat.

Fritz winked at her, prompting a laugh from Lily. "Fritz, you are such a funny guy." She bent and kissed the top of his head, and hurried back to the training room to find Bodie.

Martha handed her the leash and nodded with approval as she went through a few commands, climbing steps, making Bodie sit and then lie down on all sorts of surfaces, getting him ready for wherever he might go with his person. He resisted gravel and dirt the most, but eventually followed Lily's commands.

Her meltdown had extended their training session and it was after lunch when they returned home. Mel's car was in the driveway and Lily found her in the kitchen eating.

"Where's Wendy?" Lily asked, giving each of the dogs a treat from their cookie jar.

"Downstairs, I think. I just got home a few minutes ago and haven't seen her. I saw Poppy's Tea is looking for help. She was just putting a sign in the window when I walked by. I thought I'd tell Wendy, so she could go down there and apply before too many people heard about it."

Lily fixed herself a plate, along with a hot cup of tea, and had just sat down when Wendy came up the stairs. Her hair was disheveled and she was still wearing her robe. "I'm freezing," she muttered, moving toward the counter. She added a tea bag and hot water to a cup.

Lily nodded at Mel, gesturing toward Wendy. "There's a help wanted sign down at Poppy's Tea. You can probably be one of the first to apply if you get down there soon."

Wendy crinkled her forehead and sighed. "I guess that's better than a maid at the hotel or a cashier at the minimart. That's about all I've seen online."

"Go get ready and I'll run you down there. It's a cute shop. She sells spices and teas, and does a big business for high tea throughout the holidays." Wendy needed to do something besides lounge in bed all day, and having a job would give her a purpose, something Lily suspected she hadn't had in a long time.

Wendy shuffled toward the stairs with a heavy sigh. "I'll have to take a shower and get ready."

Lily rolled her eyes and went back to her lunch.

Mel smiled at her. "Dr. Clay says I can cut back to once a week, unless I feel like I need to see her more often, so I'm going to try it and will just go each Tuesday from now on."

"Oh, that's fantastic news." Lily added more hot water to her cup. "For what it's worth, I think seeing her has made a difference. That and going to school and your job, you seem much happier."

Mel blushed and nodded. "I think so, too. She's a great listener and doesn't make me feel weird."

"Are you going to be here this afternoon?" Lily glanced at Fritz and Bodie, asleep on the floor. "I thought I'd take Bodie uptown for a field trip, but leave Fritz with you."

"I'll be here. I've got some homework to do and can keep an eye on him."

Lily spent some time online, catching up on emails, plus composing one to Kevin to update him on Wendy's situation. Since Wendy would still be there when he came for his break, she suggested he stay in one of the cottages. The few times she had poked her head into Wendy's room, it had been a mess. Her sister was used to having a housekeeper and didn't make much effort to keep things tidy. Lily didn't need to put the cottages at risk.

After she sent the message, she pondered what to do about their trip to Victoria. She had tried to convince Mel to come with them, but she was steadfast in her desire to work through the holidays while she had so much time off school. She was more than happy to stay at the house and keep watch over the dogs.

Mac had planned to accompany them, for the two-night stay. Lily had reserved two rooms and he offered to drive, since he was familiar with the area. They had planned to consolidate the dogs at Lily's and he had asked Cyndy to stay with Mel, so she wouldn't be alone in the house at night. Now, with Wendy in the picture, it was more complicated.

Lily's stomach knotted with the idea of leaving the sweet dogs in Wendy's care, even part of the time. She'd made it clear she wasn't a fan and Lily didn't want the dogs to suffer. She texted Mac to ask if he had any great ideas about what to do.

An hour later, Wendy emerged, ready for a trip to town. She was wearing her suede jacket again. "Maybe while we're downtown, we should stop by the store and get you a jacket that will withstand the rain."

Wendy picked up her fancy purse, that probably cost more than all of Lily's clothes combined, and followed Lily to the garage. "I can only imagine finding a coat here. I'm sure it will lack any style, but be practical, like yours."

Lily didn't rise to the bait and loaded Bodie in the backseat. She backed out of the garage and turned to Wendy. "One tip, you should probably cut the attitude when it comes to knocking Driftwood Bay. Part of your job there will be interacting with the customers and being nice to them, not looking down your nose at them."

Wendy's jaw dropped. "I'm perfectly nice. I've done plenty of shopping and know how to treat customers. Believe me, I've encountered plenty of rude and inept clerks and servers."

Lily parked and pointed to Poppy's Tea, across the street along the waterfront. "Bodie and I are going to walk down to where they're setting up for the parade and tree lighting. If we're not back at the car, you can try the Driftwood Bay Mercantile for a jacket and some boots. I think you'll need them."

She attached Bodie's leash and headed down the street. "We'll see you in about an hour." After walking the first block, she couldn't help but look back, and saw Wendy still outside, staring at the storefront. For all her bravado, she didn't appear to be confident.

The city trucks surrounded the square and were using lifts to add lights to the massive tree. The loud beeping of backup indicators, along with people and equipment moving about didn't bother Bodie. They trudged on and his attention wandered, but when Lily applied a bit of tension on the leash, he made eye contact like he was supposed to. He always stopped and sat whenever Lily stopped walking, looking at her for direction.

A street sweeper went by, which was something new, but Bodie didn't flinch, just watched it as it traveled with the loud brooms circling underneath. People smiled at Bodie and many, especially children, stepped toward him, but when they saw his vest and noticed he was in training and was not to be petted, stepped back and gave them space. He was still excitable and Martha wanted Lily to work harder on getting him to greet people properly, instead of his usual exuberance.

They made a loop around the square a few times and then back down the street. She strained to see if Wendy was waiting by the car, but didn't see her, so led Bodie into the store, where dogs were permitted as long as they were leashed. They passed the aisles of home and garden supplies, and scanned the area where outerwear hung on racks.

Lily spotted Wendy's head and moved through the jackets to where she was standing. When Wendy saw her, she shook her head and pointed at the coats. "These are all just as horrible as I suspected."

Lily flicked through several hangers. They weren't that bad. She selected a few styles from the rack and Wendy wrinkled her nose at all of them. "Maybe you could take me to Seattle and I could find something there? A real city."

"You can take the bus, I think, but I'm not going to Seattle. If you want to order something online, we could stop by the drug store, where Mel said those no fee debit cards are, and then you can do your own shopping on the computer."

Wendy followed behind Lily and Bodie as they walked the few blocks. "How did you do with Poppy?"

"She said I could come in for a trial starting tomorrow and she would train me over the next week and go from there. It looks like an easy enough job, but I have to wear black pants or a skirt and a white blouse, plus an apron she provides. I'm not too pleased about that. It seems quite stifling. And can you believe she only pays thirteen-fifty an hour?"

"That's minimum wage, so yes, I can believe it. It's her business, so she can set the dress code. I'm sure you can find some inexpensive clothes like that around here." She wanted to suggest the thrift shop, but that would tip Wendy over the edge.

"I'll just find something online. Let's get the card and go home."

Bodie and Lily wandered the sidewalk outside the store, practicing sitting and quick movements until Wendy returned. From the frown on her sister's face, it was apparent reality was beginning to take hold.

While Lily put together dinner, Wendy sat in front of the computer, shopping for her new work wardrobe and a warmer coat. When Lily walked by to go to the pantry, she stole a glance at the screen and shook her head. Wendy was loading up on expensive items from a high-end store, instead of choosing something generic and affordable. It would take her a month to earn back what she was spending.

Another conversation that drifted into an argument was not what Lily was looking for, so she ignored it and went back to making enchiladas. As soon as she put the pan in the oven, she slipped into the living room and her recliner, escaping with the tree and another movie.

As the spicy aroma filled the air, Mel and the dogs came up from downstairs. Lily heard the young woman measuring out their kibble. Unlike her own sister, Mel was a joy to have around and always willing to help without being asked. Her sister could learn a thing or two from her.

Minutes later, the buzzer on the oven sounded and Lily took the bubbling casserole out, while Mel organized plates and silverware. As she stirred some salsa into the rice she was making, she noticed Wendy was still at the computer.

"You're welcome to join us for enchiladas and rice. It's almost ready."

Wendy turned from the screen. "I won't eat that. I'll have the fish."

Lily rolled her eyes and shrugged, handing Mel the spatula so she could dish up the enchiladas.

They were halfway through their meal when Wendy appeared with a shocked look on her face. "Where's my fish?"

Lily choked on the sip of water she had just taken. "I put it in the freezer, since you can't just leave it in the fridge for days." She stuck her fork into her enchilada. "And, to clear up any misunderstanding you have, I won't be cooking you separate meals. You're welcome to join us for dinner, but if you need different food, you're on your own."

With a dramatic sigh, Wendy went to the refrigerator, poked

around before slamming the door shut, scowling at Lily, and taking the apple she held downstairs, shutting the door with a bang as well.

Lily met Mel's wide eyes and began to giggle. "Having Wendy around is like getting free entertainment with dinner."

Mel smiled. "It's definitely more exciting with her here."

22

Wednesday morning, Lily dropped Wendy, whose attitude hadn't improved since her outburst last night, at the tea shop. She had hinted around at how inconvenient working was without her own car, but Lily assured her sister, she was happy to take her and pick her up or coordinate it with Mel, when she was available.

Wendy had always driven a sportscar and Lily remembered the photos on her social media of the latest Mercedes in the long line of new cars Wendy had celebrated. Gary's truck was in the garage and available, but until Lily had time to take her sister driving to practice with it, she didn't even offer it to her. Driving a truck was much different than the small cars Wendy was used to, and Lily didn't need the added problems. Lily was sure her sister would turn up her nose at the offer anyway.

Tonight, Mel would be picking Wendy up when she got off work, since Mac had invited Lily to dinner. Guilt washed over Lily for Mel's sake, but she was happy to be out of the house and not subject to what she suspected would be Wendy's foul mood when she finished her first day of work.

The dogs had been fed and Lily was admiring the tree when

she received a text from Kevin. As she scanned the message, her heart fell. Brooke and her family had invited him to join them for skiing in New Hampshire in the new year. They had a place in the mountains and offered to pay for the ticket change to allow Kevin to join them. Tears blurred her eyes at Kevin's worry in cutting his visit home short. He would be flying out on the thirtieth, but didn't want to go if it would make her too sad.

He was such a wonderful son, and although she had been counting on almost a month with him, she couldn't be the reason for him passing up a chance to enjoy such a wonderful trip. She had told herself he would chart his own path someday, perhaps find that one special person to share his life with and make a family. She just didn't think it would happen so soon. Logic told her it was natural, but the mom in her longed for the days of yesterday when Kevin was younger and she had been the most important person in his world. She plucked a tissue from the box and dabbed her eyes before typing in a reply.

Sounds like a wonderful trip and I wouldn't want you to pass it up. We'll cram in all the fun we can until you have to leave. Go ahead and change your ticket so you can get a good flight. Love you, Mom.

As soon as she sent it, he replied back with a smiley face and a heart. Watching Kevin grow up, find his own way, and make his own life, filled her with a sense of wonder and regret. Letting your child spread his wings was both the best and worst part of motherhood. She longed for the days when she would tuck him into bed and read him a story. She had loved resting her chin atop his head, sniffing in the sweet smell of him after a bath. When you're in the midst of those days, you're always waiting for something, the next milestone, and it seems like they will last forever. Now, looking back, the days of Kevin's childhood had evaporated like a puddle in the sunshine. The dogs sensed her sadness and rubbed against her legs, with Fritz putting his head in her lap, his gentle brown eyes letting her know he was there and it would be okay.

It was time to go and meet Mac. She added the alpaca scarf she loved and slipped into her coat, giving the dogs a cookie. "Mel will be back in a few minutes. And Wendy," she added grimacing. Fritz tilted his head at her, questioning her wisdom.

She drove downtown and found a parking place in front of Stillwater, a popular bistro on the waterfront. She had never been there, but Cyndy had raved about it. White twinkle lights were tucked into the shrubs and wrapped the trunks of the trees near the charming entrance. When she stepped inside, Mac was waiting for her with a warm smile and a hug.

"Our table is ready." He took her hand and led her through the lounge area and to a table in the corner, next to the fireplace.

He helped her out of her coat and pulled out her chair. "Has today been any better than yesterday?"

She took a long breath. "On the upside, Wendy has been at her new job all day. The waiter delivered a basket of warm bread with chilled butter and took their drink order.

"I can tell there's a downside by the look in your eyes. What's wrong?" He reached across the table for her hand.

"Kevin is shortening his stay here. His friend, Brooke, invited him to a ski vacation with her family in the mountains of New Hampshire." She scanned the menu, trying to find something that sounded good. "He just texted right before I came." She fanned her hand in front of her face. "I'll be fine, just disappointed and it's been a stressful week."

"Aww, I'm sorry, Lily. I know how much it means to have him here for the break."

"He'll still be here through Christmas, so it won't impact our trip. I want him to have his own life, so part of that is me letting go." Her throat clenched and she took a drink of water.

"That's easier said than done. If you can handle a bit of good news, I talked to Andy today and arranged for him to come and stay at my house when we go to Victoria. The dogs will be fine and you won't have to worry about leaving yours alone with Wendy. Andy was excited and can be trusted to look after them."

"That's a relief. If Wendy wasn't so mean-spirited toward them, I wouldn't worry, but I hate to subject their sweet souls to her. At least Mel will have another person in the house. I'll let her decide if she wants to stay at the house or go to Donna's. That was my original plan, BW."

He grinned. "Got it. Before Wendy. I was going to suggest she reach out to the woman who owns the cleaning company that services the clinic. She has most of the commercial contracts in town and is always looking for help."

Lily frowned. "She already made it clear cleaning was beneath her, but I'll keep it in mind. Hopefully, things work out for her at the tea shop."

The waiter delivered a cheeseburger with bacon relish, macaroni and cheese, and a pear and walnut salad, along with two plates, since they had decided to share their selections. As she ate the delicious food and listened to Mac, Lily's mood lifted.

"I feel a teeny bit ashamed sticking Mel with Wendy, but am happy not to be around her tonight. She's only been here four days. I'm going to have to buck up to handle the next few weeks or months."

"You'll settle into a routine soon and if she has a job, that will keep her occupied. Maybe she'll get her own place."

Lily laughed. "At the rate she spends money, it'll take her a year to save up enough to cover the costs of renting an apartment." She took the last bite of macaroni and cheese. "She literally has nothing. I feel bad, but she makes it hard to have much sympathy when she acts so arrogant." She poured a cup of hot tea and sighed. "This is all your fault, you know?"

His eyes widened and he smiled. "Do tell."

"When we were talking about family at Cyndy's before

Thanksgiving and you mentioned how with your parents gone, it was wonderful to have such a caring and close relationship with Cyndy, it made me realize I needed to make more of an effort to connect with Wendy. My wish has been granted." She smirked and took another sip of tea.

"I think a very wise woman once told me families were complicated." He collected his credit card and held Lily's coat for her. When they got outside, they walked side by side down the street, where the sidewalks were graced with trees, their trunks and branches swathed in white lights. He stopped at the entrance to one of the red brick buildings and opened the door of The Harbor Seal Tavern. "I thought we could listen to some music and have a hot chocolate or something before calling it a night."

The space was cozy and decked out for the holidays with lights and greenery, a Christmas tree in the corner near the small stage, and holiday music in the background. An ensemble was on the stage fiddling with equipment and instruments, getting ready to play. Mac followed Lily to a table and pulled a chair out for her. "I'll get our drinks. Any requests?"

"Surprise me." She watched the three men and one woman, dressed in jeans and holiday shirts, as they took their places on the raised platform. Instead of young and hip, they were middle-aged and gray. Lily wasn't a music aficionado and while she could identify drums, a piano, and a guitar in the mix, that was the extent of her expertise. She was hopeless when it came to the music category in trivia games, judging a song only by its appeal to her own tastes.

As the group began to play, Mac returned with two mochas topped with whipped cream and chocolate sauce, and settled into his chair. He pointed at the stage. "The drummer is Brian and that's Mike on the guitar, Don is at the piano and his wife, Bev, sings vocals.

The band entertained the small audience with a mix of

oldies, country tunes, and a few holiday songs. Lily tapped her feet to the familiar rhythms and for the next hour forgot all about Wendy. When they took their break, Mac turned toward her. "Are you ready to go?"

"I think so. I should get home and give Mel a break."

They walked, arm in arm, back to their cars in front of the restaurant, taking in the festive lights from shop windows and the warm glow from the colorful lights strung above the street.

When they reached her car, she hugged Mac. "Thanks for tonight. It was just what I needed to get out of my nasty mood."

He brushed a kiss across her lips, his cold nose rubbing against hers. "Spending time with you is always the best part of my day." He waved as she pulled away before getting into his car.

Having someone to talk to, someone to share things with, eased her worries. Despite knowing Mac for only six months, it was like he'd been there forever, like they were old friends. Her feelings, the ones she had tried to deny, only deepened the more time she spent with him. She didn't want to get too far ahead of herself, worrying about what might happen, so instead took comfort in having such a kind and handsome man in her life. It was wonderful to not feel alone in the world.

When Lily arrived home, she found Mel in the living room, already in her pajamas, lounging with the dogs. After hanging her coat and petting the dogs, who acted like she'd been gone for weeks and mauled her with excitement, Lily checked the office. "Is Wendy downstairs?"

Mel nodded. "She was exhausted and in a bad mood. She said her feet were killing her and went to bed as soon as we got home."

Lily eased into her recliner. "How was work today?"

Mel smiled and put down her book. "It was crazy busy. It was the best tip day I've had since working there. Everyone says

Friday night and Saturday will be even better. They told me it's usually their busiest weekend of the season."

"That's exciting. I'm sorry you'll miss the tree lighting though."

"I plan to walk down and take a look at it on my break, and the parade goes by the shop, so we'll be able to see it."

"We always had a crowd at the tree lighting at the capitol building, which was beautiful, but I'm looking forward to the parade and activities downtown this year. Mac and I are planning to stop by the coffee shop and say hello. Oh, and I've got that workshop at the arts center, so will be gone from eight until three."

"I don't go in until one o'clock so I can make sure Wendy gets to work and hang out with the dogs until I leave."

"Thanks, Mel. I appreciate you helping, especially with Wendy. I know she's a handful and can be condescending. I'm sorry and I hope you don't let it get to you."

"She's not what I expected," Mel said, with a smirk. "I imagine she's having a tough time adjusting to her life changing so quickly."

"I wish I had your patience. You're right and so kind to recognize that. I keep telling myself to be more understanding, but have had too many years of her attitude, which is why we don't speak much." She paused and stared at the tree, her eyes gravitating toward the sparkling glass ornaments. "You're such a good person, Mel. You make me want to be a better one."

"I was going to make hot chocolate and that movie I wanted to see comes on at nine o'clock. Do you want to stay up and watch it with me?"

Despite her desire to crawl into bed, Lily nodded. Being part of Mel's holiday excitement and seeing her flourish was worth missing sleep. She changed into her pajamas and cuddled under the blankets before Mel returned with their fancy hot chocolate drinks, and they settled in for another feel-good movie.

Mel had left for school by the time Wendy came upstairs Thursday morning. Lily had already taken the boys for their walk down by the beach, and was dressed and sipping her second cup of tea while the dogs rested on the deck. "Coffee's ready if you want some or hot water for tea."

Wendy grunted and poured herself a cup from the carafe. Lily opened the stack of mail she hadn't gotten to yesterday. When she slid her finger under the flap of the bright red envelope from Cyndy, she smiled. "Cyndy is having a stocking party and invited us." She frowned when she saw the date. "Oh, it's while you're working, next weekend. You would love her house. We'll have to visit on a day you're off."

With a heavier hand than needed, Wendy clunked her mug against the granite counter. "This job is horrible. People are so rude and it just interferes with everything, like Cyndy's party. The tips aren't that great, either."

"Mel said you were tired last night, I'm sorry. Give it some time, it's a big change for you. Being on your feet all day is tough. Maybe you should rethink those heels you wore."

She rolled her eyes. "I'm in great shape. Until I came here, I took seven classes a week at the gym. I always wear heels. I just hate that job. It's like I'm invisible and people snap their fingers at me, always rushing me for something. More tea, the check, to clean up some sloppy mess their stupid kid spilled at the table. I need to find something else, something more fitting."

"It's hard in a small town. Driftwood Bay is not exactly the center of business and industry. It's mostly retail."

"It's not fair. Uncle Leo left you this place, so you don't even have to work. I'm entitled to the same."

Lily choked on her sip of tea. "You have never shown any interest in this place and Uncle Leo left you a nice sum of money when he passed. What did you do with that?"

"Chad said we didn't need it and it was a nice bonus, so we used it when we chartered that yacht. Remember?"

Lily shook her head. She couldn't keep track of their extravagant vacations and seeing photos of them online grated on her, so she did her best to ignore them. "You could have put that in a savings account for yourself and then you'd have it. And for you to insinuate that I don't work is ridiculous. I've worked my whole life, retired, and now am working here. Off-season, like now, there isn't anything to do and there's no revenue coming in from the cottages, so I have to save what I make to get me through these times. You have no idea what you're talking about or what I've endured."

Tears fell from Wendy's eyes. "It's just not fair. I shouldn't have to have such a lowly job, pouring tea and serving fancy sandwiches to people who don't even notice me. I can't believe this is happening. My life is ruined."

"I'm truly sorry for what's happening, Wendy. Do you trust this lawyer, George? Is there anything he can do to help you?"

She bobbed her head. "Chad has always trusted George. I have no reason not to, but I don't know. I'll call him today and find out if there is anything else he can do. He's trying to set up a phone call with Chad, but warned me the call will be monitored, so I'm not sure how helpful that will be. George is all I have to rely on."

"Do you want me to call him?"

Wendy's eyes lifted. "Oh, yes, that would be great." She slipped her phone from her robe pocket and rattled off his number.

"Okay, you go get ready and I'll put a call in to him. I'll be home all day today, so can talk to him whenever he calls back. Hopefully I'll have more information by the time I pick you up tonight."

Wendy finished her coffee and nodded. "Thanks, Lily. I'm sorry I snapped at you. I just don't know what to do." She shuffled to the stairway, leaving her empty cup on the counter.

Lily sighed and placed it in the dishwasher. Her sister had been happy to have been taken care of by Chad, living in oblivion, spending money like crazy with no regard to saving. She slammed the dishwasher door shut, still reeling from the idea of wasting so much money chartering a yacht for months and could only imagine the amount spent on such a trip.

She tapped in George's number and left a message, explaining she was Wendy's sister.

Lily had the dogs loaded in the back of her SUV, waiting for Wendy, who came into the garage, almost hobbling on the black heels she insisted on wearing. Lily ran back inside and put a pair of her black clogs and heavy socks in a tote bag. "Here," she said, handing the bag to her sister. "I know your feet are a bit smaller than mine, but take these in case you need them. They're comfortable."

Wendy glanced inside the bag. "And ugly."

"Trust me, nobody is looking at your shoes." They made the quick trip to town and after dropping Wendy at the tea shop, she drove out to Fort Warden State Park. The colorful leaves on the ground outnumbered those on the trees, but it was still a gorgeous setting with the golds and oranges against the deep green of the grass and surrounding pines. The breeze rustled and churned them into rows along the walkway. She admired the leaves still clinging to the trees, not ready to give up the fight. She aspired to be like them, steadfast and unyielding.

As they walked, she wondered what George would have to say, if he called her back at all. At least her sister hadn't been implicated in whatever fraud and financial crimes Chad was involved with. It could have been worse, but Wendy wasn't seeing it that way and as frustrated as Lily was, she understood her sister's struggle. To have your life ripped out from under you wasn't easy. Wendy had never worked and was so dependent on Chad, it was going to be hard for her to make her own life.

Lily took a deep breath and emptied her mind, focusing on the two wagging tails in front her. She lost herself in the stunning colors of fall, her happy dogs, and the exercises she needed to practice with Bodie, vowing to be more patient with Wendy.

23

As luck would have it, George didn't call back Thursday, choosing to ring Lily as she was getting out of the car to attend the art workshop on Friday morning. She leaned against the door, while she explained her concerns about Wendy being left with no financial support and asked several questions about the status of the case.

Lily had a natural distrust of lawyers, but had worked with some wonderful ones, and after talking with George, judged him to be a straight-shooter. After chatting and confirming what she feared, she hurried to the classroom.

The instructor, Eva, was upbeat and excited to introduce the small group of women to the joys of mosaics. After introductions, Lily and her tablemate, Amy, both newbies to mosaics, admired the frames along the window, with the light shining through them. The class would be making small suncatchers using sea glass stones.

Along with those displayed in the window, including samples of each of the patterns they could choose from in class, Eva had several large pieces of her work hung on the wall. Lily was drawn to a scene of a curved beach with tall trees in the background, and another of a bridge over a river inside a huge frame. She studied the colors of the glass used in the sea and river and visualized all her aunt's jars and the possibilities.

Eva explained about the various types of adhesives and the silicone one she recommended that went on white, but dried clear. She supplied several patterns they could choose from for their projects, which were eight by ten inches. Eva suggested they use paper to draw a pattern that could be placed under the glass to guide them if they chose to make their own projects at home.

She demonstrated how to use a picture frame and went through the preparation process to get it ready for a mosaic, removing all the hardware from the back of the frame, painting it, if needed, cleaning the glass, and running a bead of silicone along the edges of it to secure it. Eva had prepared all the frames for them in advance, so they didn't have to wait for the silicone to dry.

As she showcased several of her designs, she explained that making mosaics was something she took up after losing her daughter. They had shared time at the beach and collected sea glass, and it was her way of feeling close to her daughter and occupying her mind. Her distraction soon became a beloved hobby and almost a meditative experience, and now she enjoyed sharing it with her students.

She pointed out the trays of sea glass on each table, already separated by color, and urged those who collected sea glass to set up containers that would allow them to divide pieces by color for easy storage and use.

Lily chose the lighthouse pattern and set about selecting her colors of glass. Eva pointed out some basics about design, including keeping pieces in smaller frames small, since the more pieces of sea glass, the richer the mosaic would look. She also highlighted some pieces of broken pottery and small rocks she sometimes incorporated in designs. She showed them how to secure the pattern to the back of the frame with tape and then let them begin choosing glass pieces. Amy selected a pattern of several flowers on stems, that left much of the plain glass uncovered. She was afraid she wouldn't work quickly enough to fill the entire frame.

Eva emphasized going slowly and mapping out their pattern by placing pieces that fit together nicely before gluing anything. Lily loved the feel of the smooth pieces of glass and went about selecting the colors of blue and green for the water and sky, the milky white for the lighthouse, browns and ambers for the earth, a larger oval white piece for a cloud in the blue sky, and even a yellow piece to add a light at the top of the lighthouse.

Eva stressed the importance of being neat and sparing with the adhesive, so they didn't have to go back and clean up the glass with a glass scraper. Lily's mind relaxed as she placed tiny bits of glass here and there, lining them up until she was happy. Eva stood over her shoulder to help guide her when she started the gluing process. Lily worked for hours, until she was over half done with the frame. She needed a break from hunching over and dashed to the café for a quick sandwich.

When she came back into the classroom, Eva was helping another student clean up a mess of glue before the woman took her lunch break. Lily stood and admired the samples of Eva's work. "You've inspired me, Eva. My aunt left a ton of sea glass she had collected and I've been wondering what to do with it. She also made mosaics and jewelry."

"That's wonderful. I'm glad you're enjoying it. I find it so soothing and love taking photos of the area and recreating them with glass." She was interrupted by another student, and Lily went back to her table, determined to finish so she could get home in plenty of time to change and be ready when Mac arrived.

Amy finished soon after the lunch break, and Eva showed the class the back of the frame, where blobs of white silicone were visible. "These will dry, so just leave your frame overnight, sometimes longer, until all the white disappears. Then, it will be ready to hang. The small ones can hang on a suction cup on the window easily. I like to run a wire across the frame and hang it with a wire, so it's secure. They look so pretty with the sun shining through them."

She reminded everyone she would stay until four o'clock and help anyone who was struggling to finish. Amy gathered her things and left, leaving Lily more room at the table. She had all her glass placed and just needed to finish gluing it. A quick glance at her watch told her she had plenty of time.

She put the last of the blue glass in the sky and chose a small rock to add to the corner on the back of the frame, with the date and her name, like Eva had suggested. Lily had never been crafty, or had the time to dedicate to anything like this. She admired her creation, picturing it hanging in the window at home. She'd have to stop by the store and pick up some more frames. Sorting through all that glass and finding some designs would keep her busy over the slow months. Maybe Mel and Wendy would like to try it with her.

Eva complimented her on her work and gave her a business card in case she needed more help before wishing her goodbye. Lily placed the frame in the back of the car, using the bubble wrap Eva had given them and drove home, feeling more relaxed and accomplished than she had all week.

She carried it into her bedroom and put it in the window seat to dry before taking the dogs outside for a quick walk. She knew Mel had taken them on a morning outing, but felt guilty for leaving them home all day. While she knew so many people thought of them as "just dogs," to her they were much more. They brought so much joy to her life and she wanted to make sure they had as much fun as possible. They needed some exercise before she left them again for the tree lighting festivities.

They walked the blocks around the neighborhood, before

returning home in time to eat their dinner and for her to change clothes. After fixing her hair and touching up her face, she surveyed her closet. She chose a black shirt topped with a black sweater with silver metallic threads, along with jeans, her warm boots, and silver jewelry. She took one more look in the mirror before adding her alpaca scarf and warm winter jacket. Between all her layers, she hoped to be warm no matter what the weather did. She made sure her gloves were in her pocket and added some cash, a credit card, and her keys.

The dogs rushed to the door and she knew Mac had arrived before the bell rang. He greeted the dogs with ear rubs and chin scratches, and treated Lily to a dazzling smile. "You ready?"

She promised the dogs she'd be back soon and locked the door. He led her to the waiting car. "You look sparkly and beautiful tonight," he said, making sure she was inside before shutting the door.

As soon as he got behind the wheel, he turned toward her. "How was your class?"

Warmth surged through her, happy that he remembered and cared enough to ask. "It was lots of fun. I think I've found a new hobby and a way to use Aunt Maggie's sea glass. I'm going to set up a small table downstairs and work in front of the windows. It's quite relaxing, almost therapeutic."

He found a parking spot a block from the main street and the parade route. They wandered along the waterfront to Sunrise Coffee, where they stopped to get a warm drink and say hello to Mel. The place was packed and they squeezed into the line of people waiting to order.

Lily stood on her tiptoes to get a glimpse of Mel at work. She was at the register, wearing antlers that lit up, keying in orders and handling transactions with ease, in the midst of the crowd of customers. She and her co-workers were joking and smiling with each other and customers as they worked nonstop to crank out fancy coffees and hot chocolates. When they finally arrived at the front of the line, Mel's eyes widened when she looked up to greet them.

Mac ordered hot chocolates, and Lily watched him slip a twenty-dollar tip into the jar. "Has it been this busy all day?" she asked, as Mel finished running Mac's card.

"Just the last hour or so. People getting here early for the parade and stuff. The manager is treating us to pizza tonight to thank us for our hard work. I can still give Wendy a ride and then come back."

Lily shook her head. "No, we'll pick her up. You just enjoy yourself. We'll be done with dinner by eight, so it's no problem." She pointed at the top of Mel's head. "Love those antlers." Mel waved and smiled as Lily and Mac moved down the counter to wait for their order and the next customer stepped to the register.

Mac nodded in Mel's direction. "What a difference a job and school have made. She looks so happy and does a great job keeping things organized."

"I'm so glad she has found her place in the world. She's a special young woman." Mac's name was announced by a young man with an elf hat and apron, and they took their drinks and went outside.

They strolled along the crowded sidewalks, making their way toward the fountain, where they found an empty bench. "We'll have to pick Wendy up at eight-thirty." She went on to tell him she had talked to George today just as her class was starting. "I wasn't sure if Wendy could trust him or what was actually going on, so offered to talk to him. I know she's overwhelmed."

He listened as she explained that there was no property in Wendy's name. Everything went through the company and she was not an officer. "On the plus side, she can't be implicated in any of the wrongdoing, which sounds like a solid case with Chad's partner flipping on him and leaving him to take the brunt of the punishment." She took a swallow from her cup. "Not that the jerk doesn't deserve it. He had been cheating people and laundering money. It's not going to end well for him." She blew out a long breath. "Wendy was laying a guilt trip on me last night because Uncle Leo left me the cottages and she spent all the money he left her on a charter yacht vacation."

He shook his head. "You two are really very different, you know that?"

She chuckled. "Oh, yeah. I'm not sure why, but she changed when she hooked up with Chad. Their entire life seemed to revolve around money and extravagance." She sighed and added, "Gary and I didn't have that problem."

She finished her hot chocolate. "Bottom line, George doesn't have much hope since all the assets are frozen until the case is adjudicated, but suspects it will all be seized. He mentioned Chad's sister as a possible source of help for Wendy, so I'm going to ask her about that idea. George said Chad would like to see Wendy, but knows it would be a hardship for her to fly back there and suggested his sister might be willing to help and give her a place to stay."

"What do you think she wants to do?"

Lily shook her head. "She just wants it all to be a bad dream. I don't think she understands this isn't temporary. She was complaining about her job and I don't see her hanging in for the long haul. I just don't know. I made the mistake of telling her Cyndy invited her to her stocking party and that set her off, because she has to work, of course."

"It's a rude awakening, when you've led a totally different lifestyle, I'm sure. We could include her in our dinner plans, but I don't think I'll be able to change the reservation. It's always busy on tree lighting night."

She shook her head. "No, but I'll see if I can order her something to go. Cheer her up a bit."

The parade started and their conversation was drowned out

by the loudspeaker announcing the local high school band, along with holiday entries from various groups and shops. The streets were filled with people enjoying the floats and music, along with the festive elves handing out cookies and candy canes.

Santa, riding in a sleigh, brought up the rear of the parade and took his place on a red velvet chair next to the tree. The mayor stood on a stage and welcomed the crowd to their annual celebration, leading everyone in a few Christmas carols before counting down to the lighting of the huge tree that stood in the square.

Lily gasped and the crowd erupted with cheers and whistles when the glow of the tree filled the square. Children began lining up to tell Santa their Christmas wishes. She leaned next to Mac and whispered in his ear. "It's so beautiful. What a great night." They stood, letting the wonder of it all wash over them, before leaving the square. Lily held onto Mac's arm, as he forged his way through the throng of people to the block one street away, where they could escape the crowd.

They could hear the choir singing as they walked away from the square toward the restaurant along the waterfront. There was a cool breeze coming off the water and Lily was thankful for a seat in the restaurant and the warmth of the fire that filled the space.

She scanned the menu and made her choice, requesting an order of the salmon with vegetables to go. Her glance out the window was rewarded with several boats decked out in Christmas lights, getting in the spirit of the celebration. Mac followed her gaze and tapped the window. "They're having a Christmas boat parade tomorrow night."

After another superb meal, they lingered over tea while they waited for Wendy's order, not wanting it to be cold when they picked her up from work. "I thought you, Kevin, and Mel could come over one day for a little surprise I've got in mind. We could do a meal, whatever works around Mel's schedule on a weekend."

"Sure, we'd love that. Now, I'm curious." She wiggled her eyebrows at him. "What kind of surprise?"

"The secret kind." He laughed and winked at her.

The waiter delivered the check and Lily grabbed it before Mac could, adding her card to it. "I insist, plus you don't need to buy Wendy's meal."

"I'm happy to do it, really. It's wonderful to have someone to share things with." He reached for her hand. "I've missed that and want you to know how much you mean to me, Lily. I haven't been this happy in a very long time."

24

Lily waited until Saturday morning to broach the subject of Chad's sister. Wendy had been in a terrible mood last night, and after eating her dinner, had gone straight to bed. Lily didn't mention her black clogs that Wendy was wearing, but was glad she was no longer limping.

Mel had the early shift and had already left for work. Lily had plans to meet her when she got off, so they could go to the store and pick out things to make their stockings for Cyndy's party. Mel's eyes had lit up when she saw the invitation and she was eager to put together a fun stocking.

When Lily heard Wendy's footsteps on the stairs, she ushered the dogs out to the deck, so they wouldn't add to the stress. She poured Wendy a cup of tea and motioned her to the counter. "I heard from George yesterday."

Wendy's eyes widened. "Did he have any news?"

Lily frowned. "Not much." With a gentle voice she explained that the chance of Chad getting out of the charges was slim. He would most likely be sentenced to prison and their frozen assets would be seized and forfeited. Wendy slumped lower in the chair as she absorbed the news. "He mentioned Chad's sister as a possible person you might be able to turn to? You never mentioned her, so I wasn't sure."

Wendy sighed. "Constance. She's never liked me. Thought I was beneath Chad and their family."

"George thought you might be able to stay with her and he could arrange a visit with Chad, which would be better than a monitored phone call. He assured me you won't be implicated in anything, but you also have no property. Nothing was in your name, only the name of Chad's corporation, and you're not an officer."

Tears plopped onto the counter and Wendy reached for a tissue. "I'm trying to believe he did that to protect me, but right now, it's hard to know what to think."

"Talking with him might be the best thing for you. George made it sound like he could organize a visit in the lawyer's conference room, so it would be private."

Wendy nodded. "I can call her and see what she says." She dabbed at her eyes again. "I just don't know what I'm going to do. I wish Mom and Dad were still here."

Lily grasped her sister's hand. "So do I. All the time. You'll just have to take it one step at a time. Figure out where you want to live and find a job that works for you. You can stay here, until you're on your feet. It's just not a great place to find a high paying job."

"Tell me about it." Wendy rolled her eyes and took a sip from her cup. "You were right about the shoes."

"Oh, good. I'm glad they worked. There's nothing worse than uncomfortable shoes when you're standing all day. Trust me, I've been there."

"I think I'll wait until I'm off on Monday and Tuesday, and call Constance then. I'm not sure I can handle any more bad news and keep it together at work. I'm sure I'm going to have to beg Constance to help me, and I have to work myself up to it."

Lily breathed a sigh of relief when Wendy went about

making herself a smoothie and headed downstairs to get ready. Constant turmoil was exhausting and Lily hoped Wendy could find a solution, or at least come to terms with what was happening. Hearing it directly from Chad might be what it would take.

After dropping Wendy at work, Lily put the ingredients in the slow cooker for soup, then dug out a card table and situated it downstairs. The dogs, their heads tilted, watched with interest as she unearthed the jars of beach glass stashed in the cupboards and lined them up on the counter. She made a list of supplies she would need to start her new hobby.

She set out for town and met Mel as she was getting off her shift. They stopped by the mercantile, the hardware store, the fabric store, and several gift shops, gathering supplies and finding things to stuff into their stockings. When they were picking out the stockings themselves, Mel suggested they make one for Wendy since she couldn't go to the party.

"That is such a sweet and wonderful idea. Maybe that will lift Wendy's spirits." Lily let Mel pick out a fancy velvet stocking trimmed with faux fur for Wendy, and agreed it was perfect.

They loaded their bags into Lily's car and Mel followed her home. Mel turned on a Christmas movie the moment they came through the door. The dogs sniffed and examined each of the bags, finally settling in to watch as Mel and Lily selected from the pile of small gifts they had amassed. The stockings were large and had plenty of room for the candies, teas, coffees, handmade soaps and lotions, and even a small Christmas book.

Lily left Mel to admire their handiwork, while she went about setting up her makeshift sea glass studio. After spending a couple of hours prepping some new frames, arranging trays, and separating glass, she went upstairs to find Mel fast asleep on the couch.

She tiptoed by her and checked on her suncatcher, which was looking good, with all the silicone dry and clear. She took it downstairs and added the hooks and wire to the frame like Eva had shown them, and hung it on a suction cup hook in the window. It would be her inspiration for her coming creations. The sun was setting so she'd have to wait until tomorrow to see how it looked in the daylight.

She had an idea for a couple of designs and wanted to make one for Mel for a gift. She'd have to get busy if she wanted to get it done in time for Christmas. She found an old sheet to cover the table that would keep prying eyes from seeing her surprises when she wasn't working.

By the time she went back upstairs, it was past dinner time and the dogs were staring at their bowls, signaling her it was time to pour their kibble. She stashed the stockings in her bedroom and then turned her attention to dinner. Once she had the dogs fed, she got out bowls and spoons and sliced the bread she had picked up at the bakery.

Mel came from around the corner. "Sorry I fell asleep. I guess I was tired."

While they ate, Lily told Mel about talking with the lawyer. "I'm not sure what Wendy will end up doing, but I know she can be less than kind and there's no excuse for it, but I think she's going to be even more stressed and under pressure until she figures all of this out. This week could be rocky."

Mel reached for another slice of bread. "I won't say anything, I promise. I know what it's like to feel lost. It's not easy. Honestly, without you and Donna I don't know what would have happened."

"I'm a firm believer that people come into your life for a reason. Sometimes, if you're lucky, they stay with you forever, but others are there at the exact time you need them. I think we needed each other, Mel."

She smiled and finished eating her soup. "What day does Kevin get here?"

Lily glanced at the calendar on the fridge. "Next Sunday and we head over to Victoria the day after Christmas, so you'll have to babysit Wendy for me. The dogs will be at Mac's with Andy. He's going to stay there and take care of the place." She swallowed the lump in her throat. "Kevin can't stay as long as we had planned. He's going to fly to New Hampshire right before New Year's Eve to spend a week or so with Brooke and her family."

"That's too bad. I mean, for you. I'm sure he'll have fun."

Lily forced a smile. "I'm trying to be brave and concentrate on the fun we'll have while he's here." She met Mel's eyes. "You haven't changed your mind about coming to Victoria?"

Mel shook her head and shrugged. "I'm scheduled to work, but I promise we can take the ferry over to Oak Harbor one day like you suggested."

"That would be great. We can do that after Kevin leaves. That will make for a nice outing." She glanced at her watch. "It's almost time for me to pick up Wendy."

"I'll clean up the kitchen, you go ahead." Mel began collecting the empty dishes. Lily's heart filled with pride as she watched her make sure every crumb was wiped from the counter. She wasn't sure Mel would ever understand what it meant to have her around the house. Lily couldn't imagine being alone, especially at the holidays, and now neither of them had to.

Over the next week, Lily kept busy with training Bodie, her secret sea glass projects, and playing taxi driver for Wendy. Mel spent all her time working, volunteering at the library or studying. Monday and Tuesday came and went and Wendy never said a word about Constance.

Lily wasn't going to press her. She'd either call or she wouldn't. Wendy was in unchartered waters and Lily had no idea what to expect. She knew her sister missed her old life. When she dropped her off on Saturday, Lily made a detour to the Driftwood Bay Recreation Center and inquired about exercise classes. Wendy had talked about exercising a few times. They had several options throughout the week and Lily purchased a pass for Wendy, adding it to the stocking she and Mel had made for her.

Mel came home around noon so she could change and they could get to Cyndy's for the party. The invitation had requested guests wear ugly Christmas sweaters to get in the spirit and they were all supposed to bring some type of snack or dish to share. Mel wore a red sweater with a huge reindeer on it and red and white striped arms, and Lily donned a black one with a Christmas tree, complete with actual metallic garland that was draped on it. They were both hideous and had been only a dollar each at the thrift store.

Lily had made one of her huge charcuterie boards. Along with all the meats and cheeses she normally used, she did her best to make it festive with sliced apples, grapes, pomegranates, and cranberries. Mel offered to carry it to the car and steady it on the drive over, while Lily gathered their stockings.

While Cyndy's house was always beautiful, she had outdone herself for the holidays. The aroma of mulled spices greeted them the moment they walked through the door. White twinkle lights filled every corner, decorated trees adorned each room, and her table was set with white, silver, and just a few touches of red. Candles flickered among the fresh flowers and greenery running the length of the dining table, while Christmas music played in the background.

Cyndy greeted each of them with a hug and Mel's mouth was still hanging open as she studied the tall tree near the base of the staircase. "It's like something from a movie."

Cyndy took the board she was holding as Mel's gaze never left the tree. "Come on in when you're ready. I've got some punch and hot cider ready, and I'll introduce you to the others." She turned toward Lily. "You can hang the stockings with the others on the mantle."

Mel's eyes darted from the tree to the banister, outfitted with greenery. "Wow, I've never seen anything like this."

Lily gestured with her head toward the kitchen. "Come see the rest of it."

Cyndy was busy at the island counter, making sure the food was organized. Lily hung their stockings, then joined Mel in getting a mug of cider. Cyndy made introductions around the room, pointing out her old friends, a few of whom recognized Mel from Sunrise Coffee. A few more ladies arrived. Everyone was welcoming and friendly, chatting as they filled their plates from the buffet Cyndy had organized.

There was never a moment of silence as the women visited and laughed while nibbling on appetizers and salads atop the fancy silver-rimmed plates, and drinking out of crystal goblets. A pang of sadness filled Lily's heart, knowing how much Wendy would have loved the party. With Wendy being new and the tea house staying open late during the holidays, it was impossible, but Lily wished she could have come. She was sure her sister's life had been filled with extravagant parties like this on a regular basis. She wouldn't have been caught dead in Lily's sweater, but would love Cyndy's décor.

After all the ladies had finished lunch, Cyndy guided them into the living room and explained the game they would be playing. It was the old gift exchange game most people had played, but with a twist. She had a stack of cards and after everyone chose a stocking, they had to take a card, which told them what they had to do. Directions included trading gifts with the person on your left or having everyone shift their gifts to the right, or trading a gift with someone wearing red, or someone with the ugliest sweater. It went on for a few rounds, and when Cyndy was sure nobody was holding the stocking they had brought, she ended the game.

Instead of diving into their goodies, Mel and Lily watched the two women, Nancy and Beth, who ended up with their stockings. Beth was excited about the gift card to Sunrise Coffee that Mel had included and Nancy loved the lotion and book in her stocking. Mel turned toward Lily and smiled. "I think they like them."

"Go ahead and see what you ended up with." Lily gestured to the purple velvet stocking, embroidered with snowflakes.

Mel's smile widened as she unearthed the treasures. Nail polish, plush socks, a cute hat, fig body scrub, lip balm, a snowflake bracelet, and a gift card to the bakery were among her favorites. "This is so fun," she said, reaching in to pull out the item stuck in the toe of the stocking. It was a pretty holiday mug with a pouch of tea. "This is so fun to get all these treats."

Lily slipped her hand into the gorgeous red velvet stocking in her lap, the deep band at the top decorated with gold beads, embroidery, and lace. She plucked out bath salts, shower gel, and lotion, soft gloves, a gift card for a pedicure, a leather journal and a gorgeous pen, plus a pair of earrings. Like Mel, she loved getting so many gifts.

All the women were holding up their presents and admiring what everyone had received. Cyndy interrupted the chatter with an announcement about dessert. She invited them back to the kitchen to partake and fill their cups with something warm. When the women gathered around her granite island counter, they gasped, in awe of the spread.

Cyndy smiled and gestured to Lily. "I was inspired by Lily's gorgeous charcuterie boards and thought it would be fun to do the same idea with desserts." She had used the counter to create a huge assortment of cookies, candies, mini pies, cupcakes, brownies, and cake slices, all of which were nestled among sugared cranberries, cinnamon sticks, and orange slices, with some sprigs of greenery to give it a holiday look. Like everything she designed, it was perfect.

The women filled their dessert plates, admiring the sinful treats. Cyndy's signature laugh rippled through the room. "Since all of these are bite sized, you can sample one of everything without feeling guilty."

As they enjoyed the sweets, they continued visiting and Mel discovered several of the women were in a book club and was over the moon when they extended an invitation for her to join them. Cyndy had provided take home containers and insisted they all help themselves to the leftovers. Lily loved hearing the excitement in Mel's voice as she talked about getting the book they were reading so she could join them at their meeting in January. Mel grabbed a container and pitched in to help box up some food to take home. Lily doubted Wendy would eat much, but added helpings of several salads, hoping she would try them. Mel concentrated on filling a container with desserts.

She looked up at Lily and shrugged as she pressed the lid onto the top, careful not to squish the pretty cookies. "I figured Kevin will help us eat all this when he gets here tomorrow."

Lily put an arm around her shoulders. "He'll love them. I'm so glad you came today and even happier you found some new book friends." When Lily met her eyes, she noticed a tear leak from them.

Mel smiled at her. "I'm so excited for Christmas this year. Somedays, like today, I can't believe it's all real. If you hadn't given me a place…a home, I wouldn't have all of this."

Lily hugged her close and said, "Let's go home. We have time to watch another movie before I have to pick up Wendy. You can make us some hot chocolate and we'll snuggle with the dogs."

25

Sunday morning, Lily was up early, excited about Kevin's arrival. Mac had volunteered to drive Lily to meet Kevin's plane, and Mel would make sure Wendy got to work on time. His plane arrived just before noon and once he had been hugged numerous times and Mac took charge of his luggage, they hit the road. Just past Tacoma, they got off the busy freeway and onto the quieter highway that would take them to the Kitsap Peninsula.

Forty-five minutes later, Mac pulled into a cafe promising the best views in Gig Harbor. Lily smiled at him as she grabbed her purse. "I take it you know this place, the way you drove straight to it?"

"I've been here a few times. Great food and service and they're right about the view, especially in warmer weather when you can sit on the deck."

Kevin followed them inside, holding the door for both of them. It wasn't busy and they had their choice of tables next to the windows. Kevin's eyes lit up when he saw they served breakfast all day. Lily didn't even have time to give Kevin the latest update on Wendy before their platters of food arrived. An omelet, eggs benedict, and cinnamon raisin bread French toast covered the table and the enticing aroma made Lily's stomach growl. She had been too excited to eat anything before they left and was starving.

Mac shared a bite of his decadent French toast with each of them, smiling as he watched them savor it. "I told ya, it's the best thing ever." He chuckled and dipped his bacon into the warm maple syrup on his plate.

"So, Wendy's situation is up in the air, but you're free to relax and take it easy. We don't have anything planned until the day after Christmas when we go to Victoria. It will just be the three of us. Mel is working."

Kevin nodded, as he scooped up another bite of his eggs benedict. "I'm looking forward to just hanging out with the dogs and you."

"Your mom said you're going to do some skiing up in New Hampshire. Do you do quite a bit of skiing?"

Kevin's cheeks reddened and he glanced at his mom. "We went a few times when I was younger, but I'm not much of an expert. Brooke assures me it will be fine, but I'm sort of nervous about it. It sounds like they are a family of avid skiers."

Mac nodded. "If you want to get in some practice, we could run over to Hurricane Ridge. It's where you and your mom visited when you went to Olympic National Park."

Kevin's eyes brightened and he grinned. "That would be great. Are you sure you have time?"

Mac met Lily's eyes. "I have plenty of time and I'm determined to use it for fun." He turned his attention to Kevin. "As long as your mom trusts me with you. It's been a long time since I've been skiing."

Kevin laughed. "Good, then I won't feel bad when I mess up."

After finishing their wonderful meal, Mac and Lily leaned against the railing, admiring the waters of Gig Harbor while they waited for Kevin to use the restroom. "You're sure you're okay with me taking him up to Hurricane Ridge?" he asked.

"Of course," she said, lacing her fingers through his. "I can't tell you how much it means to me that you would take time off to spend with Kevin, especially when you're already taking time off to drive us to Victoria." Tears filled her eyes. "Thank you, from the bottom of my heart."

He squeezed her hand and gave her a quick kiss on the cheek. "I'm happy to do it. It will give me some time to get to know him, just the two of us. I think you'll both love Victoria."

Moments later, Kevin emerged and they piled back into the car for the rest of the journey to Driftwood Bay.

As excited as Mel had been to make a special stocking for Wendy, her reaction to it was less than enthusiastic. Mel had presented it to her on Sunday night, when she got home from work. Kevin and Lily remarked on each of the little gifts, trying to elicit a response from her, but she just stuffed them all back into the stocking and went downstairs.

Kevin and Lily distracted Mel by letting her choose a Christmas movie and they played a board game while they watched it. The sound of them laughing made Lily's heart swell. No matter Wendy's attitude, it would be a wonderful Christmas, with Kevin home and Mel enjoying her first holiday in what Lily guessed was years.

Tuesday morning, Mel was already at work and Kevin still sleeping when Wendy came upstairs, looking happier than she had since she had arrived. "I just talked to Constance and she's agreed to let me come and stay through the holidays so I can meet with Chad and will even pay for my ticket. I booked a flight for next Monday. I can't wait to get out of here." She grinned, looking quite satisfied with herself.

"Wow, that's great news." Lily didn't bother to clarify if she meant about being able to stay with Constance or that she was leaving. "So, you won't be here for Christmas?"

Her sister waved her hand in the air as she went to pour a cup of coffee. "No, I should leave even earlier, but figured I'd have to endure another lecture from you about leaving Poppy stranded."

"Good for you. It wouldn't be right when you committed to working for the season." Maybe there was a glimmer of hope that Wendy would grow up one day soon.

"I've got to be at the airport super early Monday, so I reserved a spot on that shuttle again." She rolled her eyes. "As horrible as it is." She took a sip from her cup. "Constance is sending her car service to collect me, thank goodness."

Lily ignored the jab. "Good plan on the shuttle. It's what Kevin does when he's got an early flight." She checked her watch. "I've got to get the dogs loaded and go to training. I'll see you when I get home." She couldn't stomach another minute of her sister's attitude.

They were early for training, so she took a detour to the park, giving herself a pep talk while they strolled the pathways. She just had to get through the next five days with Wendy. She could do that; she'd survived much worse. But it pained her to see how selfish her sister was. Just as difficult, guilt nagged at Lily for not trying harder.

She hated being judgmental, of both Wendy and herself, but couldn't seem to help it. She should be happy to have her sister with her for the holidays. They were all that was left of their small family, and yet she couldn't deny the ripple of happiness she felt knowing Wendy would be back in Texas soon.

All she could do was maintain her patience and let Wendy know she always had a place to stay. Though she wanted her sister to be kinder, Wendy was the only one who could make that change, and Lily beating her head on that rock would only result in making her miserable.

Their mom would be so disappointed.

Lily spent the rest of the week working on her mosaics and planning the food for Christmas Eve. Instead of an elaborate dinner, she decided to make appetizers and scoured recipe groups she found online for ideas. Mac had taken a weekday off and picked up Kevin for a trip to Hurricane Ridge for some skiing. He then ended up working most of the weekend, since he was taking time off after Christmas, and she and Kevin lounged around the house for most of it.

Monday morning, Wendy left, without much fanfare. Lily made sure Wendy understood that she always had a place to stay, and asked her to let her know when she'd be coming back. She tried to hug her sister goodbye when she dropped her at the shuttle stop, but Wendy was in a hurry and offered her an air kiss instead. She then watched with dismay as Wendy instructed the driver how to place her luggage and warned him not to scratch it. Her recent experience had not humbled her in the least.

When Lily returned home, she saw the special stocking Mel had made for Wendy sitting on the counter, along with the wrapped gifts for her that had been under the tree. She had been in such a hurry to leave, she must have forgotten about them. Either that, or she didn't care about them at all. Lily tucked them all back under the tree as far back as possible, so Mel wouldn't notice. She'd save them for when Wendy came back from her visit.

She occupied herself with her mosaics, while Kevin spent most of his time sleeping or watching movies.

With all her presents wrapped and ready Wednesday afternoon, with Christmas music playing, Lily was puttering in the kitchen putting the last-minute touches on the charcuterie boards she had put together for Christmas Eve.

Kevin sat at the counter, sipping hot cocoa, the dogs at his feet. "Mac is pretty cool, Mom. We had so much fun skiing. He's nice and funny. I'm glad you found him."

She stopped fiddling with the garnish and looked up at her son. The boy she loved more than anything. "I'm so relieved you like him. I've been nervous wondering how you would feel about him."

"He's great. You're so much happier now, which helps me not worry about you. I wasn't sure about you moving so far away, on your own, not knowing anyone, but you've got some great friends."

She smiled. "I feel the same way. I wasn't too sure myself, but *something,* I like to think maybe it was a combination of your dad and Uncle Leo, pulled me here. I miss being closer to you, but I'm better here."

"Well, I just wanted you to know, I think he's great and I know Dad would have liked him." He slid off the chair and hugged her in a tight embrace. "I'm going to go get changed." His words were like a healing balm to her heart. Young men weren't known for sharing their feelings, but in his few words and matter-of-fact way, he had succeeded in letting her know he supported her.

He made for the stairs and the dogs bounded after him. She checked her watch and finished the last of the garnish before changing her clothes, expecting Mel to be home in a few minutes. Then Cyndy and Mac would be arriving, along with Jeff and Donna, Nora and Bree. Andy had promised to stop by and visit before their family dinner.

When she emerged from her bedroom, she found Kevin entertaining Mac and Cyndy, who were in the kitchen nibbling on appetizers. Mel joined them, changed from her work clothes, and wearing a pretty new sweater Lily had urged her to buy. It wasn't long before the others arrived and the house was filled with laughter and conversation.

Bree and Mel had their heads together laughing and snacking, while Andy and Kevin spent most of their time surrounded by the dogs while they chatted, with Andy teaching Kevin some sign language.

Lily stood against the wall, taking it all in, her thoughts drifting to Gary and her parents, wishing they were here. She didn't linger long in the past, urging her mind to the present and the happiness right in front of her—the new memories she was making. Warmth flooded through her when she caught Mac's eye and he winked at her, waving her over to join him and the others. The wise words of Margot and Jean echoed in her head. She would never replace Gary or forget him, but the man smiling at her, his eyes full of love and kindness, was here right now. She would be foolish to throw away a chance at happiness, a second chance at love.

After everyone had left, and Kevin and Mel took the dogs outside, Mac lingered and gave Lily his gift to her. She opened the card first and discovered a gift certificate for a complete spa day at the fancy hotel on Orcas Island that Izzy had mentioned when they had visited. "Oh, how thoughtful. I can't wait to go."

Next, she opened the beautiful foil-wrapped box. A small blue velvet box nestled inside of it. Her heart pounded and her fingers trembled as she lifted the lid. She breathed a sigh of relief when she discovered a gorgeous pair of earrings nestled against the satin lining.

"Do you like them?" Concern laced Mac's voice.

"I love them." She held the shimmering moonstone drop earrings out up to the light. "They're lovely. I've never had any moonstone jewelry."

"Something about them made me think of you and our walk in the moonlight. I wanted you to remember that special night."

She took out the earrings she was wearing and put in the new ones, giving him a kiss. "I will never forget our night on that moonlit beach."

Christmas morning, and the house was quiet, with Mel and Kevin both taking advantage of the holiday and sleeping in. It wasn't like when Kevin had been a boy, charging through the house at dawn, looking for what Santa had left him under the tree. Memories were tricky and poured out at times like a sweet elixir, and other times, like today, a tart lemonade. Her mom always told her how precious time was, but she never understood it until it was too late.

She wanted to go back in time and relive those idyllic years, when she had been a child, surrounded by the love and affection of her parents and the magic and wonder of Christmas. She hadn't appreciated it at the time, but longed for that bubble of security, when nothing tragic had touched her, she hadn't experienced loss, and all she had known was happiness. She and Gary had done their best to create that type of childhood for Kevin, and as a mother, those loving memories of their early years, when Kevin's eyes filled with the excitement of the holidays, brought her the most joy.

Two wet noses against her leg jogged her back into the present. After feeding the two pups, she opened the fridge and went about prepping a special holiday breakfast board she had planned for the three of them before they were due at Mac's. By the time she had arranged the sliced fruit and mini muffins, plus the almond croissants she had picked up at the bakery yesterday, Kevin had ambled up the stairs.

"Merry Christmas, Mom," he said, kissing her on the cheek. "Mel's in the shower." He eyed the spread. "Oh, that looks great. I'm starving."

"Help yourself. We can open presents when Mel gets up here." She filled the kettle and added a croissant and fruit to her own plate.

They were in the midst of eating when Mel came up the stairs. "Oh, fancy," she said, surveying the selection and helping herself to a plate.

They weren't due at Mac's until two o'clock, so had plenty of time to relax and open their gifts. Lily delighted in watching Mel open the mosaic she had made her. It was in a square frame and depicted one of the cottages, along with Fritz and Bodie in front of it and the blue water behind it. Mel rushed to hug her as soon as she opened it. "I love it. I can't believe you did this. It's so pretty."

"I wanted you to have something to always remember us by." Like Kevin, Lily knew at some point Mel would find her own way and perhaps move or get married and have her own family. She hoped she would always remember she had a home here. "You don't get much sunlight in your bedroom, but you can put it in the window downstairs and when you get a house of your own someday, you can take it with you so you always remember Glass Beach Cottage."

"I could never forget you or Fritz and Bodie." She lifted it toward the window to admire it again then opened her other boxes, revealing new clothes and a pretty bracelet that she promptly put on her wrist. "Thank you, Lily. I love everything."

Kevin was excited to open his new tablet and the gift of a year's worth of a movie streaming service, along with a subscription to a cookie club that would send him homemade cookies each month. He hugged his mom and went about plugging in the tablet so he could charge it up and test it out.

Lily loved the personalized mug Mel had given her that featured a woman, with hair the color of Lily's and two goldens beside her, sitting on a dock, looking out over the water. All their names were painted on the mug. Lily embraced Mel.

"Thank you. I'm going to have a hard time letting Bodie go when it's time, so will cherish this."

She opened the package from Kevin and found a beautiful silver necklace with charms on it, engraved with Bodie and Fritz's names, along with a cute tiny paw print. It was perfect and she put it around her neck. Kevin smiled, and added, "I guess this is the year of dog themed gifts for you."

"I love them, thank you both very much." She handed each of them a stocking. "There are a few little gifts from Santa in your stockings." They tore into them like excited kids, unwrapping candies, toothbrushes, pens, socks, and snacks.

After another helping of breakfast, Lily put the leftovers away and got ready, making sure she added her new earrings to her outfit. They were stunning with the black sweater she wore.

The dogs were excited to load into the car and when she mentioned they were going to see Sherlock, their tails swished even faster. She put Mel and Kevin in charge of holding onto the gifts for Mac and Cyndy and they headed down the road.

Mac met them as soon as they pulled into the driveway, Sherlock at his side. Kevin unloaded the dogs and let them run to greet their best furry friend. He studied the house and grounds while Lily gathered the gifts. Mac took Mel's hand and said, "Close your eyes. I have a surprise for you."

She giggled and complied, letting him lead her around the back of the house to the pasture. Kevin and Lily walked behind them, Lily depositing the gifts on the back deck on their way. Kevin's eyes widened as he took in the huge deck and overlook. "Wow, this is some place. What a great view and it's so nice and quiet."

She nodded. "Wait until you see his llamas." She watched as Mac positioned Mel at the fence. Two alpacas stood nearby with the larger llamas behind them.

"Open your eyes," he said.

Mel squealed with delight. "Oh, you got them. I was hoping

you would find some after seeing those photos you brought back." She reached to pet them. "They are so cute and soft."

"I thought you could do the honors and name them."

Her eyes widened. "Really? Wow, I'll have to give it some thought."

"There are a few fruits and veggies I cut up for them, if you want to give them all a treat. Margo and Coco, too." He pointed at a plastic container.

Kevin approached the fence line and petted the two new arrivals. "They are super cute." He helped Mel feed them chunks of carrots and apples, while Mac and Lily made sure the dogs were secured before they headed back to the house.

He carried the bag of gifts inside, letting the delicious aroma of whatever Cyndy was cooking greet them. She hollered out a cheery "Hello, come on in. Merry Christmas, Lily."

"Something smells beyond yummy," said Lily, selecting a gift bag and putting it on the counter. "Here's a bit of Christmas cheer for you."

Cyndy turned away from the beautiful apple salad she was prepping and wiped her hands on a towel. She appeared unable to resist opening the bag and seemed to love the wine inspired gifts, including a set of wine infused salts for cooking. "I brought you a little something. It's under the tree."

Mac led Lily into the living area, where a huge tree stood, decked out with gorgeous ornaments and draped with sparkling ribbon. It had Cyndy's fingerprints all over it. Mac handed her a gift.

"Before I open Cyndy's, I want you to open mine." She held out a gift bag.

He smiled as he took out the large bubble wrapped frame. Once he unwrapped it, he gasped. "Oh, it's beautiful." He hugged her close and kissed her cheek. "I love it." He held it up to the window and the sunlight exposed the beautiful mosaic of Sherlock, his smiling face easy to recognize in the amber sea glass pieces. She had used the aqua and darker blue pieces in the background.

"I had to cheat and buy some darker glass for his nose and eyes and to define his jawline, plus the pink and red for his tongue, but I thought it captured him." She smiled as Mac admired the piece.

"I'm going to hang it right by the back door, so I see it each time I leave and come home."

"There's one more treat in the bag," she said, shaking it.

He dug into the bottom and brought out a card. Enclosed with the heartfelt message was a gift card for golf in the San Juan Islands. His eyes lit up when he saw it and he encircled her in a long embrace. "Great minds, huh? We both chose gifts focused on our next trip together. I find that to be a good sign."

She laughed and nodded her head. "I'm so looking forward to it."

Cyndy's voice echoed through the house. "Tell the kids dinner's about ready."

She felt his lips against the side of her neck and it sent a thrill through her. "I see you're wearing the earrings. They look gorgeous on you."

He took her hand as they made their way back to the kitchen. "This has been my best Christmas in decades and it's because of you."

She rewarded him with a brush of her lips across his cheek. "I feel the same way."

Kevin and Mel came through the door, smiling and laughing, talking about the alpacas. While they were all there, she opened Cyndy's gift. Inside the beautifully wrapped box was a set of customized ornaments, three of them painted with the cottages, one of Fritz, and one of Bodie. "Oh, these are so cute. I love them. That's so thoughtful of you." She gave Cyndy a hug.

"I work with an artist through the shop and she does wonderful work. Mac helped me by taking some photos for me to share with her. I'm so pleased you like them." She untied the strings from her apron. "Let's eat while everything is hot."

They gathered around the table, decorated like it had come straight from Cyndy's shop, and enjoyed her delicious glazed ham, applesauce, buttery potatoes, and all the side dishes she had made. While they ate, Mac asked Mel if she had decided on names for the two new additions.

She smiled and glanced at Kevin. "We think Lucy and Ethel." Mel loved watching the old episodes of *I Love Lucy,* so her choice wasn't a surprise. Everyone laughed, agreeing it was an excellent choice. "This is the best Christmas I've ever had," said Mel, her voice fading as tears filled her eyes. "Thank you for making it so special."

Lily noticed there wasn't a dry eye around the table and didn't trust her own voice. She glanced at Cyndy, who raised her glass and said, "Here's to remembering the joys of the season and carrying them with us throughout the coming year. Merry Christmas."

26

Holding on to the fun memories from their time in Victoria, Lily hugged Kevin, not wanting to release him, but knowing she had to let him get into the shuttle. No matter the knot in her stomach and everything in her body screaming at her to hang onto him, she had to let him get on a plane and fly across the country today. It had been a wonderful visit, but like all of them, much too short. Watching him go, brought back all the doubts she had about moving so far away. Her heart ached as she watched her sweet son slide into a seat and wave goodbye.

He couldn't hide his excitement at getting to see Brooke and she would never deny him the chance of finding someone special. She waved to him until the van disappeared, tears streaming down her face. If she had stayed in Richmond, he'd still be going to New Hampshire, so that wouldn't have changed today. She reminded herself, the only difference would have been the geography, making for a shorter distance to see each other.

Mothers never knew if their decisions were the right ones; they just had to do the best they could and hope their choices wouldn't scar their children. She had trusted in all the prayers she had uttered and the signs, including the bequest from Uncle Leo that led her to Driftwood Bay. If she had stayed in Richmond, she would still be miserable, trudging along, surrounded by memories of all she had lost. She would have never met Mac or Cyndy or Bodie or Andy…or Mel. Thinking of them comforted her and made her realize she had made the right choice, but it didn't soothe the pang in her heart that came with Kevin's absence.

She got back in the car, where the dogs were anxious to greet her, sensing her sadness. She detoured to get a hot tea and then stopped by the park so the dogs could get some exercise. Tomorrow was New Year's Eve and she had to shake off this funk so she could enjoy the festivities with Mac. It wasn't fair to him for her to be down in the dumps.

With Christmas over, she had expected to hear from Wendy and made a mental note to call her in the afternoon if she hadn't gotten in touch. Lily had run into Poppy at the market a couple of days ago. With the tea shop cutting back to their normal winter hours and Poppy not offering to extend Wendy's employment, she'd have to find something else. That wouldn't be easy during the off-season.

She cleared her mind, determined to focus on the dogs and nature. There was no point in putting too much effort or concern into what Wendy would do. She hated seeing her sister suffer, but had learned long ago that Wendy would do what she wanted, with or without her input. As she wandered the pathways with the dogs, she avoided focusing on Kevin flying. It never failed to fill her with dread, her mind always happy to play worst case scenario with her. Losing her mom had only amplified her own tendencies to anticipate the worst. That trait served her well in law enforcement, but was a drag in real life.

Instead, she focused on the wonderful few days they had enjoyed in Victoria. Along with all the gorgeous decorations and millions of festive lights gracing the domes and outlining the massive buildings, plus the private tour she had arranged of the Parliament Building and the fun horse and carriage ride they had enjoyed, Mac had driven them to Butchart Gardens. Instead of the gorgeous flowers they were famous for, during the holiday season they wowed their guests with light displays throughout the fifty acres. Even Kevin was impressed with the stunning effect. She had taken hundreds of photos and couldn't wait to visit in the spring or summer when the flowers would dominate.

After several loops around the park, she led the dogs back to the car and home. She took refuge at her work table, sorting and finding pieces of glass for a new project. She had ordered a round mirror from the mercantile and had been rifling through her aunt's collection of glass to make a border around it, starting with shades of brown and sandy tones around the bottom and then gradually changing the colors from lighter aqua to a deep blue. It was a challenge, but a welcome distraction for the winter.

As she had worked on the pieces for Mac and Mel, it struck her that much like her own life, she was taking bits of broken pieces of glass and putting them together to make something new, something beautiful. While the pieces would never resemble what they used to be, they were transformed into something different, something that would bring joy and happiness to her life. All those broken shapes, smoothed by the power of the sea, were essential and would live on in her new creations. Maybe it was the same way with her memories. She'd never have exactly what she had lost, but she could have something new and wonderful.

Mel was at work and the house was quiet, save for the sound of the dogs snoring and the scrape of glass against the plastic trays. Lily stretched her shoulders and back and made her way upstairs for a late lunch break. She couldn't resist taking her snack and a cup of cocoa into the living room to enjoy the tree while she ate. Kevin wouldn't be here to help her take it down this year. The days after Christmas were always filled with melancholy, but without Kevin it would be worse.

She felt hot breath on her leg and the weight of Fritz leaning against it reminded her she wasn't alone. His soulful eyes were full of love and understanding. She reached out to pet the top of his head. "You're a good boy, Fritzie." He rested his head on her thigh, relishing the attention.

Her phone buzzed and she almost toppled her mug, reaching for it. Kevin had landed in Chicago and had a short layover before the final leg to Manchester. She let herself relax a bit, knowing the longest part of his travel was over. Once he took off, it was just over two hours to New Hampshire. He would be there by her dinner time.

She texted him a reply, reminding him to drink lots of water and to send her photos of the mountains. She finished her lunch and sunk back into her recliner, covering herself with her blanket and petting the dogs until they stretched out next to her. Her finger hovered over Wendy's name on the screen of her phone. The last week had been nice, without the tension between the two of them. She wished they had a better connection, one that made it easy to be together. One like Mac and Cyndy had. Regardless, she had made up her mind to do the right thing, which meant making sure Wendy knew she could stay with her, as long as it took to get on her feet. She just hoped that wouldn't mean forever.

She hit the green button and after several rings, Wendy's voice greeted her. "Hey, how are you doing?" asked Lily. "Any news?"

"I was going to call you. I've just been swamped."

Lily's eyebrows rose. "Really, what have you been doing? Did you get to see Chad?"

"Oh, yes. George set up a couple of visits, so that was good and Chad had asked George to talk to Constance, so that helped. She's agreed to let me stay in her guest house until Chad's trial is over. It's not ideal, but I can't handle living out there in the backwoods with no conveniences, forced to do some menial job. I honestly don't know how you do it, Lily. I don't think I could survive and told Chad that."

Her tone and words stung, but Lily focused on the silver lining. "I'm sure you'll be happier there, closer to Chad, and George can keep you more informed."

"And I don't have to get a job. Constance promised to cover everything while I'm here, so I can just relax. She's got a pool and she lives in a different area, so I don't have to face all our friends."

Lily could only imagine what she would do if Chad ended up in prison, but the trial wouldn't be happening anytime soon. "I'm glad things are looking up for you, Wendy. I hope you had a nice Christmas."

"Oh, it was wonderful. Constance treated me to a shopping spree and she had a lovely catered affair. She also has one of those blenders I wanted and someone does her shopping and food prep, so it's so much less stressful. I finally feel like I have my life back."

Lily's eyes rested on the stocking and packages Wendy had left behind, still under the tree waiting for her; one from her and one from Mel. It was hard to fathom how someone raised by parents like hers could be so heartless and self-absorbed. It had crushed Mel when Wendy left so abruptly and didn't even bother to take the gifts Mel had taken the time to get her. Without any prompting, she had spent her own money on a smoothie recipe book, luxurious foot cream, and fluffy socks.

Lily shook her head as she contemplated sending the gifts to her or just returning them. She doubted Wendy would take the time to acknowledge them, which would be worse for Mel than returning them. She might as well get her money back or enjoy some of the items herself.

"Sounds like it's perfect for you." Lily rolled her eyes at Fritz and Bodie. "You do know you left your gifts from me and Mel behind?" She couldn't resist the jab.

"Oh, that's right. I was in such a rush to leave I didn't even think about it. Tell her I'm sorry. I'll send you guys something."

"There's no need to send us anything, Wendy. Mel used her own money, which she has very little of, to buy you some things she thought you would like. It's a shame you can't be a bit more thoughtful."

Wendy groaned. "I don't need a lecture right now. My life is in shambles if you haven't noticed. I'm worried about what's going to happen to me, so pardon me if I don't have time to coddle the poor little homeless girl you've taken in."

Lily's heart pounded in her chest as her temples throbbed and her blood boiled. "Mel is a wonderful young woman who has had to overcome more than you or I will ever know. You belittling her only highlights your own character flaws, not hers. I'm glad you've found a solution to your problem, since I was going to let you know you were welcome to stay here as long as you need. Welcome may be too strong of a word, but I would never let you go without a place to stay. I truly hope things work out for you and Chad."

Lily took a deep breath. "You know, Wendy, Mom would be so hurt knowing how distant we've become. Family was always so important to her and Dad and I hate the fact that we've grown apart and no longer have a close connection. We're lucky to have each other and I don't want to look back on our relationship with regret. Don't you think Mom would be sad to know we don't even talk much?"

"I just think we're very different people. I don't think about Mom that much and I think we just lead such separate lives, I'm not sure we have much in common any more. Maybe we never really did."

Lily's shoulders slumped at her sister's words.

Garbled sounds in the background competed with Wendy's voice. "I've got to go. We're heading out now. Constance is hosting a New Year's Eve party tomorrow and we need to pick up a few things. I'll call you later." She disconnected before Lily could say goodbye.

She let out a long breath and then took in another, hoping to calm her racing heart. Typical Wendy. More concerned about parties and her luxurious lifestyle than anyone with real problems. She knew one thing—she wouldn't be sending Wendy any of her gifts.

Why did it have to be so hard? Lily had never had many close friends, perhaps because it was often too much work, too much drama, and she craved calmness. Wendy was right that they live opposite lives and she couldn't force her sister to have a relationship. She wished they could have a closer one, one where they could tell each other things and rely on one another, but it took two people to build such a connection. Just because they were related didn't mean it would happen.

Her heart felt heavy, knowing someday Wendy would regret her focus on money and extravagance rather than family. It made her sad to know Wendy didn't think of their mother often. Maybe it was too hard. Although deflated, Lily knew she would never turn her back on Wendy, but she wasn't going to subject herself to the constant rudeness and rejection. She'd always be there for her, but Wendy had to live her own life and maybe someday she would understand the value of family.

Lily glanced at the garbage and remembered she needed to take the trash can out to the curb. She started to collect it and then stopped, opened the freezer and took out Wendy's blasted fish and tossed it into the bag, before gathering it up and taking it outside. She took great delight, maybe a little too much, in heaving that bag with the frozen fish into the green container and shoving it to the curb.

With that chore done, Lily padded into the kitchen, filled the kettle and set about brewing a cup of tea. The ritual calmed her, centered her, and she understood why all the characters in her favorite British shows sipped tea during a crisis.

~

Mel was working the late shift and once Lily heard from Kevin, who had arrived in New Hampshire and was waiting at baggage claim with Brooke and her family, she relaxed and went back to working on the mosaic. She had been at it for more than an hour when Fritz and Bodie dashed up the stairs and moments later the doorbell rang.

She put the sheet over the table and hurried upstairs, surprised to find Mac and Sherlock at the front door. He held up takeout bags from Noni's. "I figured you could use a little pick me up tonight."

Sherlock darted by her as she rushed into his arms. She swallowed hard, trying to control the sobs that threatened to rise from her throat. "I'm so glad to see you," she whispered.

He put an arm around her, still holding the bags in his other hand. "Let's go inside and we'll figure out what's wrong."

She leaned against his arm as they walked through the door. The dogs huddled together near the tree, watching them as they passed by to the kitchen. He plopped the bags on the counter and took her in his arms. "Is Kevin okay?"

She nodded, murmuring into his shoulder. "He's fine. He got there and is with Brooke and her family."

"Oh, that's good. It's not easy, letting them go."

She cleared her throat. "It's partly that and then I made the mistake of calling Wendy. She was a beast." As she talked and told him about their conversation, she pulled out plates from the cupboard.

He grimaced as he added pasta to his plate and uncovered the garlic bread. "It might be a blessing in disguise, you know? I could tell how much she stressed you out when she was here. I'm not sure it would get any better."

"My head agrees with you. I'm just trying to wait for my heart to catch up. I've been spending too much time thinking about her, about our parents, what they would think. Having Kevin here helped mask all the sadness I always feel this time of year. Talking to Wendy brought it to the surface and it bubbled over."

"It's going to be okay. I promise." He reached for her hand and squeezed it."

She nodded and made an effort to smile. "I'm just wallowing. I'll be fine. I just feel like I've lost the last bit of my family I had left. After my parents died, it was the three of us for so long and I put all my hope in our tight circle. Gary and Kevin shielded me from the unending sorrow of that time in my life. Then, when Gary was killed, I honestly wasn't sure I'd make it. If not for Kevin, I would have given up."

His caring eyes filled with tears, as he rubbed a thumb across the top of her hand. She licked her lips. "I know I'm not telling you anything you haven't experienced first-hand. The pain is so powerful, it's like a paralytic agent. Coming here, meeting you, taking in Bodie and Mel, changed all that. It gave me a glimmer of hope, a possibility of a new future, a purpose, you might say."

He nodded and smiled. "I feel the same way about meeting you. I was on the hamster wheel, running and running, focused on work so I didn't have to think about my life, being alone, Missy, all of it. But then I met a beautiful woman in my exam room, along with her loyal golden, and in a split second, my life changed. I think Fritz and Bodie knew what they were doing when they brought us together." He brought her hand to his lips and kissed each of her knuckles.

"I'm so lucky to have you in my life." Lily leaned against his shoulder. "Thank you for making me feel better about everything. Sometimes I spend too much time in my own head."

He chuckled. "I know the feeling." He pushed the container of pasta toward her. "Let's eat and then maybe we can talk Mel into making us some hot cocoa when she gets home."

27

New Year's Eve, Mel was working the late shift at the coffee shop and then attending a movie and pizza party with her coworkers. Mac worked, but took off earlier than usual and arrived at Lily's with Sherlock. He'd be joining his two furry friends to spend the evening together. Mel would be home before ten o'clock and had offered to watch over the three pups.

Lily wasn't sure what to wear on the dinner cruise Mac had booked, but had settled for a sparkly top with a velvet jacket over jeans and boots, along with her new earrings. She suspected it would be chilly on the water and wasn't into skirts or dresses, so opted for warmth with a bit of glitz.

She and Mac left the dogs with a promise they'd be back soon and headed for the marina. The town was still decked out in her holiday best, with twinkling lights everywhere and the tall tree visible in the town square. People were out and about, ready to ring in the new year at local eateries.

The cruise company had partnered with a local restaurant, where the evening started with appetizers and drinks along the waterfront. Mac, as always, ran into a few people he knew. In between snacking on delicious nibbles, he introduced Lily to a couple of pet parents he knew from their longstanding relationship at the clinic.

Soon a crewman addressed the group and announced it was time to board the *Moonlight,* and directed them to the yacht. Lily knew next to nothing about boats, but thought the name was a sign and liked the look of the sleek white vessel waiting at the dock. It had two enclosed levels with dark windows along both sides and an open deck in the front and back. The top section of the yacht was open and strung with festive lights.

They followed the other couples and a few families, as they lined up for entry. Mac presented their tickets and they were taken to an intimate table for two on the lower deck. A waitress appeared with a basket of warm bread and dipping oil and took their drink orders.

Once everyone was aboard, the captain's voice boomed over the loudspeakers and welcomed them, gave them a run-through of the safety procedures, and explained their route and that they would be positioned to enjoy the best view of the fireworks later in the evening.

The engines hummed and the yacht glided forward. It was dark, so there wasn't much to see beyond the festive lights along the harbor, which soon faded as they made their way further out to sea. The scrumptious meal was served at a slow pace, letting the diners enjoy the ambience. A delicious heirloom tomato salad along with filet mignon and lobster, cheesy potatoes, and fresh vegetables left them stuffed. The waiter let them know dessert would be served later, closer to midnight.

Music from a live band, situated on the second deck near the popular open bar, drifted throughout the yacht. The captain announced the dance floor was open. "Are you a dancer?" Mac asked, gesturing toward the other couples making their way upstairs.

She laughed. "No, not even a little. High school would have

been my last attempt."

"Whew," he wiped his hand across his brow. "I'm a rotten dancer and avoid it at all costs." The waiter returned with a pot of hot tea. "I like listening to music, but have zero rhythm."

"Just one more thing we have in common." She selected a tea bag and poured water over it. "This has been lovely. Thanks for treating me. I had planned on snuggling with the dogs, binging movies, and stuffing myself with cookies tonight."

He grinned. "Yeah, I haven't been out for New Year's Eve since Jill." His smile faded. "I don't think it's a great holiday when you're single."

She reached for his hand. "I'm pretty happy not to be single."

His eyes brightened. "Just for the record, I'd be content to eat cookies, watch movies, and snuggle with the dogs, and you, of course. Maybe that could be our plan for tomorrow?"

He waved his hand across the table. "This is not my usual thing, but one of my patients raved about it so much and I thought you deserved something special after Kevin leaving early and everything with Wendy. Plus, the fireworks should be something else from out here on the water."

While they chatted, the waiter returned with a platter loaded with desserts. He placed it in the center of the table and let them know the fireworks would be commencing soon.

They nibbled on the mini desserts, which reminded Lily of Cyndy's huge spread. She chose a tiny chocolate layered cake and Mac opted for a cheesecake with strawberries. They savored the sweet confections, but agreed Cyndy's were better and then sampled a couple more bite-sized treats.

The captain asked the guests to make their way to an outer deck or the top deck for the best viewing options. Mac pointed to the outside deck on their level. "Let's try that one, away from the crowd." Lily agreed and took his arm. They were indeed alone and the yacht had made its way back toward the shore, positioning them with a perfect view of the waterfront. The captain helped the cruisers countdown to midnight and as the new year officially arrived, Mac leaned closer to her. "Happy New Year, Lily." As his lips met hers, she shivered. The spark of electricity moving through her all the way to her toes.

Her eyes closed, she breathed in his scent, a mixture of sandalwood, leather, and lemons. Engulfed in his arms, she felt safe, needed, cherished. All the things she didn't think would ever be possible again. When she moved to Driftwood Bay, she never would have dreamed she'd be in the arms of a man she treasured, celebrating a new year. So much had changed over these last months…and all for the good.

Mac stood behind her, cradling her against him, as the first fireworks launched. They watched with amazement as the sky filled with colorful bursts, sparkling against the dark sky and lighting up the harbor below. Collective gasps sounded from above as the fancy gold lights sizzled and then twinkled as they fell, disappearing, as if glitter had been shaken into the sea. The sky exploded with color, again and again, as did the water below with the stunning reflection. The festive display went on for over twenty minutes before the grand finale.

Breathtaking was a word that came to Lily's mind as a canopy of stunning colors bloomed above them. Huge pink explosions that resembled fountains, green starbursts, and twinkling gold light filled the dark blue canvas. It was a gorgeous way to celebrate the last day of the year and welcome the new one.

As the yacht moved toward the dock, she turned to face Mac. He grinned and met her eyes. "I'm not sure what this year will bring, but I know I want you by my side no matter what. Until I met you, I'd given up hope of ever finding someone I could imagine spending the rest of my life with."

Lily gulped, her eyes widening and her mind scrambling, not ready for what she thought he might ask.

He chuckled. "I can see the fear in your eyes. Don't worry,

I'm not popping the big question." He winked at her. "Not yet, anyway. I just want you to know how much you mean to me. I daresay, I've fallen in love with you. We agreed to take things slowly and I'm still on board with that, but this is serious for me. I want you in my life."

She swallowed the lump in her throat, wishing she had taken the wait staff up on the glass of champagne. She squeezed his hand in hers. "I feel the same way. I know whatever joy this year brings will be increased because I'll be sharing it with you and whatever burdens come my way, will be eased because you'll be there with me. I'm better with you and grateful because I assumed I'd always be alone. With you, I have a partner again, and while a part of me hopes this is forever, I need to be careful and sure. There's more than just the two of us involved."

Lily smiled to herself. She'd wondered what they had for so long, and now she knew. It might be too soon to know what the future would bring, and she couldn't help but worry about Mac's daughter rejecting him even further because of Lily, but she and Mac had love between them. And they had tomorrow. Right now, that was enough.

The bump of the hull against the dock, shifted them against each other.

He kissed her again, slowly, purposefully, and when he finally let her go, he looked into her eyes and touched her forehead with his. "We have each other and I'm not planning on going anywhere."

The captain announced their arrival and wished them all a good night. As they walked down the dock, Mac squeezed her hand and pointed at the almost full moon high in the sky, reflecting off the water. "Join me in the first walk of the year on the beach? There's nothing better than a moonlit beach with a beautiful woman." His brows wiggled, full of mischief.

She rested her head against his shoulder. "There's no place I'd rather be and nobody I'd rather be with."

EPILOGUE

Lily hopes you enjoyed the second installment of her story in the Glass Beach Cottage Series. If you haven't yet read BEACH HAVEN, it's the first book in the series and available at all book retailers in digital formats and print.

If you're a new reader to Tammy's books, the characters in *Moonlight Beach* took a trip to the San Juan Islands and met up with the characters from her Hometown Harbor Series. This is a bestselling series and you won't want to miss reading the six books. Each tells the story of a different heroine and like this book, they all include dogs.

If you've missed reading any of the Hometown Harbor Series, here are the links to the all the books. All but the prequel are available in print and eBook formats.

Prequel: Hometown Harbor: The Beginning (prequel novella eBook only)
Book 1: Finding Home
Book 2: Home Blooms
Book 3: A Promise of Home
Book 4: Pieces of Home
Book 5: Finally Home
Book 6: Forever Home

ACKNOWLEDGMENTS

During 2020, I've written more books than any other year I've been writing. It was a great escape from the sad and troubling news of the pandemic that dominated everything in 2020. I've immersed myself in my writing, which much like reading, offers a wonderful escape. In this second book in the series, I thought it would be fun to do a cross-over and allow readers to meet the characters in my Hometown Harbor Series. If you're already a reader of mine, I'm sure you noticed, but if you're a new reader, it will give you a glimpse into the characters I've come to think of as friends in that series and I hope you'll try them.

My thanks to my editor, Angela, for finding my mistakes and helping me polish *Moonlight Beach.* Like my other covers, I love this one and especially love the purple door. All the credit goes to Elizabeth Mackey for creating such an inviting and gorgeous cover. I'm fortunate to have such an incredible team helping me.

I so appreciate all of the readers who have taken the time to tell their reader friends about my work and provide reviews of my books. These reviews are especially important in promoting future books, so if you enjoy my novels, please consider leaving a review. I also encourage you to follow me on major book retailers and BookBub, where leaving a review is even easier and you'll be the first to know about new releases and deals.

Remember to visit my website at http://www.tammylgrace.com and join my mailing list for my exclusive group of readers. I've also got a fun Book Buddies Facebook Group. That's the best place to find me and get a chance to participate in my give-aways. Join my Facebook group at https://www.facebook.com/groups/AuthorTammyLGraceBookBuddies/

and keep in touch—I'd love to hear from you.

Wishing you tea, books, & happiness,

Tammy

FROM THE AUTHOR

Thank you for reading MOONLIGHT BEACH. Like my readers, I've fallen in love with the characters in this series and enjoyed writing this installment of Lily's story. There is one more book planned in the series and I'm hoping to have it out in 2021 or early 2022.

If you enjoy women's fiction and haven't yet read my HOMETOWN HARBOR SERIES, I think you'll enjoy them. It's a six-book series, with each book focused on a different female heroine. They are set in the gorgeous San Juan Islands in the Pacific Northwest and you'll recognize some of them from the trip Lily and Mac took in Moonlight Beach. You can start the series with a free prequel that is in the form of excerpts from Sam's journal. She's the main character in the first book, FINDING HOME.

If you're a new reader and enjoy mysteries, I write a series that features a lovable private detective, Coop, and his faithful golden retriever, Gus. If you like whodunits that will keep you guessing until the end, you'll enjoy the COOPER HARRINGTON DETECTIVE NOVELS.

The two books I've written as Casey Wilson, A DOG'S

HOPE and A DOG'S CHANCE have received enthusiastic support from my readers and if you're a dog-lover, are must-reads.

If you enjoy holiday stories, be sure and check out my CHRISTMAS IN SILVER FALLS SERIES and CHRISTMAS IN SNOW VALLEY. They are small-town Christmas stories of hope, friendship, and family. You won't want to miss any of the SOUL SISTERS AT CEDAR MOUNTAIN LODGE BOOKS. It's a connected Christmas series I wrote with four author friends. My contribution, CHRISTMAS WISHES, is the third book in the series and is a heartwarming, small-town holiday story that I'm sure you'll enjoy. The series kicks off with a free prequel novella, CHRISTMAS SISTERS, where you'll get a chance to meet the characters during their first Christmas together.

I'd love to send you my exclusive interview with the canine companions in my Hometown Harbor Series as a thank-you for joining my exclusive group of readers. You can sign up www.tammylgrace.com by clicking this link: https://wp.me/P9umIy-e

MORE BOOKS BY TAMMY L. GRACE

HOMETOWN HARBOR SERIES

Hometown Harbor: The Beginning prequel

Finding Home

Home Blooms

A Promise of Home

Pieces of Home

Finally Home

Forever Home

Hometown Harbor Series Books 1-3

COOPER HARRINGTON DETECTIVE SERIES

Killer Music

Deadly Connection

Dead Wrong

Cooper Harrington Detective Novels Books 1-3

CHRISTMAS STORIES

A Season for Hope (Christmas in Silver Falls Book 1)

The Magic of the Season (Christmas in Silver Falls Book 2)

Christmas in Snow Valley

Christmas Sisters (Soul Sisters at Cedar Mountain Lodge Book 1)

Christmas Wishes (Soul Sisters at Cedar Mountain Lodge Book 3)

GLASS BEACH COTTAGE SERIES

Beach Haven

WRITING AS CASEY WILSON

A Dog's Hope

A Dog's Chance

Don't miss the **SOUL SISTERS AT CEDAR MOUNTAIN LODGE**, a

connected Christmas series centered around a woman and the four foster girls she welcomes into her home.

Christmas Sisters, Book 1, by Ev Bishop, Tammy L. Grace, Violet Howe, Judith Keim, & Tess Thompson

Christmas Kisses, Book 2, by Judith Keim

Christmas Wishes, Book 3, by Tammy L. Grace

Christmas Hope, Book 4, by Violet Howe

Christmas Dreams, Book 5, by Ev Bishop

Christmas Rings, Book 6, by Tess Thompson

If you've enjoyed Tammy's work, please consider leaving a quick review on retailers, Goodreads, or Bookbub. They are so very helpful and essential to authors wishing to market their books. Just a quick sentence is enough! To the readers who have taken the time to leave a review, Tammy sends her heartfelt appreciation.

Tammy would love to connect with readers on social media and her website at www.tammylgrace.com. Remember to subscribe to her mailing list and you'll receive the fun interview she did with the dogs from her Hometown Harbor Series as an exclusive gift only available to her subscribers. **Subscribe here: https://wp.me/P9umIy-e**

Connect with Tammy on Facebook and click over and follow Tammy on BookBub and retailers by clicking the follow buttons on those pages.

ABOUT THE AUTHOR

Tammy L. Grace is the *USA Today* bestselling and award-winning author of the Cooper Harrington Detective Novels, the bestselling Hometown Harbor Series, and the Glass Beach Cottage Series, along with several sweet Christmas novellas. Tammy also writes under the pen name of Casey Wilson for Bookouture and Grand Central. You'll find Tammy online at www.tammylgrace.com where you can join her mailing list and be part of her exclusive group of readers. Connect with Tammy on Facebook at www.facebook.com/tammylgrace.books or Instagram at @authortammylgrace.

facebook.com/tammylgrace.books
twitter.com/TammyLGrace
instagram.com/authortammylgrace
bookbub.com/authors/tammy-l-grace
goodreads.com/tammylgrace
amazon.com/author/tammylgrace

Made in the USA
Monee, IL
22 January 2025

10624116R00156